Autumn's Child

Books by Kathleen Gilles Seidel

STAND TALL series
THE FOURTH SUMMER
THE LAST SNOWFALL
AUTUMN'S CHILD

Autumn's Child

Kathleen Gilles Seidel

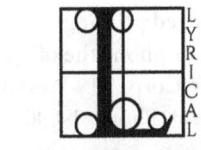

LYRICAL PRESS
Kensington Publishing Corp.
www.kensingtonbooks.com

LYRICAL PRESS BOOKS are published by

Kensington Publishing Corp.
119 West 40th Street
New York, NY 10018

All Kensington titles, imprints, and distributed lines are available at special quantity discounts for bulk purchases for sales promotion, premiums, fund-raising, educational, or institutional use.

Special book excerpts or customized printings can also be created to fit specific needs. For details, write or phone the office of the Kensington Sales Manager: Kensington Publishing Corp., 119 West 40th Street, New York, NY 10018. Attn. Sales Department. Phone: 1-800-221-2647.

Lyrical Press and Lyrical Press logo Reg. U.S. Pat. & TM Off.

First Electronic Edition: November 2019
ISBN-13: 978-1-5161-0735-3 (ebook)
ISBN-10: 1-5161-0735-7 (ebook)

First Print Edition: November 2019
ISBN-13: 978-1-5161-0738-4
ISBN-10: 1-5161-0738-1

Printed in the United States of America

To Max Tedford and Aseem Nambiar, my daughters' happily-ever-afters.

Chapter 1

Mrs. Norton W. Ridge IV could name every bride in town who had given birth to a "premature" baby seven months after the wedding. She never forgot who had fallen in arrears on their country club dues. And the young man who had come to tee off in baggy cargo shorts…wouldn't his grandfather be rolling in his grave right now, just *rolling*? Mrs. Ridge, the former Miss Eleanor Alexandria Burchell, was a good old-fashioned Southern…ah…difficult woman with exacting standards and an unforgiving spirit.

"Why are people so afraid of her?" a granddaughter's boyfriend had asked.

"She's lonely," the granddaughter had answered, trying to explain what she wasn't willing to say, that her grandmother was a sharp-tongued, rich old lady who had chosen being powerful over being loved.

Mrs. Ridge had spent her married life in Carlsville, Georgia, a once well-mannered town north of Atlanta. Like many small towns in the South, Carlsville had faded. The young people moved to Atlanta. The country club first opened its restaurant to non-members, then the golf course, and finally had to shut its doors altogether. Miss Dessy's Shop for Ladies closed. The Ridges were the only one of the old families who had held on to their money. Eleanor Ridge had accepted the impoverishment of her town, the declining affluence of her friends, and her own aging with matriarchal grace. Wasn't decay the natural course of things in the South?

What Mrs. Ridge had proved unable to endure was the reverse, the sudden improvement in the town's economy. A massive pork-processing plant had gone up on the grounds of the country club, running two shifts a day, providing many, many jobs. New people came to town; new stores opened; all the rental properties were taken. There was money in town. Homeowners were getting ahead of their own bills by leasing out rooms in their basements. The high school football team had new uniforms; the public library had money to buy new books.

But it wasn't elegant money. The country club was not reopening; Miss Dessy's Shop for Ladies remained shuttered.

The new people were immigrants, speaking languages that Mrs. Ridge did not understand. The new grocery store stocked foods she had never seen. She could not pronounce the names of the people serving on the school board and the town council. The town had suited her when it was fading, when the paint on the white porches weathered and peeled, when the wisteria vines grew thick and heavy and the honeysuckle toppled the fences.

But the rusty cars with loud mufflers, the plywood skateboard ramps, the Catholics renting space in the Baptist church for their ever-growing Sunday school offended her. Her friends were moving to the city to live with their grown children, but Mrs. Ridge had more resources and options than they did. She announced that she would start living year-round at her summer home in the Blue Ridge Mountains of Virginia. She was still invited to bridge luncheons up there. The historic inn in the nearby village still had white tablecloths in the dining room, and its parking valet always retrieved her car first even if other people were waiting in line. Up there she was still treated as she expected to be.

Her daughter and her older son had objected to the expense involved. The house would have to be winterized, a first-floor bath installed. Mrs. Ridge had replied that she was not accountable to them for how she spent her money. They had fretted about how many valuables she would be leaving in the vacant Georgia house. She responded by taking everything with her. Two interstate moving vans carried boxes of china figurines and chests of sterling silver flatware. Rugs were rolled and swaddled in plastic. Artwork was boxed in custom-built wood crates. Less than half of this would ever get unpacked.

Her lawyers, Timothy Healy and his son Ryan, had wanted to do an inventory of those valuables while they were being packed. Mrs. Ridge's will had a years-old, pages-long attachment listing individual family heirlooms. The Healys wanted to be sure that the items on the list could be matched up with the actual possessions. Mrs. Healy announced that that was nonsense. Surely everything was still there—why would anyone in the family have ever sold anything?—and as for knowing what was what, who couldn't tell a Dresden Rose fruit bowl from a Les Cinq Fleurs vegetable dish?

She had arrived at the lake in late December and quickly realized that the ladies she had played bridge with weren't there. They were summer residents, just as she used to be. She had no one to lunch with, no one to complain about, no one to bully. By March, out of isolation she would never admit to, she announced to the Healys that she was agreeable to an inventory. But no, they couldn't hire someone local. How could she be expected to have a stranger in the house? They needed to send someone she knew, someone she could sit down to dinner with.

She had spent more than eighty years making sure that she got her way. She wasn't going to stop now.

* * * *

Of Mrs. Ridge's three children and six grandchildren, only one, her younger son's daughter Colleen, had any sympathy for her.

"Try to understand," Colleen said to the two friends she had invited to spend spring break with her at her grandmother's lake house. "She will criticize you for violating rules of etiquette that you never knew existed, but it will make her happy."

"I don't like the sound of this," Colleen's fellow-teacher Amanda said from the front seat of the car. "I'm from Missouri. We have character, not manners."

Amanda's boyfriend, Jason, was driving. "You two teach in a private school." Jason worked in the fund-raising office of the University of Virginia. "What can be worse than private school parents?"

"My grandmother can be."

"And we teach in a parochial school," Amanda corrected. "Our families are nice. At least most of them."

* * * *

Ben Healy looked out his window on Friday afternoon. Mrs. Ridge had assigned him a room at the front of the house, and he could see the driveway that curved down to the fortress of spruce, white birch, and aspen trees that protected the property from the stares of passing motorists. He would be able to see the car drive up.

This was some kind of crap-ass joke.

Ben had been a professional snowboarder. He had had a great run, he and his two closest friends training together as kids, sharing a chalet at a resort in Oregon as adults. But he was realistic enough to know when his competition days were ending. Having always been analytical and interested in details and systems, and being one of the few snowboarders with a college degree, he had done a "boot camp" in software engineering and was now working on a master's degree in cyber-security.

The program was mostly online; he had a lot of flexibility about timing and location. The faculty did take a spring break, so he decided to take a week off as well. He had offered to go down to Georgia and help out for a week. He had assumed that he would be cleaning out the garage or something, but his mom had said that her garage was clean. His dad and brother said that if he truly wanted to help, he could supervise the inventory of an elderly client's valuables. She wanted someone from the family to come. Ben said that he could do that.

Oh, and she was now living in her summer place in southwestern Virginia.

That was okay. Ben had nothing against southwestern Virginia.

And the client was Mrs. Ridge.

Mrs. Ridge was a piece of work, but if they needed him, he would go.

Then his father said, "And there's no reason to think that Colleen would be there."

Wait. What? "Why would Colleen be there?"

"I just said that there was no reason that she would be."

"Yes, but you said it. If there really was no reason to think she would be there, if she were in the Peace Corps or manning a mission to Mars, you wouldn't have said anything at all."

"She lives in Charlottesville. She teaches French at a high school there."

Charlottesville was about ninety minutes from Mrs. Ridge's new home. There were suddenly all kinds of reasons why she might be there.

Snowboarders need to be fearless; it helps if they are insanely so. Apparently leaving the pro circuit had robbed Ben of his manly courage. He checked Charlottesville's public school calendar. Their spring break was a week after Mrs. Ridge was commanding his presence. If Colleen was coming, it would be after he had left. Mrs. Ridge probably wanted to spread out her visitors.

He had been greeted at the door by an elegant woman who introduced herself as Leilah; she was Mrs. Ridge's "house manager." Ben had no idea what a house manager did. He had never heard of such a job. Mrs. Ridge was resting, Leilah said. She would show Ben to his room. She waved him toward the wide front staircase, but didn't offer to take his suitcase. Apparently house managers weren't footmen.

"We're expecting the other houseguests to arrive shortly," she said as they reached the landing. "Mrs. Ridge's granddaughter is bringing two friends with her."

Granddaughter? Ben forced himself to take a breath. There were two granddaughters, weren't there? Colleen had a female cousin. Ben couldn't remember her name. Maybe it was her.

No, it wasn't her, whatever her name was. Colleen was the only one of her generation who paid Mrs. Ridge any attention. But what about the school calendar? Spring break wasn't supposed to start until a week from Monday.

For the public schools. He hadn't thought about checking the private school calendars. She could be teaching at a private school or a parochial one. The Ridges in Georgia had been Episcopalian for generations, but Colleen and her brothers had been raised in Chicago as Catholics. She could be teaching in a Catholic school with a different schedule.

So she was coming. He was a big boy, wasn't he? He could handle it. What was the big deal? They had had a summer fling four years ago. It hadn't lasted. End of story.

Except no one else would let it end. Everyone had adored Colleen. And not just Seth and Nate, his two closest friends, but all their families too. His own family had known Colleen her whole life. Nate's parents, Mr. and Mrs. Forrest, had been employing her at their resort that summer, and they thought she was just as marvelous as Ben's own family did. Seth's family, the Streets, had never met her, so you might think that they wouldn't have a strong opinion, but the three moms talked to each other way too much, and so the Streets also thought that Colleen was the torch on the top of the Statue of Liberty.

When you were with a woman like that, after a while you started to wonder what she was doing with you. Why would Colleen Ridge, even-tempered and generous, glowing and vibrant, gifted at languages, stick around with a guy like him?

He must be fooling her, he finally concluded. She must not realize that he wasn't as good a snowboarder as Seth and Nate. He didn't have Seth's style or Nate's muscle. He had as many medals as they did because he was consistent. On his own, he could earn bronze medal after bronze medal; silver and gold came only when someone else screwed up. He had made as much money as anyone, but only because the sponsors liked the way he looked in their clothes, not because little kids wanted to grow up and be Ben Healy. His green eyes and Irish cheekbones were more valuable than his McTwists.

Surely Colleen would dump him the minute she saw the real him.

So it had been easier to be a dick.

Once the summer was over and he was back on the pro circuit and she was on the East Coast, he had become the Disappearing Boyfriend from Hell. He would return her phone calls with a text. He would wait two days before answering her texts. He would discourage her from coming to events, saying that all the spectators would be drunk. He would answer all her questions with monosyllables, and when she would push, trying to recapture the magic of the summer, he would say even less. Then he would lie and say that everything was fine, that nothing had changed. Of course she had eventually broken up with him. He hadn't given her much choice.

He cringed at the memory of how badly he had behaved. He tried not to think about that time. It wasn't really Colleen he dreaded meeting, but the person he had been to her, the self-defeating, self-sabotaging moron.

* * * *

The house was a few miles south of the little village that had the lake's only commercial establishments. Colleen sat forward, telling Jason to look for the third break in the dense wall of trees. Two stone pillars flanked a narrow drive. The pillars were not marked. One had a mailbox recessed into it, but there was no name, no address. *If you haven't been here before,* the pillars seemed to say, *why are you coming now?*

The drive immediately made a sharp curve so that from the road no one could see any of the property. Beyond the curve the trees opened up to a narrow meadow of sweet clover and wildflowers, trout lilies that would bloom early and asters that would come late in the summer. Anchored by its stone foundation, the big, old house flowed across the earth. Sided with weathered cedar shingles, it was as welcoming and informal as a large house could be. Bay windows, deep recesses, and broad eaves etched out spaces for rocking chairs and wrought-iron gliders, and the narrow third-story dormers promised a world of cozy secrets.

The house had always been slightly seedy in a casual old-family way. Colleen remembered weeds sprouting in the gravel driveway, garden hoses left in a careless tangle, and broken canoe paddles abandoned by the side of the boathouse. The house was rooted in nature; the sloping grounds and the trees were a part of summer. Why would the ivy and periwinkle be confined to neatly edged beds?

That was how it should be, how it had always been. But it wasn't like that now. Everything had changed. The property looked like something from a magazine. The railings and the trim around the windows, once an indeterminate light color, were a glossy ecru; the shutters were a perfectly chosen mossy green. The gravel had been bulldozed off the driveway and replaced with a fresh ribbon of silvery black asphalt. The bushes, previously a tangled mass along the stone foundation, were pruned and thickly mulched.

This was strange. Her grandmother couldn't have ordered this. The shining paint and meticulous landscaping looked so nouveau-riche, so new money, and new money was yet another thing that Mrs. Norton W. Ridge IV did not approve of.

Colleen didn't sneer at new money; as a foreign language teacher in an era of funding cuts, she was happy to have any money at all. What she didn't like was change. So much had already changed in the last few years—her mother dying, her father remarrying, her brothers wanting to spend the holidays with their in-laws. The lake couldn't change.

She had grown up outside Chicago, and during the school year they had all been so busy, Dad with his dental practice, Mother driving the boys to their sports and Colleen to her lessons. But every summer they had the two weeks at the lake. She would play in the water with her brothers, the three of them balancing themselves on the gunnels of the wood canoe, trying to jar the other ones off. As her brothers grew and she remained small, she would splash up to stand on Sean's shoulders. Finn would count. On "two" Sean would bend his knees, on "three" he would jump; an instant later she, too, would jump, pulling herself into a tight tuck, seeing how many times she could somersault in the air before cannonballing into the water. They would play croquet on the lawn, the game having an Alice-in-Wonderland madness because of the sloping course. Sometimes their grandmother would play with them; her strokes were elegant, her strategy ruthless. At night everyone would gather around the library table to play games.

That was the lake. That was what happened at the lake. It couldn't change.

A little red Prius was parked under the portico by the kitchen door. It belonged to Leilah, her grandmother's one full-time employee. Her grandmother's big Lincoln was angled into a space across from the front door. A nondescript car was next to the Lincoln. Colleen didn't know who it belonged to. She suggested Jason park next to it.

She and Amanda got out of the car, never thinking to wait for Jason to come around and open their doors. For a moment, she saw a person in one of the front bedroom windows, but whoever it might be stepped away almost instantly. Amanda had seen the figure too, and English teacher that she was, started making comparisons to *Jane Eyre* and the first Mrs. Rochester, the madwoman in the attic.

"That's not the attic. The attic is up there." Colleen pointed to the dormer windows under the roofline. "My brothers and I sleep there." Those rooms were small, having been designed for servants, but Colleen loved them. The cozy, oddly shaped spaces seemed quaint and endearing. She had spent her Christmas vacation here this year to help her grandmother settle in. Even though only the two of them had been in the house, Colleen had slept in the attic.

She had a key to the front door, but as soon as she saw how bright the brass lock was, she knew that her key wasn't going to fit. Another change.

Wanting to be a dutiful granddaughter hadn't been the only reason she had spent Christmas here. Her brothers were spending the holiday with their in-laws. Her father had been going to California with his new wife to see her son and his family. Of course she would have been welcome at either place, but she would have felt like a guest. She didn't want to feel like a guest at Christmas. As difficult as her grandmother could be, coming to the lake had felt easier.

Colleen rang the doorbell. Leilah, the house manager, opened the door.

Slender, as tall as Amanda, with the lithe, grounded bearing of a yoga instructor, Leilah was dressed in a collarless shirt and soft trousers in a wheat-colored linen. Her hair was the same light golden brown color as Colleen's, but without Colleen's exuberant texture. Leilah's hair was glisteningly smooth. Everything about her seemed refined and elegant. Colleen couldn't imagine anyone, even her grandmother, calling Leilah a maid.

When Colleen had come in December, she had been fascinated by Leilah. She was like the elegant priestess who glided across the waiting room of an expensive spa, handing you a thick white robe, escorting you to the luxurious mysteries that awaited in the dimly lit, scented rooms.

But after a while Colleen had grown uneasy. Leilah was obviously well educated. Her vocabulary was precise; her sweaters were cashmere. Why would such a woman, seemingly in her mid-thirties, take a job that had low pay and little future? There were many possible reasons—she could be a poet or an artist; she could need a year of quiet after a difficult divorce. But whatever her story was, she was not sharing it with Colleen. Colleen's first few questions—routine questions about where Leilah was from and the like—had been so deftly evaded that Colleen stopped asking.

In fact, as she began to introduce Leilah to Amanda and Jason, she realized that she didn't even know the woman's last name.

"Do come in," Leilah said graciously. "I will show you to your rooms. Mrs. Ridge will meet you in the library for cocktails."

"Is there someone else here?" Colleen asked, wondering about the rental car.

"Yes. Mrs. Ridge is undertaking an inventory of her family heirlooms. One of her lawyer's sons has come to supervise."

"Her lawyer from Georgia? Mr. Healy?"

"I believe so. One of his sons."

Tim and Marianne Healy had four sons, and the oldest, Ryan, was a lawyer in practice with his father. He would be the one who was here. That was fine. She knew Ryan; she liked him. It would be strange because he and Ben looked a lot alike, but she could handle that. No problem.

At the top of the stairs, Leilah turned right. The stairs to the attic were to the left. Colleen supposed that made sense. She wouldn't be putting Jason and Amanda up in the attic. Once they got settled, Colleen could find the back stairs on her own.

The doorway to one of the second floor bedrooms opened. Sunlight spilled into the hallway. A man stepped out, the sunlight behind him, outlining his shape, obscuring his features.

Yes, Ryan was built like Ben...and like Colleen's own brothers, their birth families, and all her mother's relatives. Their shoulders were sturdy, their torsos long and lean, and they didn't have much extension in his forearms and thighs. All these people were Irish-American with the build of people who had, for generations, trudged up and down Ireland's green hills.

"Amanda, Jason," Leilah was saying, "I'd like you to meet our other guest, Ben Healy."

What? *What?* This was supposed to be Ryan, the older brother, the lawyer.

But Leilah had said Ben. Colleen didn't know where to look. She couldn't look at him.

The floorboards creaked; someone was stepping forward to shake someone's hand. Words, accents, Maryland, central Missouri, north Georgia, and then "...how nice to see you again..."

Was that her? Had she spoken? Of course. She was poised; she was polite, and the tip of her tongue was still touching the roof of her mouth just behind her teeth, the "n" from "again."

Nice...Had she really said that it was *nice* to see him again? It wasn't nice at all, it was...She didn't know what it was.

She had to look at him. She couldn't resist—his hair dark and auburn-tinged, thick and rumpled; his lower lip full and soft; his eyes deeply set beneath dark eyebrows, all that wild Irish beauty. Ben.

Nice...oh, no, it was something quite different than nice.

It had started so randomly four years ago. He had happened to look at a list of Norwegian interpreters, a list that was lying on a desk in the office of the Endless Snow resort. *Hey, I know that girl. I played with her brothers when we were kids.* He lived with two other guys in a chalet on the grounds of the resort. *Hire her. She'll be fun to have around.* So she had gone to Oregon for the summer to interpret for two Norwegian snowboard coaches.

Oh, the memories—the sun sparkling off the ice-frosted snow, the orange-red flames in the depths of a stone fireplace, chalet windows bright in the soft twilight. Ben had tried to teach her to snowboard. She fell. And fell again. Her laughter had been light and clear, his deep and throaty while he reached his hand down to help her back up.

She had known that she was more sure about the two of them than he had been, but she had assumed that it was that Irish-Catholic worldview that if anything could go wrong, it would. She had been confident that he would get beyond that.

He hadn't. *You never knew how much I loved you. I told you and told you. You never believed it.*

Leilah was gesturing her into one of the lakeside rooms, saying that she hoped Colleen had everything she needed. The door closed. Colleen found herself sitting on the bed, staring at her suitcase, a quilted duffel, its fabric tumbling with sweetheart roses and blossoming peonies.

I loved you, but I hated myself.

She knew what the books said. She had read them, struggling to understand what had happened between them.

It had turned into a distancer-pursuer relationship, the books said. She was the pursuer, begging him to call her more, talk to her more. That wasn't who she was. She was a confident, competent person. She knew that she was physically appealing, that she was smart with a gifted ear for languages. She was helpful; she was kind. People liked her.

But waiting two days for him to answer the simplest text had made her needy and desperate. She couldn't bear to think about how pathetic she must have seemed back then. So now Ben wasn't simply an ex-boyfriend. That she could have handled. He was the ex-boyfriend who had turned her into a person whom she could not respect.

She heard a sound, a little rap. It was a knock on the French door that led to the balcony overlooking the lake. What was she doing in this room? This had been her parents' room.

The knock came again. She could see Amanda through the glass, waiting for Colleen to open the door. Colleen got up. She might not be able to open the door. It used to stick. Her father would have to jerk hard on it, and then it would pop open, sometimes making him almost lose his balance. She might have to ask Amanda to push from the outside. Besides teaching English, Amanda coached the girls' field hockey and lacrosse teams. She was tall and strong.

But there was no need for Amanda's muscle. This time the door glided open, soundlessly and easily.

"This is fun," Amanda said as soon as Colleen let her in. "Our rooms connect through the balcony. Does this mean I can creep into your bed in the middle of the night?"

"If you want."

"Speaking of creeping into people's beds, I take it that that was *the* Ben," Amanda said. "You never mentioned how good-looking he is."

"Really?" She would have thought that she had told Amanda everything about him.

"He is pretty memorable. How do you feel about him being here? You weren't expecting it, were you? It seems odd that your grandmother didn't mention it."

"My grandmother likes catching people off guard."

"That sucks. But seriously, this place is unbelievable. It's like staying in a fancy resort. I don't think I brought the right clothes. I don't think I *own* the right clothes. Do people really live like this?"

Colleen looked around the room. The walls were pristine with new ivory paint; the floors and the oak trim around the windows and doors had been newly sanded and stained. The closet was empty except for matching padded hangers and two new white bathrobes. Next to the dresser was a folding luggage rack, and on top of the dresser was a little basket of toiletries.

No was the answer. At least not anyone Colleen knew. Even in the more formal Georgia house, the closet in the best guest room was full of the family's out-of-season clothes. This wasn't a home anymore. It was a resort, a B&B for paying guests.

Except at a resort, she wouldn't be expected to sit down to dinner with an ex-boyfriend and a ghost of her worst self.

"By the way," Amanda continued, "I'm not getting a signal on my phone. Is there a wi-fi connection?"

Colleen shook her head. That was one modernization that hadn't been completed. "You can get a phone signal at the end of the dock."

"There was a dock out there?"

"Of course."

They went out onto the balcony. Below them, a lawn, green with new spring growth, sloped in a widening vee to the water's edge where the boulders protected a strip of sand big enough for children to play. Set off to one edge of the property was a two-story boathouse, sided with shingles like the house. Boats would always slow down as they passed, envying the sunlit lawn, wondering at the wealth and comfort of people who called it home.

Despite the lawn, the boulders, and the boathouse, there was no dock. "Oh, that's right," Colleen remembered. "It's not going in until Monday."

"*Monday?*" Amanda looked a little sick.

"This is the lake, Amanda. You don't need the internet."

Amanda did not look convinced.

Chapter 2

The upstairs hall smelled of lemon-oil wood polish. Colleen looked over the banister into the front hall. The house faced east, and this late in the day not much natural light came through the leaded-glass fanlight over the big front door. A small arrangement of fresh flowers sat on the round, leather-topped center table. As Colleen came down the stairs, the scent of the lemon oil gave way to the flowers' powdery sweetness.

"The Nats could do with some of the Braves' hitters, that's for sure."

It was Jason. Colleen couldn't see him. He must be at the far end of the front hall.

"Yes, but the pitching staff could use a better closer."

Ben. That was Ben, a hint of a north Georgia accent warming his voice.

He had an effortlessly attractive voice. It was low-pitched and confident, expressive and resonant, rich in the undertones. It had served him and his sponsors well.

She had a nice voice too. She was going to need to use it. She was going to have to talk to him, make conversation, be polite, gracious, welcoming, all that. She was at the base of the stairs now. She took a breath and turned.

Suddenly a memory—a bed and a room lit by scented candles, their swirling fragrance encircling her and him, shutting out the world. All that mattered, all that existed, was the graceful movement of his body as he raised and lowered himself above her. Their breath, his and hers, was the only sound. His breath had grown richer and slower, coming from deep within him; then it would quicken, becoming shallow and catching in a sharp gasp.

What was she doing remembering how he breathed during sex? It had been four years. She should have forgotten. There hadn't been that many other men, but she couldn't remember how any of them breathed.

Only Ben.

"Has my grandmother emerged yet?" she asked them. Amanda was with the two men. Clearly they had all been waiting for her.

"No," Jason said. "But Leilah said that the drinks are in the library and we should help ourselves."

Along the front of the house, the side that faced the road, were the formal living room, the spacious front hall, the dining room, and the kitchen. Across the back of the house were the room her grandmother now used as a bedroom, a long sitting room, and a paneled library. These rooms faced the lake, and the sitting room, with its three sets of glass-paned French doors, was washed with the late afternoon light. The library was a darker, wood-paneled room. A minute later Colleen's grandmother swept into the room.

No one could make an entrance like Grannor. She was always perfectly groomed, and her posture was nearly as good as in the portrait from her presentation at the Christmas Cotillion nearly seventy years ago.

Colleen hugged her and gestured for Jason and Amanda to come nearer. Colleen and the others in her generation called their grandmother "Grannor," a combination of Grandmother and Eleanor, but Colleen introduced her as "Mrs. Ridge." Probably no one under the age of seventy called her by her first name.

A rimmed silver cocktail tray was on the mahogany center table set with mixers, bottles of spirits, differently shaped glasses…and wine. Knowing that she alone could tease Mrs. Norton W. Ridge IV, Colleen said lightly, "Wine as a cocktail, Grannor?" Her grandfather would not have approved. Wine was to be enjoyed with a meal and only with a meal. Cocktail hour required spirits. "What has happened?"

Grannor waved a hand. "Oh, your grandfather and his rules. Aren't we women supposed to think for ourselves these days?"

"When have you ever not thought for yourself, Grannor?"

Grannor found that amusing. "I am afraid that your uncle Norton does not value my independent thinking. Now, Colleen, go over and make dear Ben feel welcome while I become acquainted with your two friends."

"Dear" Ben was in front of the window bench, its worn tapestry cushion newly re-covered in a sage-green chintz. He nodded politely as she approached but said nothing.

He really was an exceptionally good-looking man. She had gotten used to it during their summer together; she had loved him, not his looks. But his etched cheekbones, his thick coppery-black hair, his deep-set green eyes...

Four years ago, the gang at the resort had been playing around with an app that split photos of people's faces and then mirrored each half so you could see yourself as if you had two right sides or two left sides. One of Colleen's eyes was slightly farther from her nose than the other, something that no one had ever noticed before or since.

When it was Ben's turn, everyone thought that the app wasn't working. It turned out that his face was as perfectly symmetrical as the gorgeous movie stars in the sample photos. No wonder he got more endorsement deals than some of the guys who had many more medals than he did.

Those perfectly spaced eyes seemed cool now, not really looking at her. He was always comfortable standing quietly, but she was not good at silence.

She took a breath and reminded herself that they had more in common, more shared history, than that one summer. Their families were friends. The Healys lived in a slightly larger town ten miles from Carlsville, Grannor's former home. Ben's grandfather, father, and now brother had done much of the Ridges' legal work. The two families didn't socialize except when Colleen's family visited from Chicago, and Grannor wanted Colleen's high-energy brothers slamming doors at someone else's house.

Their mothers, Mary Pat Ridge and Marianne Healy, had only seen each other once a year, but both had had hearts as warm as their red hair. Colleen's mother had grown up in a big, noisy Irish-Catholic family, and that was the kind of home Marianne Healy had created for her family. The eight Healys ate in the kitchen, consuming platters of soda bread and lamb stew, big pots of potato soup, and barge-like cuts of corned beef. Mary Pat Ridge was happy to drive the ten miles to the Healys' rather than have her children spend too much time entombed in a home where there was still a bathroom in the garage for the help.

"It was good of your parents to come to Chicago for my mother's funeral," Colleen said to Ben now. *We still have this, families who go to each other's funerals.*

"They thought the world of her, especially my mom. How is your father doing?"

"Very well. He has remarried."

"Oh." He thought for a moment. "I guess I did hear that."

"She was one of my mother's closest friends. I still think of her as Mrs. Sisson."

"That has to be strange."

"It is."

She supposed it was odd, her saying only two words, not going on and on as she usually did. "I hadn't heard anything about this inventory," she continued. She wanted to sound like herself. She didn't want him to think that she was uncomfortable. "I'm sorry. I could have started it when I was helping Grannor unpack in December."

He ignored that. "I take it that you didn't know I would be here."

That was direct. "No, I didn't. I'm surprised that Grannor didn't say something. I talked to her yesterday. She must have known that you were coming."

"Oh, she didn't just *know.*" He was looking down at his drink, twisting the stem of the glass. Then he looked at her, his eyes glinting beneath his dark eyebrows. "She arranged it. Once she knew that I was coming, not Ryan, she insisted that it be this week."

"You're joking! Why did she want that? What was she thinking?"

He shrugged. "You know her better than I do."

Colleen had never talked to her grandmother about her summer with Ben, but Grannor made it her business to learn such things. So what was Grannor doing, making sure that the two of them were at the lake together? Was she trying to remind Colleen of her failure? Grannor never thought that anyone was adequately aware of their failures. The moral composition of the universe required Mrs. Norton W. Ridge IV to dose out guilt and shame.

But me? Why would you want to torture me?

* * * *

The dining room had never been Colleen's favorite room. The roofed octagon porch kept the room dark, but the new color embraced the darkness. The walls were a deep blue-green, the color of Norway pine in the late afternoon. The plate rail that used to have a few dusty plates now bore silver trophies, platters, and punch cups whose sheen reflected the light from the chandelier and wall sconces. Colleen was willing to admit that this was an improvement.

Only five places had been set at the table. Amanda looked at Colleen uneasily. "Leilah reminds me of my college music-theory professor," she said softly. "Is she going to be our waitress?"

"I assume so," Colleen answered.

Grannor directed Amanda and Ben to sit on one side of the table with Jason and Colleen facing them. Ben pulled out Grannor's chair for her.

The women who had been Ben's fellow competitors on the pro circuit probably would have belittled this kind of gallantry. Grannor wouldn't; she expected to be treated with old-fashioned courtesy.

Colleen unfolded her napkin. "When it's just you and Leilah, Grannor, do you eat together?"

"Why, no, of course not." Mrs. Ridge answered with an exaggerated sigh. "I suppose that your father, Colleen, would say that I am a terrible snob. He is always criticizing me for that. But to pretend that Leilah and I are friends would be unpleasant for her. If she were a friend, she would have to entertain me and listen to me ramble on like some old person yammering about things that happened ages ago, and that is not part of her job."

Leilah served dinner in courses. She brought out a leek soup in delicate two-handled bowls. Mrs. Ridge, in a lightly patronizing tone, told Amanda that the bowls were called "ecuelles." "They are really for drinking broth, but I don't know anyone who serves broth before a meal anymore, but you did like them as a child, Colleen."

That was true. Sarah, her grandparents' maid, had once had to put together a soup with less than an hour's notice because Colleen had seen and liked the ecuelles. Colleen was touched that Grannor remembered that. Grannor usually didn't pay particular attention to other people's preferences. Surely her own could set a standard for the rest of the universe.

"All these things"—Amanda gestured to the two corner china cupboards and the massive glass-fronted sideboard so crammed with china and silver that it was impossible to distinguish one piece from the next—"do people use them?"

Mrs. Ridge shook her head. "The girls, the brides, don't anymore, but we used our pretty things. Of course, we all had maids who didn't mind polishing the silver. Your father, Colleen, always said that they didn't mind because it was their one chance to sit down. He always talks as if we mistreated them."

Colleen was not going to answer that. Her father was appalled by his parents' snobbery and racism. Grannor tried to make light of her younger son's disapproval because, Colleen felt sure, she secretly minded it a great deal.

After the soup course, Amanda and Colleen stood up to clear the ecuelles. Leilah stopped them at the swinging door to the kitchen. "I'm sure Mrs. Ridge wants her guests to enjoy themselves."

But I'm not a guest, Colleen wanted to protest. *I grew up in this kitchen.* She had made ginger snaps with Sarah and had learned to fry chicken from Nancy, Sarah's daughter. Reluctantly she sat back down at the table.

She was finding it difficult to sit across from Ben. He was sitting as he always had, back in his chair, his chest broad and open, his arms held lightly away from the sides of his body. When Amanda said something amusing, he smiled without actually smiling, his dark eyebrows going up, his green eyes glowing, his face opening.

You used to look at me like that.

He had claimed that he didn't like small talk, but he was doing fine now. He asked Amanda questions about herself and easily replied to hers about him. Yes, he had always been interested in technology, and once it was time to stop competing professionally, he had studied software engineering and had then gotten interested in cyber-security.

There was *so* much more to the story than this. People had always said that Ben was going to be a better coach than he was a rider. He was analytical and observant, and he could make people understand what he saw. Although he would never be an Olympian himself, everyone believed that one day he would be coaching the Olympic team.

But then—Colleen had learned all this from the internet—more than two years ago he had suddenly come out criticizing the snowboarding establishment's training programs. Kids were being pushed too fast; parents were being given false hope about their children's eventual earning potential. The half-day classes that resorts offered for kids who wanted to have fun were fine, but the programs for the promising juniors...no, they were dangerous. Owners of such programs had felt betrayed by what Ben had said. He made enemies, and a lot of doors had been closed.

It was such a stupid act of self-sabotage. He had destroyed his career just as he had destroyed their relationship.

This wasn't the time to ask him why he had done that. Colleen sat back and listened while he told Amanda that he hoped to continue studying a couple hours a day while he was at the lake.

"But here?" Amanda asked. "Without the internet? Colleen said we won't be able to get a cell signal until Monday, and then we'll have to stand at the end of the dock."

Ben admitted that "working from anywhere" did not encompass standing at the end of a dock. He turned to Grannor. "I hope you'll excuse me after dinner, Mrs. Ridge. There's a little town a few miles north, isn't there? If I can get a signal there, I can download what I need through my phone."

"You young people use those little phones of yours too much," Grannor announced. "But I don't imagine that you are going to listen to me about that. If I can impose on you to take Colleen with you, she can return my library books. I'm sure Jason and Amanda will enjoy watching the sunset, but Colleen has seen it before."

Jason and Amanda looked as if they would enjoy finding the internet connection.

"I'll return your books," Ben said. "You don't need to bother Colleen."

"Oh, she doesn't mind," Grannor declared.

Colleen followed her grandmother into the bedroom to get the library books. They were Mary Stewarts and Phyllis Whitneys, so old that the library had had them rebound in pebbly buckram. "Do you want me to get you some more?" Colleen asked.

"That dinky little library isn't going to be open at this hour. You'll need to put these in the book drop."

And why couldn't Ben have done that exhausting chore? Colleen flipped one of the books open. It was due April 1, more than a week away. "Grannor, I don't truly think that I need to do this." She wasn't going to jump through a lot of hoops for her grandmother. If she did, her grandmother would only raise the hoops higher. "I'll go give the books to Ben."

"Well, have it your way, missy." Grannor sniffed.

Colleen set the books down on the leather-topped hall table while she got a coat from the closet. Through the side light of the front door she could see that Ben had backed his car around and was waiting for her so that he could open the door. The shadows were long, and the mountain air was growing chilly, but he wasn't wearing a coat. He and his snowboarding friends didn't feel the cold like normal people did.

He was leaning back against the car, his hands linked behind his head. The gesture pulled his blazer up and open.

She would have once taken the open blazer as an invitation to slip her arms underneath it, pressing her check against his shirt, feeling his lean, hard muscles, hearing his heartbeat. His arms would have closed around her, and he would have nudged her hair with his chin, getting her to tilt her head back so that he could kiss her.

She suddenly yearned to be back in those days when his green eyes always scanned a room looking for her. The longing was velvety blue, the heart-piercing plea of a lonely violin.

He straightened as soon as he saw her, and his jacket fell back in place. She had been about to hand him the books when suddenly, impulsively, she pulled them back. "I'm ready whenever you are."

The village was only a few miles away, and even before they reached the mini-golf course, their phones were picking up signals. Ben said he would turn his into a hot spot and download the documents onto his computer that way, but it might take a while. He parked in front of the library. Colleen put the books in the book drop and crossed the street to walk through town.

The village's Main Street ran parallel to the lake with a public beach on one side and the shops and restaurants on the other. Most of the shops had closed early as it was between seasons. The arcade with its pinball and skee ball machines was still open. Her brothers had loved that place. She hadn't. She wasn't any good at games like that.

What she had been able to do was spell. Third grade was the first time she had won the schoolwide spelling bee, beating even the sixth graders. She hadn't cared that much about winning. What she had loved was the way that Sean and Finn had been rooting for her. Sean had been in fifth grade, and Finn, her almost twin, had also been in third. They had competitive natures, and they had loved seeing their delicately built sister wiping the floor with the big kids.

What happy memories. She peered into the arcade. Most of the machines were still the same. The same blaring robo-voice blasted out "SPIN...TO... WIN," drawing out the 'n' sounds like a dying engine. She did see two desktop computers on a counter in the back. An overhead sign declared that it was an internet café. She would have to tell Ben.

He was sitting on a park bench when she came back up the street. His computer was open on the bench between them. She didn't see his phone.

"Did you get a wi-fi signal?"

"The library has a guest network. The password is 'guest.' I got it on my second try. 'Patron' was my first one."

"At least they had a password," she pointed out.

"A lot of people are way too careless about internet security."

Colleen hoped he never found out that she used the same password for everything. "Do you see yourself working with ordinary people who have clicked on a bad link or with big companies or the government?"

"Corporate and federal work can be the most interesting, but my dad and brother and my grandfather before them have always helped regular people." He shrugged. "I just wish I were better at it. I don't have the intuitive feel for it that other people do."

His intuition about snowboarding and how to teach it to others had been great. Colleen decided to jump in the deep end. Playing from her heart was one of her strengths; restraint wasn't. "So why don't you do what you are best at? Isn't that the best way to serve, by using your gifts to their fullest potential?"

"I assume you are talking about coaching. 'Service' seems like pretty church-y language to be using."

"Keeping children from getting injured and their parents from being exploited...maybe that is the service that you were meant to do."

"Maybe, but it's not an option open to me anymore. You must have heard about my big flame-out."

"But it was two years ago," she said. "Haven't people forgotten about it by now?"

"No, and I still believe it. I wouldn't want to work in any of those programs even if they would have me, which they won't."

"Don't you miss it?"

"Sure," he said easily. "Who doesn't miss some parts of being a kid? You're so thrilled to see your name in the standings that you don't care where you are."

He was talking about competing, not coaching. She had been asking about coaching. But he was talking about himself; she wasn't going to risk him shutting down. "The three of you did have wonderful times together."

"Yes, but that sort of 'no girls allowed' treehouse isn't much of a long-term strategy. Seth and Nate are both married now."

As her father and brothers were. "Do you feel abandoned because of that?"

"No, not at all—"

So they weren't in the same place about this. Colleen did feel abandoned by her family.

"—but remember, I went first. I was the first to truly fall in love and realize that that was better."

Colleen could never hide her feelings. He must have seen how astonished she was.

"You didn't think I was going to mention it, did you?" He was still speaking easily. "Maybe it is a form of penance. I could say a rosary every day for a month, or I could tell you that even if I did throw it away, what we had mattered." He glanced down at his computer screen. "Oh, it looks like I am done. Are you ready to go?"

She had no idea how she answered.

Had she given up too quickly on him? She had told all her friends about him not calling. Of course she had. That's what she did. They had all encouraged her to break up with him. *No one should treat you like that... You deserve better...*

She had kept making excuses for him. He was in the midst of competition season. That had to be all-consuming. And his steady stream of bronze medals and hearing himself labeled as "all technique, no passion, no style" had to be demoralizing.

When she got birthday cards from his two friends and not even a call from him, she had known it was time to give up. Then she had waited another month, hoping, not sleeping, then finally did what her friends had been urging.

Was it possible that this week would be a second chance?

* * * *

When she had declared that she would live here at the lake year-around, Colleen's grandmother had sensibly decided that she should start sleeping on the first floor. A bedroom and bathroom had been created in the large corner room on the opposite end of the house from the library.

Colleen stopped by the room to say good night. Even with the bathroom taking up part of the room, it was still big enough for a pair of love seats opposite the bed. Grannor was sitting in one of them. She waved a hand at the one across from her, and obediently Colleen sat down.

"I can't believe how much you've gotten done on the house since Christmas," Colleen said.

Grannor sighed and shook her head. "We had workmen in the house every day. One day we had five painters and four landscapers. We couldn't use the driveway for three days. And the deliveries, there were so many deliveries. It was difficult, beyond what you can imagine."

Colleen imagined that her grandmother had been only slightly inconvenienced by these labors.

"Now, child," her grandmother continued, "let's have a good gossip about these friends of yours. Have you ever thought about hinting to dear Amanda that she should not wear a knit top to dinner?"

"No, I haven't." And she never would.

This was one of Grannor's numerous Southern-belle commandments. Knits were for sports. As long as it had sleeves and a collar, of course you could wear a knit shirt to the tennis courts or golf course. But anywhere else? Absolutely not. "In my day," she sniffed, "we would never wear a sweater to a luncheon, much less in the evening. A nicely tailored jacket is so much more flattering on the female form."

Colleen had heard this before. "This is how people dress now."

"I know, and even I wore a sweater in the evening this winter. Oh well, let's talk about the Healy boy. He's always been the quiet one in that family. His mother was hoping he would become a priest."

"*What?*" Ben? A priest?

Certain of Colleen's memories did not correspond very well to the priesthood.

"I don't think there was much chance of that. Those Irish boys can be naughty, naughty, naughty, although the Healys, they all settled down just fine. Now, if you want my advice, child, you will make sure of him before someone else gets there first."

"I beg your pardon?" Colleen spoke stiffly.

"Don't get prissy with me, young lady. You can talk all you want about times having changed, but you can be sure that the Healys are thinking about it."

"Thinking about what?"

"About you. They must want you for one of their boys. You're a Ridge and a Catholic. Your mother and his talked about it when you all were in your cradles...although I suppose they were thinking about one of the other boys, as Ben was supposed to be a priest."

Colleen couldn't get her mind around the notion of Ben being a priest... or any of the rest of what Grannor was saying. She was just starting to like the idea of a second chance with him; actually she was starting to like the idea a lot. But "making sure of him"? Their mothers planning weddings?

"That was just talk about babies," she said, "what mothers sometimes do. I don't want to be disrespectful, Grannor, but people do *not* think that way anymore."

Her grandmother's laugh was almost a cackle. "Oh, my dear child, they do. They certainly do."

So this was what Grannor was up to. She wasn't trying to punish Colleen; she was trying to make a match between her and Ben. Apparently she had decided that at twenty-seven, Colleen was too decrepit to find a husband on her own.

Matchmaking seemed out of character. Surely Grannor was more likely to relish breaking people up than getting them together. In either case, she would be demonstrating power, and more than anything Grannor loved proving that she had power.

There probably was at least some goodwill behind the effort. Colleen knew that she was the one person whose happiness Grannor might actually care about. She was Grannor's favorite. Grannor talked with glee about how her own daughter, Colleen's aunt Laura, had "ruined herself" with all her divorces and affairs. If Cousin Kim hadn't been from a "good family," she would have been "trash." Grannor had disliked all three of her son Norton's wives. Her references to Colleen's father were needling, and she never spoke about Colleen's mother at all…probably because if you couldn't say something nasty about someone, there was no reason to speak at all.

* * * *

He had done it. At dinner, sitting across the table from her, she looking and smiling so exactly like he remembered her, he decided that the honorable— the gentlemanly—thing to do was admit that she had been important to him, not ask for her forgiveness, that was too much, but just let her know. He hadn't quite managed to tell her that she was the only woman he had ever loved, but he had gotten closer than he thought he would be able to.

Back at the house he decided to walk down to the lake. Jason and Amanda were in the library. The glasses and liquor bottles had been put away, and Colleen's two friends had pulled up chairs around the center table. Playing cards were spread out in front of them.

"Oh, Ben, come save me," Amanda called out. "Can you play bridge? Colleen and Jason can. Mrs. Ridge says she needs a fourth."

He was definitely going down to the lake now. "Sorry," he said, and then, trying to sound very Mrs. Ridge–like, "I'm sure you will enjoy learning."

She made a face at him.

That was the sort of thing Colleen would have done. No wonder they were friends.

He went out to the flagstone patio that spanned the back of the house and then crossed the sloping lawn to the lake. Two Adirondack chairs had been placed near the water's edge. He sat down.

So, what now?

She was still everything that he had once liked—once loved. She sparkled. That was the only word for it, sparkle. She was the sort of person who always wore costumes to a costume party, and she would seem to be having such a good time in whatever absurd getup she had rigged up for herself that after a while, even if you weren't the costume-type, even if you were *so* not the costume-type, you started to regret that you hadn't worn one.

And to wonder why someone like her was with someone like you.

She wasn't perfect. She would have worn a costume because she didn't want to hurt someone's feelings. She was always worrying about other people's feelings. That was fine in small doses, but she could never say no to anyone in case she might hurt their feelings.

She also never did anything alone. Everyone loved her and would want to be included in whatever plans she was making. It was exhausting, this being with other people all the time. He wasn't insensitive. He wasn't a hermit. He liked people...just not all of them all the time. When his high-spirited family got together, there were always three people talking at once with everyone else breaking in and interrupting them. Whom were you supposed to listen to when everyone was talking at once? Being a "people person"—that was high praise in his family. *People who love people* and all that. But sometimes he had to wonder—how could you call yourself a "people person" when you talked all the time? Wouldn't an individual who was genuinely interested in other people sometimes shut up and listen?

Colleen Ridge was a really great person, she was probably an amazing teacher—who wouldn't memorize French verbs to try to please her?—but they were completely wrong for each other. He would frustrate and disappoint her. She would drive him nuts. End of story. Whatever Mrs. Ridge had in mind by making her go into the village with him was not a good idea.

A faint trace of pink lingered above the tree line on the other side of the lake. As it disappeared, lights came on across the water, glowing pinpricks among the mass of trees. Some of the lights flickered; others were steady beacons. A number of the docks were already in. A few were outlined in light; the rest had a single lamp burning at the end.

A flutter of something pale caught his attention. He turned his head. It was Leilah, going to her apartment on the second floor of the boathouse. Her light-colored clothes were almost ghostly as she crossed the dimly lit lawn. He gripped the arms of the chair, preparing to stand up, but as she came closer, she held up a hand, stopping him. *Don't get up.*

He didn't.

She circled around to the staircase on the far side of the boathouse. In a minute, a light on the second floor flicked on, then a second one. Their glow spread out around the small building, turning the nearby grass a silvery green and outlining the pilings for the still dismantled dock. The windows became hard-edged slabs of empty light.

The Adirondack chairs had been set at a slight angle. Ben could watch the boathouse's two side windows as easily as he could watch the water. Leilah appeared first at one window, then the other, lifting her arm to close the curtains.

But the curtains were filmy. He could still see movement and shape. So he leaned back in the chair, his hands linked behind his head, watching her undress.

Sometimes it was easier to be a dick. And a whole lot safer.

Chapter 3

The back stairs were a narrow dark tunnel zigzagging from the little attic rooms on the third floor down to the kitchen. One summer Colleen's older brother Sean wasn't allowed to go into the lake for three days because he had told Colleen and Finn a story about the stairs. It had so terrified them that they couldn't go up to their bedrooms at night. He had also had to write each of them a letter of apology. When her father and Mrs. Sisson had moved, Colleen had found hers. If she had had to choose between that letter and any of her grandmother's valuable silver, she would have held on to the letter.

Your big brother scaring the socks off you was part of a family summer.

That's what brothers did. They cheered when you won the spelling bee; they came and picked you up when you went to the wrong party; they told you scary stories…and then they got married and cared more about their wives than you.

Which was right, of course it was. Colleen wouldn't have it any other way. She shouldn't have even been thinking about it. Families changed.

As did sleeping arrangements. Did she really miss staying in a room where half the drawers were full of clothes belonging to people she had never met? Was she sorry that the closet in her room didn't smell musty, that she didn't have to hang up her clothes on a mismatched tangle of wire hangers?

That was a lot to be said for bedside lamps that worked, for a new mattress with an expensive pad. It was fun to look through the little basket of toiletries; there were individually wrapped toothbrushes and products scented with lavender just as Grannor's bedroom in Georgia had been.

So what if it seemed like a luxury bed-and-breakfast? Was that really so bad?

She was astonished at how late it was when she woke up. She remembered waking up at her usual time, glancing at the clock—there had never been clocks in the bedrooms before—and snuggling back into the deep memory foam of the mattress pad. She must have gone back to sleep. It was almost nine o'clock.

She dressed leisurely, enjoying the clear Carolina blue of the sky. As she was coming down the wide front stairs, the scent of the lilies in the flower arrangement drifting up to her, she heard voices in the dining room, Ben's and Leilah's.

Ben was standing on a battered metal stepstool, reaching into the back of a china cabinet. A moss-and-buff tattersall check shirt rippled along his torso and was threatening to come untucked from his jeans and broad leather belt. Leilah, in a long butter-colored skirt, was next to him, her hands up, waiting to receive what he would hand to her. On the dining room table was a little colony of oddly shaped drawstring bags made of dark tarnish-proof felt. Ben's laptop was open next to a neat stack of papers.

"Let me get some coffee," Colleen said quickly, "and I will come help."

Ben bent to hand Leilah a long flat object, its tarnish-proof bag drooping from its hard rectangular shape. It must be a tray. Leilah took it and after finding a place for it on the table, brushed a wrinkle out of her skirt. Only then did she answer Colleen. "It's good of you to offer, but my instructions are clear. I am to work with Ben and no one else. The breakfast service is set up in the library. Would you mind helping yourself?"

"No, of course not."

Jason and Amanda were in the library. Amanda, red pencil in hand, was grading papers; their school was traditional enough to have students submit some of their work on actual paper. Jason had a pile of letters printed on University of Virginia stationery. He was adding a handwritten note to the bottom of each. Colleen supposed that fund-raising professionals did a lot of that sort of thing.

"We did offer to help in the dining room," Amanda said, "but Leilah said no."

"Is the inventory for your grandmother's will?" Jason asked.

"Probably," Colleen answered. "But I really don't know. I suppose it could be for insurance."

"Do you know what's in the will?"

Colleen was surprised. That seemed like a tacky question.

"I'm sorry," he apologized quickly. "I am a development officer. We don't like it when there are surprises in people's wills."

Colleen could see that. How messy it would be if people thought that they were going to inherit a bundle only to find out that it was all going to charity.

She looked down at the silver coffeepot in her hand, its handle warm from the heat of its little oil-fueled silver lamp. Covered with deep repousse Baroque decoration, it belonged to an elaborate service that Grannor had always used at holidays. In addition to the heavy tray, coffee- and teapots, creamer, and sugar dish, the service also had the warming lamp, a lidded butter dish, and a spoon jar, all of it sterling, its total value probably equivalent to the down payment on a starter home in the better part of town.

It was traditionally passed from grandmother to granddaughter. Grannor had gotten it from Colleen's great-great-grandmother, and the first owner had been Colleen's six-times-great-grandmother. It was as old as the nation itself and had been buried in an apple orchard during the Civil War.

Would it go to Colleen or to her cousin Kim? Kim was older, but Grannor didn't think all that much of Kim or, for that matter, Kim's mother, Grannor's only daughter, Laura. Colleen would have liked this set for its history, but in truth, some of the other family tea services were more to her taste…not that her current high-school-teacher lifestyle needed a sterling tea service very urgently, even if it had survived Sherman's March to the Sea.

"I assume," she told Jason, "that except for a few specific things, she will leave everything equally to her three children—my father, my aunt, and my uncle."

"It's also possible," Jason said, "that she's skipping them and leaving everything to your generation. Do you have first cousins?"

Colleen nodded. "My uncle has two sons from his first marriage. We don't know them very well because they grew up in California with their mother and stepfather. My aunt has one daughter, and I have my two brothers."

"So it makes a big difference if the distribution is *per stirpes* or *per capita*."

"I have no idea what you are talking about."

"If your grandmother leaves her property equally to her three children," he explained, "then eventually, assuming that they don't spend it all—"

"Which is a big assumption," Colleen pointed out. "My aunt is a spender, and my uncle is on his third marriage. My dad is the most stable one of the lot. He probably won't touch much of Grannor's money. He made enough on his own." Her father was a dentist, and his practice had been successful. "He didn't share a lot of his parents' attitudes. That's why he left Georgia."

"Then whatever happens to your aunt and uncle's share," Jason said, "you and your brothers are likely to eventually inherit one-ninth of the estate."

"My dad is sixty-one. I hope I won't be inheriting anything for a very long time."

"Some people do skip a generation." Jason was interested in this. "If your grandmother leaves assets to her six grandchildren *per capita*, each would get a sixth, but if she wants to preserve the original ratio, she can leave it *per stirpes*, and you and your brothers would get one-ninth, and your aunt's daughter would get one-third."

Kim would like that. "Is this what development officers have to know about?" Colleen asked.

"Yes. My boss is working with a lady who doesn't understand her own will," he answered.

"I'm sure that my grandmother understands every word of hers."

"But how does any of this explain why Colleen can't help count the forks?" Amanda asked.

No one could answer that.

* * * *

Colleen and Amanda had pledged to each other that they would have their grading done by Sunday night so that they could enjoy the rest of the week. Amanda had her stack of research papers to read; Colleen had translations for two of her French classes and exams for the Latin students. She joined Amanda at the library table, and together they begin the ascent up Mount Grademore.

Colleen started with the translations, as she found them the most discouraging to grade. The students understood the French well enough, but their ear for fluent English diction had apparently been eaten alive by their cell phones, and they punctuated sentences according to fleeting wisps of random inspiration.

Grannor came in to say "good morning" and then went into the dining room. Although she would never admit to having any hearing loss whatsoever—hearing aids were for old people—Ben and Leilah both raised their voices. Colleen could hear the conversation. Grannor was helping them reconcile the paper inventory with the actual items. They were dividing things into "Group A" and "Group B." Colleen had no idea what that was about, but more things were going into Group A.

Taking a break from grading, Colleen peeked into the dining room. Grannor was sitting at the head of the table. Ben would hand her a silver piece. Grannor would announce what it was and whether it belonged to Group A or Group B. Leilah found the listing on the inventory and then checked it off. Ben put the things from Group A on the table. The Group B items were on the sideboard.

There were many more pieces on the table; Group A was much larger. A number of the Group B pieces had clean mid-century lines—mid-twentieth-century—but beyond that, Colleen couldn't figure out why which things were in which group.

With Grannor's permission, Leilah served lunch in the library, but Grannor expected the evening meal to be in the dining room. Ben, instead of joining the others for cocktails, helped Leilah clear off the dining room table and lay out the place settings. When Leilah was ready to serve, Grannor swept into the dining room, Colleen, Amanda, and Jason following her like obedient ducklings.

"Whatever people say about me," Grannor announced, "I do keep up with the times. Jason, Ben, if you boys trade places, then dear Amanda can sit next to her beau."

Colleen forced herself not to look at Amanda, who was undoubtedly also struggling not to laugh at the idea of having a "beau." By the time she was sure of her composure, her grandmother was seated, and Ben was standing next to Colleen herself. He had pulled out her chair and was waiting for her to sit down.

That summer they had been together, he had never made a big show of the manners he had learned growing up down South. He didn't stand up when she came into a room; he didn't make a thing about walking on the outside of the sidewalk. That would have felt tedious and embarrassing, out of place in the snowboarding world. But there had been little things. If she came in to lunch late, he would hook his foot under the rung of a chair, pulling it forward to her. When he was ready to leave a bar, he would get off the bar stool and stretch, his shoulder blades contracting, his chest opening, then he would reach out his hand for her, a silent announcement that he was not leaving without her.

He might not have been great with words, but his body had spoken for him. *You matter. You are special.*

And that body, the effortless strength, the unending stamina, the lithe flexibility. No other man had ever been built like Ben had been.

The Ridges had always used their beautiful things. Some of the porcelain plates had chips along the rims; some of the handles of the teacups had veins of yellowing glue. The sterling platters had little scratches cross-hatching the gleaming silver, and the Old Sheffield plated pieces had softened to a warm golden as generations of polishing had worn the layer of silver so that the copper glowed through. Colleen had been taught that this made them more beautiful than anything shiny and new.

Would a second chance be like that? More rich and glowing because it wasn't new?

As a first course, Leilah served a smoked fish mousse with toast points, the sort of dish that had been elegant when Grannor was first married.

"How is the inventory going?" Amanda asked Ben.

"Surprisingly well," he answered. "We're halfway through with what I now know to call hollowware. Then we are on to the flatware—the knives and the forks—which are apparently all a jumble. The art stored upstairs shouldn't take long. My father had the movers take pictures before they crated it. I don't know about the carpets."

"They are rugs, Ben dear, not carpets," Grannor reproved. "And you can't blame me for the flatware mess. I used the Burchell family sterling—we had Francis I—and I kept my grandmother's separate from my mother's. My husband's aunts put all that Whiting Lily in the same chest. You're going to have to look at the monograms to get it all straight."

"Is that how it works?" Amanda asked. "That a family has one silver pattern, and a bride doesn't get to pick her own?"

"It is a very good system. When I got married, my great-aunt was no longer giving large dinners, so she gave me six place settings. They were enough for a few years, as I could always borrow from my mother. Then, just when I really did need more, I got my grandmother's and the rest of my great-aunt's, and no one ever had to buy anything new." She said the word "new" as if it had an odor. "But it's not like that anymore. Colleen's sisters-in-law, Patricia and Elizabeth, chose their own patterns."

"Why do you have your husband's family's silver?" Amanda asked. "Didn't his aunts have their own children?"

"None that survived. Between couples who didn't have children and the only sons who got themselves killed in the wars, it's one spindly family tree on both sides. So girls would marry, get their own hollowware, take some of the family pieces, but when they died without heirs, it would all come back. And their jewelry too. I've got a little tin box with three diamond engagement rings. There used to be a piece of paper somewhere that says whom they belonged to. I suppose my grandsons William and Jeffrey should each get one if they ever get around to finding the right girl…although since they live in California, who knows what they will bring home?"

Colleen decided not to speculate about who was being slurred by that reference to California. But why had Grannor only mentioned giving the rings to Will and Jeff? Sean and Finn had bought Patty's and Liz's rings themselves. Grannor had been the one to tell the two brides to select new flatware patterns; she had given each of them twelve place settings of sterling. It had been an exceptionally generous gift, but Colleen imagined that Patty and Liz both would have been happier with new kitchen appliances. Why hadn't Grannor given them some of the family silver? God knows there was enough to go around. Why make this distinction between her cousins and her brothers? Grannor hardly ever saw Will and Jeff, while she had seen Colleen and her brothers for a week each spring and for two weeks in the summer. Furthermore, once Sean and Finn had gotten serious about Patty and Liz, they had each dragged their future fiancées down to Georgia for a painful weekend at the old family mansion. They weren't as attentive as Colleen, but they were certainly much more so than the other three grandchildren.

So, what was the reason? Maybe it was that Grannor saw so little of Will and Jeff that she had nothing to disapprove of. The only other reason Grannor could be saving the family diamonds for Will and Jeff—and this made no sense; it was flat-out crazy—was because Colleen and her brothers were adopted.

When Ned and Mary Pat, Colleen's parents, had finally acknowledged that they needed to adopt if they were going to have children, they had registered with agencies whose waiting lists were discouragingly long. Mary Pat's mother, Colleen's Grammy O'Connell, hating to see her daughter so unhappy, had prayed for her every day…and had called parish after parish and then each one again until she found the Bannings, a nearby family with a daughter "in trouble." The family had had two conditions for a privately arranged adoption, that the child be raised Catholic and that there be some contact. That child became Sean, Colleen's older brother.

Then a year and a half later, the Bannings had called Ned and Mary Pat. Their second daughter had not learned from her older sister's mistake. There would be another baby; did Mary Pat and Ned want that one? Of course they did. So biologically Colleen's brothers were first cousins. With open adoptions, they had their birth parents' medical histories; they knew their much younger biological half-siblings. Whenever Mary Pat took her children to see her family in St. Paul, they also visited the Bannings.

The Bannings were Irish-American, just as the O'Connells. Even though neither Sean nor Finn had facial features resembling Mary Pat's, they looked as if they could be her offspring. She was Irish; they were Irish. They were from the same gene pool.

When the Bannings called about the baby who would become Finn, Ned and Mary Pat had already made contact with a lawyer. He was representing another family whose daughter was due to deliver in a few weeks, six months before the Banning girl. Ned and Mary Pat decided to take both babies. That was why Colleen was only six months older than her younger brother, why they called each other "almost twins."

But the adoptions were different. Colleen's was as closed as possible. All she knew was that she had been born "somewhere in the South," that her parents had gone to Georgia to pick her up, and that a priest had brought her to them at her grandparents' house. The one condition her birth family had placed on her adoption had been that no one ever attempt to make contact. Ever.

In sixth grade, Colleen started to learn French, and she had instantly been sure that she must be French. The language came so easily to her; it felt so natural in her mouth. But a year later her mother got a new cleaning lady whose first language was Spanish, and Colleen discovered that she could learn Spanish just as easily. When the high school foreign-exchange program sent her to Norway, she picked up Norwegian even though her host family spoke excellent English. She was good at learning languages. Once she heard a sound, she could repeat it perfectly and then never forgot it.

There was nothing about her that suggested a definite ethic origin. She didn't have the broad planes of a Scandinavian face nor the sturdy build of one of the Germanic tribes. She didn't have the etched cheekbones of the Slavs nor the olive skin tones of Mediterranean people. Her hair was between honey blond and golden brown, her eyes were hazel, her features were even. She was melting-pot American.

Whenever the willowy, ginger-haired Mary Pat was out with her two tall redheaded sons and her petite light-haired daughter, people would exclaim that Colleen must look like her father's side of the family. "Colleen looks exactly like herself," Mary Pat would always say, "and we wouldn't want it any other way."

It didn't matter that she was adopted. Or if it did matter, it only made her and her brothers more special. Grammy O'Connell had always said that the three of them were a gift from God. Grannor would never use that language, but surely she had to see that Colleen and her brothers were far more attentive grandchildren than Will, Jeff, or Kim.

Chapter 4

Ben was one of the few professional snowboarders to have a college degree, having cobbled together the credits from online courses and summer classes. When the other guys had grimaced at his books, he would blame his parents, saying it was important to them that all their kids had degrees. That was true, but he had really gotten his education for himself. He liked learning new things and was glad not to be completely clueless about differential calculus and the Boer War.

It didn't take a bachelor's degree, however, to see what Mrs. Ridge's game was. By Sunday noon it was clear that she was trying to fix him and Colleen up. What a shame. If the old lady cared about anyone, it would be Colleen, and here she was trying to arrange for a lifetime of frustration and disappointment.

We tried it, ma'am. We're too different. It won't work.

At least Colleen was awake to the scheme and able to outmaneuver her grandmother.

"Why, Grannor," she had said when Mrs. Ridge had suggested that the two of them go down to the lower level of the boathouse and check the boat before the dock was put in, "Jason grew up in Annapolis. He's been around boats his whole life. He'll know lots more than Ben or me."

Then Mrs. Ridge had asked Ben to take her winter coats upstairs. Colleen would show him where the cedar closet was. "Are you really suggesting," Colleen had said with a laugh in her voice, "that I can't carry three coats up one flight of stairs?"

Sometimes the old lady's moves weren't worth countering. On Monday he and Colleen worked quietly side by side, counting all the cards in each deck of aging playing cards, making sure that each one had fifty-two cards and two jokers. She had a pale-pink natural-looking polish on her fingernails. Four years ago she hadn't worn nail polish.

Mrs. Ridge asked them to take some old prints out of the frames. The frames were dusty. Colleen happened to touch her hand to her face. There was a smudge on her cheek. He wanted to wipe it off, but he didn't.

After a while it did seem pointless to pretend that they didn't both know exactly what was going on.

"Why is your grandmother doing this?" he asked as they were doing yet another invented chore. "You must be able to get your own boyfriends." Surely all she would have to do would be to walk into a bar and smile.

"I manage," she admitted. "But apparently my grandmother thinks that at twenty-seven, I am over the hill. She was married at nineteen."

"But guys must have proposed."

"Actually, no. Whenever I sense anything close to that might be on the horizon, I head them off. I don't want to make someone hear a no."

Who were they? He suddenly wanted to know. *Were they good enough for you? Could they have made you happy?*

But was that any of his business? He had already declared himself not good enough for her, unable to make her happy. He needed to shut up and count cards and dust picture frames.

* * * *

Although it took a day longer than they had hoped, Colleen and Amanda had conquered Mount Grademore by Monday evening. They would have been finished by noon, but once the dock was in, they took long breaks to go out and check their email and texts.

After lunch on Tuesday, Grannor decided that Jason and Colleen should take her out in the boat. The afternoon was warmer than they had expected, and Grannor asked Colleen to run back into the house and get her a lighter jacket.

"Why didn't she just unbutton the one she was wearing?" Amanda asked as she helped Colleen look through the front hall closet.

"Because she doesn't have to." Colleen had decided that because she was resisting her grandmother on her matchmaking schemes, she would give in on the other requests, no matter how irrational.

"Maybe she wants to talk to Jason behind your back."

"No doubt," Colleen agreed. "But if he tells you anything, don't tell me. I don't want to know." She did enough for her grandmother. She wasn't going to be bullied into changing her shirt, her nail polish, her accent, her manners, or whatever else Grannor was disapproving of today.

She draped the coat over her arm and paused to look in the dining room. Ben was alone, sitting at one end of the table, a large piece of green felt unrolled in front of him. It was covered with little stacks of silver flatware. A gooseneck reading lamp was plugged into an extension cord, and he had tilted the brass apothecary shade so the light pooled on the green felt. He was looking through a magnifying glass at the handle of a cake fork.

"Are you having to do that for every piece?" she asked.

"Yes, but don't ask me why." He had set down the fork as he spoke, and as if he was suddenly noticing that the room had grown warm, he unbuttoned the cuff of his left sleeve, turning it back over and over on itself until it was up to his elbow. The light from the reading lamp reflected against the narrow gold lines on the case of his watch.

She had not seen this watch before. It was elegant, having a black alligator strap and a gold case; the face was white with slim black Roman numerals. A gold second hand swept around a small circle inset near the "VI." Snowboarders didn't wear watches like this. She couldn't imagine Ben buying such a watch for himself even though he had plenty of money. And it didn't look new. The strap was, but the gold had a rich matte patina that comes with age and use.

"That's a nice watch," she said.

He had been rolling up his other sleeve. He stopped and glanced down at his left wrist. "It belonged to Judge Rutherford. I was named after him. I inherited it when he died."

"Judge Benjamin Rutherford?"

"Yes. I use 'Ben' on everything because marketing people said that 'Benjamin R.' sounded too stodgy for the cool dude I was supposed to be, but the judge was one of my grandfather's oldest friends."

"He signed my adoption papers."

"The judge did? I didn't know that." Ben picked up another fork. "It makes sense. If my grandfather or father helped with the paperwork, they would have taken it to Judge Rutherford."

He tilted the handle of the fork to the light to see the monogram, going back to work as if there was no big deal.

But it was. He had been named after the man who had signed the papers making her herself, Colleen Marie Ridge. In fact, when the judge had signed the papers, he might have been wearing the very watch Ben was wearing right now.

She knew that she could be sentimental, but she loved the idea that this was a sign that they were supposed to be together. This watch was on its second owner; it was having its second chance. Why couldn't they?

The door to the kitchen swung open, spreading natural light into the room. Leilah came in, carrying a stack of photographs. Colleen knew that there was no printer in the house. Leilah must have gone out to the boathouse to use her own.

"Your grandmother was wondering where you were," she said to Colleen and then put the pictures in front of Ben, leaning so close to him that her breast almost brushed his shoulder.

Colleen froze. Leilah? Leilah and Ben?

There was something compelling, even erotic, about Leilah's controlled elegance. When she moved, her clothes floated with liquid grace; when she was still, they draped about her in a marble statue's graceful folds. She carried herself with self-possession and mystery, elegance and control. She was the White Goddess, alluring and dangerous.

She was a force out of Jungian myth, and she made Colleen feel trivial, a force out of *Pat the Bunny*.

* * * *

The deep sleep that had embraced her each night in this luxurious room had abandoned her. She was restless, turning off her light when she thought she was ready to sleep, then having to turn it back on ten minutes later. At 4 a.m. she woke up with her light on and her book open on the pillow. She turned off the light, but then couldn't go back to sleep. With the light still off, she got up and went out on the balcony.

Charcoal clouds hung low in the night sky, and the dank-smelling fog was heavy. Even the light at the end of their dock was blurred, and those across the lake were nothing more than yellow smudges against the single black mass that the lake and trees had become.

A light came on in the second floor of the boathouse. Colleen was surprised. Leilah did not come over to the main house until six. Why would she get up so early? A few minutes later a figure emerged. It wasn't Leilah.

It was Ben. His broad shoulders, his easy walk…Ben.

Colleen jerked back, pressing herself against the cedar shingles. No, *no*. Ben and Leilah together…in the dark, in bed…her hair spread across a pillow, his hands on either side of her naked body…the two of them together.

The wall was hard against the back of her head, the shingles rough against her arms. She couldn't move.

What we had mattered. He had said that. Didn't it matter anymore?

Had Leilah laced her fingers through his thick hair to guide him, to show him what she wanted?

Air sat heavily in the base of her lungs, strangling her. The fog from the lake must have surged up to the balcony in some kind of nightmare wave. It was a heavy, choking, poisonous fog; she couldn't see, she couldn't breathe.

Had they undressed each other? Colleen remembered watching his long fingers working the buttons of her blouse. What of his would she have taken off first? His shirt?

Or the watch. Leilah would have taken his hand and turned it over, slipping her fingers under the wide band and tugging at the strap, freeing it from the prong. Colleen was imagining herself doing that.

I wanted us to have a second chance. But he must not have. This hurt. It hurt so much.

What about all the connections? Judge Rutherford's watch, their mothers wanting her to marry a Healy...didn't that mean something?

If it did, it wasn't something that he wanted. He hadn't wanted it four years ago; he didn't want it now.

Why, Ben, why?

* * * *

Leilah had smiled that little smile of hers and brushed his hand away. She was not going to let him take her nightgown off. He could ease the delicate strap off her shoulder, exposing her breast. He could run his hands up her thighs, the silk of the gown riding up along his forearms. But the nightgown stayed on.

"I won't lock the boathouse door," she had said to him Sunday afternoon. She was mysterious and seductive, but not coy.

She had already been in her floaty nightgown when he had come that first night, and the sex had been focused but leisurely. She had been on top, and after he was finished, she had slipped her hand between her legs, her orgasm accompanied only by a flutter of her eyelashes and a slight jerk in her torso.

The second night she did have a bottle of wine opened, and they sat out on the balcony, saying only a word or two about the moon. He knew very little more about her than he had when first shaking her hand Friday afternoon.

* * * *

"So you've been jilted."

"*Gran!*" Colleen was so shocked she couldn't get out more than the one syllable. How did Grannor know? Colleen had not said anything to anyone about what she had seen before sunrise. It was unlike her not to instantly tell all her friends everything, but she had known what would have happened if she had told Amanda. Amanda would have been so outraged on Colleen's behalf, attacking Ben so harshly that Colleen would have felt compelled to defend him. That's what had happened with her other friends four years ago.

"I suppose you aren't used to that, a pretty thing like you."

"Ben did not jilt me. We were not a couple."

Grannor's laugh was almost a crackle. "Is that what they call it now, 'being a couple'? I don't imagine that he plans on marrying her."

Marry? "He hasn't even known her for a week."

"I hope you have a plan. If you want him, you'll have to fight for him."

It was after lunch on Wednesday. Colleen and Grannor were supposedly going on a short walk, but her grandmother had gone directly to the Adirondack chairs angled away from the shore line. Colleen waited until her grandmother was settled in one. "I'm not willing to think about relationships in such combative terms."

"Don't think big words can change anything, missy," Grannor scoffed. "I told you that you needed to act quickly, and now you see what happened when you didn't. I imagine the Healys are going to be none too pleased when they hear about this."

What about me? Don't you care about how I feel?

No, probably not. Any normal grandmotherly concern was entrenched behind Grannor's prickly fortress. Colleen had thwarted her. Colleen hadn't taken her advice. Colleen was now another exhibit in Grannor's museum of grimly gleeful "I told you so."

Why do I put up with her?

Colleen knew the answer to that. *Because she needs me.* Her maternal grandmother, her mother's mother, was easy to love, easy to be with, but having had eight children of her own, Grammy O'Connell had many granddaughters, five of whom lived near her in St. Paul. But whom did Eleanor Ridge have? She, Laura, Kim, and Norton's wife all brought out the worst in each other. Colleen was the only one who could deal with each of them without turning into—her mother wouldn't like her saying this, but the phrase fit—a white-hot Southern bitch.

Her grandmother was a bigot and a snob. She was arrogant. She had no interest in other people's opinions. But Colleen did have good memories. Sometimes, when her mother and brothers were escaping to the familiar carnival of the Healys' home, Colleen would stay in Carlsville with her grandmother. Together they would go through the china closets and select what dishes to use at dinner. Then they would go into Grannor's shaded, lavender-scented bedroom with the high four-poster mahogany bed. Grannor would take out her jewelry and let Colleen play with it. The fox-head brooch with its glittery diamond eyes scared her, but she loved the rest of it, looping pearls around her neck, topping them with a garnet necklace and a set of lapis lazuli beads, turning herself into a Christmas tree. She would cover her arms with heavy bracelets, cloisonné cuffs, silver bangles, and gold charm bracelets. She would have to spread her fingers wide to keep the bracelets from slipping off her narrow wrists.

As a child, Colleen had loved her grandmother; as an adult she felt sorry for her. But if Grannor was going to be nasty about Ben, that would be nearly unforgivable.

* * * *

The punishment for not following Grannor's advice started on Thursday evening. The inventory was almost complete. A lid to a chafing dish, a sterling water pitcher, and a few stray pieces of flatware could not be found. Only two of the sets of china were completely intact, but Grannor said that some of those pieces had been broken even before she herself had been born.

As usual, Colleen went into her grandmother's room after dinner.

"That young man of yours—"

"If you are referring to Ben," Colleen interrupted—and no one ever interrupted Mrs. Norton W. Ridge IV—"he is not *my* young man."

Grannor ignored her. "That class he has been working on, whatever it is that he went into the village for Friday night, he said that he didn't have to actually sit in a classroom."

"A lot of instruction happens that way now."

Grannor was shaking her head as if online classes were yet another way that the world was going to hell in a golf cart. "Tell him he can stay on to do it here after you all leave. He can have dinner with me and keep me company, at least until the bridge ladies return."

"Wait. You want him to stay here?"

"Yes. We should invite him to stay here while he works on that. He doesn't have other plans, does he?"

"You want him to stay on here? At the lake?" *With Leilah?*

"Isn't that what I just said?"

"But he can't work here," Colleen countered. "He needs an internet connection."

"He has managed so far, hasn't he? Leilah says that she gets some kind of dial tone in the boathouse. That's why he hasn't had to go back to the village."

"Leilah can get a cell signal?"

"Signal, dial tone, it's all the same, isn't it? Leilah says that it isn't, and she is making a plan to bring some kind of wire into the house. It seemed like nonsense to me, but I told her to do what she likes. You should also tell him that he can clear his comings and goings with her."

Nonsense wires and Colleen telling Ben something? What was happening here? "Are you saying that it's all right for Ben to stay in the boathouse?"

"My dear child, what would ever make you think that I would dream of intruding on such a private matter?"

Only every breath that you have ever taken. "Then shouldn't Leilah have some say in this?"

"The invitation needs to come from the family, honey lamb. You should know that."

"Then shouldn't it come from you? Why bring me into it?"

"But it is from me. I'm merely asking you to deliver it."

Why? "Is this some kind of test, Grannor? To see if I can hold up my head, act like a Ridge?"

"And if it is?"

Then figure out a better one. A poorly designed test enraged the students and then was impossible to grade. Colleen had learned that her first year in teaching.

But whatever the test, Colleen liked getting As.

Jason and Amanda said that Ben had gone to the second floor to inventory what was stored there. Colleen could hear Leilah working in the kitchen, so she went up to her grandparents' old bedroom at the far end of the second floor. It was being used as storage for the bulkier items that Grannor had brought up from Georgia.

Ben was sitting on one of the rolled-up carpets, a pile of crumpled newspapers at his feet. He was unwrapping Royal Doulton toby jugs, pottery vessels fashioned in the likeness of the heads of famous personages—pirates, presidents, Henry VII's six wives, the Three Musketeers. There were ten or so already lined up. Colleen hadn't known that her family had them. They were ugly. She hated them.

The one he was unwrapping was a woman wearing a white Tudor-era headdress. A brown stick-thing was leaning against her head forming the jug's handle. It was an axe. This must be Anne Boleyn. Oh, lovely.

She should look on the bright side; she liked looking on the bright side. Ben might not want her, but at least he couldn't chop off her head. How was that for sunny optimism?

"I have a message from my grandmother. She really does appreciate how much time you've spent on these inventories."

That was a lie. Grannor was gracious when people did things for her. Her manners were appreciative, but actual appreciation, awareness of what sacrifices had been made on her behalf...no, Eleanor Ridge took other people's helpfulness for granted.

So why was Colleen lying? She didn't like to lie. She hated it. And why, of all people, was she lying to him?

Because I don't want you to know how much you hurt me. Not ever.

She knew that she had the world's worst poker face. She could never hide how she felt. Her brothers used to tell her that they won card games because they were so good at calculating odds. Finally her mother had told her that she either needed to quit playing with them or stop squirming every time she pulled a good hand. She hadn't done either one. She had gone on playing, squirming, and losing. She hadn't minded losing.

She minded now. She was losing now.

"It was no trouble," he said.

Now he was lying too. Of course it had been trouble.

"She says that you are very welcome to stay while you work on your degree." Colleen rushed her words. She needed to get it out.

"What?" Clearly he had not expected this. "Stay here? I would not want to impose on her."

"You don't have to worry about that. My grandmother only lets people impose on her when she wants to have something to get outraged about." That, at least, was the truth.

Ben was standing now. Colleen didn't remember him getting up. She used to find his posture sexy. His collarbone held his shoulders broad and straight; his hips were trim and tucked. Now it made him seem aloof, like the sort of guy who stopped returning your calls or didn't remember your birthday.

"She is being very generous," he said. "I will think about it."

This was the right place to end the conversation. Yes, she had told a white lie, but she hadn't gotten weepy or whiny. It was time to stop.

Except she wanted to punish him. She wanted to make him pay for what he had done. *I know,* she wanted to say. So much for having a poker face. *I know about you and her. I saw you on the lawn. I heard your footsteps in the hallway.*

"So she says," she continued, her voice as even as before, "you can clear your comings and goings with Leilah." *I know.*

She wanted him to suffer. She wanted him to feel guilty.

And what exactly would that accomplish? It wouldn't make her feel any better, and this wasn't about her. It was about her grandmother. Grannor would never admit it, but she had made a mistake coming here during the off season. "Grannor's lonely, Ben. She doesn't care what you do with the rest of your time. She wants someone to have dinner with."

"I'm not good at chitchat. You know that."

"Then don't chitchat. If you can get her off that gossipy, bitchy thing, she's an interesting woman. I suppose you'll have to talk to Leilah, but please think about it. Please."

Was she begging again? Pushing him, pressuring him? Well, maybe. But how could it be wrong to ask someone to help a lonely old woman?

Chapter 5

As soon as school started again, Colleen got two pieces of disappointing news. She and Amanda had applied for a grant to develop a high school foreign-language curriculum for the kinetic learners, the athletic kids, drawing on the research done for the primary grades. The committee praised their application, but the three anticipated grants had been cut to one. Colleen and Amanda didn't get it.

On top of that, her summer plans fell through. She was supposed to spend a month touring Singapore, Australia, and New Zealand with a group of Norwegians, then traveling on her own for another three weeks, but the organizers of the Norwegian tour decided that there were enough young people in the group that they didn't need an interpreter.

She never relied on her summer income to pay her regular bills. She saved that money, half in her retirement account, half in her travel fund. Subletting her apartment provided even more money for those two savings accounts.

Not only did losing the summer gig make it impossible to reach her savings goal for the year, but it also meant that she would need a place to live. She approached the couple who were going to sublet her apartment. Oh, yes, they were still coming to Charlottesville for a summer program and were so looking forward to living at her place. Colleen didn't push them. She wasn't the sort of person who made awkward requests of others.

She could go to Chicago and live rent-free with her father and his second wife, but Genevieve would try so hard to make Colleen feel welcome that it would exhaust both of them.

Grannor, on the other hand, wouldn't do a thing beyond telling Leilah to set another place at the table. Colleen would go there. Surely Ben would be gone by then. Once the other summer residents returned, Grannor was likely to start hinting that his time was up. But when Colleen turned in her students' final grades on a Thursday afternoon, he was still squatting in the boathouse, having dinner with Grannor every night that she didn't have other plans.

He couldn't be staying because he enjoyed those evenings. Leilah must be like the sirens in the *Odyssey,* the beautiful, mythic creatures whose irresistible songs lured sailors into drowning themselves.

Grannor seemed pleased at the idea of Colleen coming for the summer. In fact, she encouraged her to bring friends. "I like having young people about, and you teachers aren't busy in the summers, are you?"

How little Grannor knew of the real world. Colleen didn't have student loans, but most of her friends did. They had to work in the summer. Amanda was the assistant manager of the athletic camp that used the school's facilities. Other friends taught in various summer schools. But the Fourth of July would be a long weekend this year, so Colleen was able to invite a few people to come to the lake.

The weeks passed. Colleen proctored the AP exams; Ben was still at the lake. She wrote her own final exams; he was still there. As she calculated the final grades, she was resigned to the notion that he was going to be there. With Leilah.

She celebrated the end of the school year with her friends Thursday evening and the next morning finished packing and organizing her apartment for her renters. Her phone went off continually. People were hoping that she would stay for the weekend. Some wanted her to change her mind and come to their parties. Other people who, being incapable of making social plans for themselves, were calling to hint that if she was doing something, maybe she could invite them to come along.

Being the person whom everyone liked took a lot of time.

She was trying to close her extra suitcase when the phone went off again. *Dum...dum...*her breath caught.

It was the Olympic fanfare. That had been Ben's ringtone. Four years ago he had jokingly programmed it into her phone, saying that he might as well be her Olympian since he would never be America's. But that had been four years ago. She had upgraded her phone at least twice. The data must have transferred automatically. Her phone, pathetic little creature, had never lost hope that he would call.

"Ben?"

"Where are you? Are you still at school?"

"Yes."

"I'm glad I caught you so you don't have to backtrack. Your grandmother's had an episode of some sort, and we are at the hospital in Staunton."

The hospital? "What do you mean an 'episode'? Is she okay? What happened?"

Grannor would hate being in the hospital. She had bragged that she hadn't been admitted since the birth of her youngest child sixty years ago.

"She's still in with the doctors so I can't tell you much." Both he and Leilah had been with her when it happened, he said, and by the time the ambulance arrived, she was conscious again. "You should come straight to the hospital. You were planning on coming today, weren't you?"

"Yes, yes…Of course, I'll come straight there." Colleen looked around frantically. How much did she have left to do?

"She seems stable," Ben was saying. "There's no reason to drive like a crazy person."

"I won't."

Staunton was on the east side of the Blue Ridge Mountains about forty miles from Charlottesville. Colleen's phone continued chirping as she drove west on interstate 64, but driving was one of the few times she ignored phone calls. She did pick up when she heard the children's song "Brush Your Teeth."

"Hi, Dad. I'm in the car so I've got you on speaker."

"Then I'll be quick. You shouldn't talk on the phone while driving. You're going directly to the hospital?"

So he had heard about Grannor. "How did you find out?"

"Ben Healy called. I'm on my way to the airport now."

"You're coming? Right now?" Things must be worse than Ben had told her.

"Genevieve is out west with her son's family, but your brothers will probably get in Saturday morning."

"Sean and Finn? They're coming?" This must be really serious. Colleen had been about to move around a slow-moving horse trailer, but decided not to. Now was not the time to get fancy with the driving.

"I don't know exactly when they'll arrive, but don't you worry about that. You focus on driving carefully."

"Yes, Dad."

Her father didn't usually lecture her about road safety. He was upset.

This should have prepared her, but she almost didn't recognize the small, white-haired woman in the hospital bed, IV lines snaking into her arm, a nasal cannula feeding oxygen through her nose. Was she in the wrong room? No. The man rising up from the bedside chair, folding up his newspaper, was Ben.

Ben...*Ben*...For a moment she saw nothing else. The room, the world, swirled and dissolved, leaving only him. How incredible he looked, with those cheekbones and green eyes, that copper-black hair. Suddenly everything that had happened—Leilah, his footsteps in the dark hall, the awkward conversations—none of it mattered. He was here, waiting for her.

Except he wasn't waiting for her in the sense that she wanted him to be. He was simply waiting for someone to relieve him at Grannor's bedside.

Why, Ben, why? Everyone else likes me. Why don't you?

"I was hoping you'd get here before I had to leave," he said. "I knew that you wouldn't want her to be alone."

Colleen forced herself to look back at her grandmother. "She looks so old."

"She is eighty-six."

"Tell me what you know." She wanted to hear his voice.

He claimed not to have much news. He and Leilah had given her aspirin as soon as they could in case she had had a heart attack, but the doctors thought it was more likely that she had had a stroke. They would do more tests in the morning. Ben was afraid that he might have broken her sternum during CPR, but the ER people hadn't thought so.

"You had to do CPR?"

"Not for long and just chest compressions. It probably wasn't necessary, but when I couldn't get a pulse immediately, I started right away."

"You know CPR?" She wanted to keep talking to him.

"When you do any coaching, they want you to have it. My certification's probably not current, but whatever." He flicked his hand, dismissing any possible heroics. "I'd better shove off. I told your father I'd pick him up at the airport."

"I could have waited in Charlottesville for him." That was the closest big airport. Ben was having to go right back to where she had come from.

"I knew you'd want to be here. I don't mind. And that little cooler...it's got food for your dinner. Nothing fancy, just something from Subway."

"How nice of you."

"Leilah has a lot to do at the house, getting ready for people. Otherwise she would have brought you something better from the lake."

"This is fine. This is more than enough."

"There's tuna or turkey for you. Ham or Italian deli meats for your father."

"That's great, Ben. Really." *Are you having trouble leaving? Why? You didn't want me.* "It has been good of you to spend so much time with Grannor. She enjoyed it."

"You were right. She is an intelligent woman, and she actually enjoys having people disagree with her. She likes to argue."

"Most people are too afraid of her to do that, but you're used to doing things other people find scary."

He shrugged. "It comes with the job, at least with my old job." He turned his arm and looked down at his elegant watch. "I suppose I should be leaving."

"Yes."

"But the room's cold. I'll leave my sweatshirt."

He tried to hang it on the corner of the bed's footboard. It fell. Colleen bent to pick it up. When she stood up, he was standing with his hands in his pockets, still unable to leave. *This is where you belong. With me.* She dropped the sweatshirt on the chair and stepped forward. Putting a hand on his shoulder, she stood on her toes to kiss his cheek. His skin was rough against her lips; he hadn't shaved. "Thank you for everything."

For the briefest moment, she felt a warmth, a hand, at the small of her back. It was the lightest of touches.

"It was nothing," he said. "I was glad that I was there."

How nice he had been. Did he just feel sorry for her? She had seen it at parent-teacher conferences, the single mom and the happily remarried dad. The men were often very courteous to their ex-wives, deferential and solicitous…because they could afford to be. *I was a shit to you once, but now I am going to be nice because I'm happy and you're not.*

Colleen would rather have Ben not care at all than be nice because he was happy and thought that she wasn't.

Before the room could feel empty, a nurse came in. Colleen asked question after question. The nurse kept saying that the family would need to speak to the doctor, but clearly Colleen had been assuming too much from Ben's calm. This was indeed serious.

"Is she going to be impaired?" Grannor would loathe that.

"It is too early to answer that, but some patients do make remarkable strides during rehab."

Remarkable strides? Did that mean that Grannor had something remarkable to stride away from?

The room was bright with a harsh white light. After the nurse left, Colleen realized that she was cold. She had warmer clothes in the car. Should she go get them? No, Ben had left his sweatshirt for her. She had been sitting on it. She pulled it out from under her. It was a thick, soft cotton fleece, charcoal gray with a hood and a kangaroo pocket. She recognized the black and red Street Boards logo. That was the family company that his friend Seth was now helping to run. She pulled the shirt on over her head, scooping her hair free from the neck. The heavy fabric fell to the middle of her thighs. She could have worn it as a dress.

"You would *not* like seeing me in this," she said to her grandmother.

Over Grannor's left shoulder was a little forest of equipment mounted on chrome poles that sprouted from heavy wheeled bases. Green LCD lights flashed numbers that changed constantly, but their values varied only a little. Colleen assumed that a big change would bring people rushing in.

The chair was a padded vinyl recliner. The headrest was a little high for her. She reached behind her neck and rolled the hood of Ben's sweatshirt. It made a nice little pillow.

She felt cozy in the thick fleece, cozy and taken care of. People didn't usually think of her needing to be taken care of. It was nice.

Grannor had told her that she should have fought for him. What did that mean, fighting for someone? It wasn't like she could have drawn her sword and forced him to love her. You could fight for things to happen, but not for people to change how they felt.

Sweet, but fierce, little Grammy O'Connell had known that.

Colleen's mother had believed that God had put her on earth to raise her three children, these three and no others. Maybe that was true. If so, God had worked through her mother's mother. Grammy O'Connell had called parishes throughout central and southern Minnesota, up into the Iron Range, and across the borders into Wisconsin and Iowa. Grammy had fought to make sure her daughter had children to raise. That was fighting.

Some of the ladies answering the parish phones must have gotten sick of hearing from her. "No, Mrs. O'Connell, we've already told you, none of our girls would ever…there's no reason for you to keep calling."

But Grammy, sweet, kind Grammy, had ignored the rejection and had gone on calling. Was that what Colleen should have done with Ben? If so, that was a more important lesson than the one about not wearing knits at the dinner table.

Colleen tucked her knees up under the sweatshirt, pulling the hem down over her legs. She suddenly asked herself a question that she had never asked before.

If Grammy had found Sean and Finn, who had found Colleen? Who had made the calls that had brought the priest to her grandparents' porch in Georgia? Grammy wouldn't have called parishes in the South.

It wouldn't have been Grannor. She didn't have Grammy O'Connell's empathy for someone else's pain, not even her own child's. Moreover, she was a snob. Catholics had too many children and machine-made lace curtains. Grannor would have never called the secretary of a Catholic parish...unless it was to complain about weeds on the church's sidewalk.

But someone must have.

* * * *

Ben dropped her father off without coming inside; Dr. Ridge would use Colleen's car to get back to the lake.

"You should come too," her father said. "There's no reason for you to stay here all night."

"I want to stay, Dad. I'm going to."

"Ben said that you would feel that way and there was no point in fighting you on it." He put his arm around her. "You're a good girl, Colleen. I wish my mother deserved it."

"She's family, Dad."

"Now, don't *you* go Southern on me. But speaking of family, I talked to my brother. He wants to know if there is a DNR order."

A DNR was a "do not resuscitate" order, instructing the health care professionals not to perform heroics to keep a person alive. "I don't know," Colleen answered. "Mr. Healy had her update all her papers last fall. So I assume she has one. I'm sure she would have wanted one."

"Of course she would have, but Norton wants to have it rescinded."

"Why? Is he concerned about how small the hospital is?" She herself had already wondered if they should transfer Grannor to a more sophisticated facility.

Her father shook his head. "I wish it were that. No, my charming brother and his wife—his third wife—have separated, and he doesn't want your grandmother's estate to be a part of the divorce settlement."

Colleen made a face. There wasn't anything to say to that.

Her grandmother woke up while her father was still there. She recognized them, but her speech was slurred and the right side of her face drooped. Colleen's father was surprisingly comforting, taking her hand in his, telling her that she had had a little "event," that she was in the hospital for observation. There was nothing to worry about, and Colleen would be here if she woke up again.

You do love her, don't you, Dad? Somewhere beneath all your disapproval and hostility, there is still love.

"You were the best of the lot, Neddy." Grannor seemed unaware of how impaired her speech was. "That wife of yours…is she here? She is so pretty, that red hair of hers."

Colleen saw her father flinch. Genevieve, his current wife, kept her hair stylishly light. But his voice was still as soothing as before. "No, she couldn't make it."

A few hours later, after her father was gone, Grannor woke again. "Your mother, Mary Pat, she passed, didn't she?" Her speech was still slurred.

"Yes, Grannor."

Grannor sighed and shut her eyes. She didn't like being wrong. "Is Will here?"

"Will?" It took Colleen a minute to figure out who she was talking about. "My cousin Will? Uncle Norton's son?" They hardly ever saw Uncle Norton's sons by his first marriage.

But Grannor had already dozed off again.

Her father returned in time Saturday morning to talk to the doctor. The news was discouraging. When he called his brother and sister to confirm their arrival times, Colleen had him tell Norton that Grannor had been asking for Will.

In the middle of the morning, her brothers arrived. Colleen had told them what to expect, so they didn't even ask Grannor how she was doing. They instead pulled up chairs and started to reminisce about summers at the lake and spring vacations in Georgia. Colleen had heard it all many times before, but her brothers could tell a story. She was like a toddler with a favorite picture book. If either of them had skipped any part of a story, she would have wanted them to start over.

When an aide came to give Grannor a sponge bath, she, her brothers, and their father went out to the hall.

There were four of them. Suddenly she was no longer a child being comforted by family stories. Four wasn't the right number. They had always been a family of five. Five plates, five forks, five seat belts, five tickets.

Except they weren't even a family of four. There was Genevieve, Patty, and Liz. And Genevieve's son, daughter, daughter-in-law, and little grandson. Colleen had spent Christmas with her grandmother because her father and brothers were with their wives' families.

Did she want her father to be lonely or her brothers not to have married? No, of course not. She just wanted to feel like she still had a family.

As soon as the door to Grannor's room closed, Sean spoke. "I have marching orders from my wife. I am to forget that I am the older brother. I am to do exactly what Colleen tells me to do."

"Patty said that?" Colleen couldn't help being pleased.

"Yes, she said that at a time like this, the women need to be in charge."

"She's absolutely right," Colleen's father agreed.

"But me? Not Aunt Laura? Shouldn't she be in charge?"

"Oh, children," her father sighed. "Whatever happens, we are *not* taking orders from my sister. And not from my brother either. I talked to Tim Healy this morning. I have your grandmother's health care proxy, not Norton. And I can't do anything as long as she is competent, which she seems to be."

"What's this about?" Finn asked.

Colleen's father explained his older brother's situation. "I'm sure that the three of you hope for your grandmother's complete recovery, but we all know that she wouldn't want to live if she were in pain or had severe cognitive impairment. Unfortunately, my brother wants her to be kept alive under any condition."

Sean stretched and linked his hands behind his head. Finn folded his arms. Colleen knew that both of them were disgusted, but like her, they had been brought up not to criticize their elders.

"In the next few days," Dr. Ridge continued, "even with the best possible outcome, my brother may want to talk about your grandmother's estate. I don't know exactly what's in her will—she did a major overhaul of it several years after she became a widow—but I assume that most of it goes to my siblings and me. It's possible that there will be some specific bequests to Colleen, silver and jewelry and such, but—"

"I hope that there are a lot of specifics for Colleen," Sean interrupted. "She deserves more than the rest of us."

"I agree," her father continued, "but it's less about Colleen herself than the fact that our family gives things to the girls. There will probably be other such bequests for Kimberly. I mention this in hopes that your wives won't feel slighted."

"Liz and Patty? Slighted?" Finn was surprised. "They won't expect a thing."

"And you should have known that, Dad," Sean added.

Their father's lips tightened. Then he nodded apologetically. "You're right, son. Just because my blood relatives will behave badly doesn't mean that other people will too. Let me say one more thing on the subject, and then we will not speak of it again. If I do inherit a third of my mother's estate, it is my intention to disclaim my share and pass it directly to the three of you. I don't need it, and in fact, I don't want it. I have some ambivalent feelings in play here."

The additional tests and the conversations about rehabilitation wouldn't happen until Monday. Her uncle, then her aunt arrived, departed, then came back again. Colleen took Ben's sweatshirt off, then put it on again. She got more ice for the sandwiches in the cooler. The local Episcopal priest stopped by. She ate the turkey out of one of the sandwiches. Flower arrangements were delivered. Her father returned, bringing her car back.

By mid-afternoon everyone was urging her to go back to the lake. She would have liked to have taken a shower, eaten a decent meal, and gotten a little rest, but no one offered to stay at the hospital in her place. She tried not to feel like a martyr. None of them felt that it was necessary to have someone in the room. Why should they inconvenience themselves to live up to her standards?

She didn't have an answer for that...except that if it were Grammy O'Connell in the bed, the aunts, the granddaughters, the neighbors, person after person, would have considered it an honor to be the one to stay with her.

Where were Sean and Finn? They would feel uncomfortable, being here alone, helping with the pillows and the bedpan, but if Colleen asked, they would each take a shift. When they had left for lunch, they said that they would be back, but they hadn't come.

She got out her phone to send Sean a text, but remembered that if he was at the lake, he wouldn't get the message.

Finally at around eight, there was a light rap on the door. It was the youngest member of Grannor's bridge club—a gal in her early seventies. She was wearing comfortable clothes and was carrying her knitting bag. She had heard that Colleen had been in the hospital for more than twenty-four hours without a break.

"You go home and don't you worry about me," she said. "I couldn't sleep anyway, not until I figure out where I went wrong on this sweater pattern."

Colleen kissed her.

* * * *

Lights were on all over the house. Colleen paused in the sitting room to speak to her aunt and uncle and then went into the kitchen. Leilah had a cookbook open on the counter; she seemed to be making up a grocery list.

The kitchen had been painted last winter, but it had never been updated. The narrow pine cupboards were probably original to the house; the linoleum floor was yellowed and cracked; the appliances were all from different eras, having each been replaced whenever it could no longer be repaired.

Grannor had spent almost no time in the kitchen; she hadn't cared what it looked like or how well it functioned.

Colleen felt awkward. Didn't fighting *for* Ben mean fighting *with* Leilah? *I'm out to take your man.*

"I'm sorry." She couldn't help starting with an apology. "I'm sure you're sick of people wandering in and out—"

Leilah held up her hand, stopping the flow of apologies. "I knew that people would be grazing all day. Do you want to eat here in the kitchen?" Her tone was surprisingly down-to-earth.

"Please."

Colleen sat down at the old metal-rimmed kitchen table, relieved not to be treated like the Spoiled-Brat Princess anymore. Of course, Aunt Laura genuinely was a Spoiled-Brat Princess, and even Leilah, despite all her serene competence, might be finding that one such creature was enough.

Colleen watched Leilah take a ham out of the refrigerator. "I saw my aunt and uncle. Where is everyone else?"

"Ben went back to Charlottesville to get your cousin Will. Your brothers are in the cellar. Your father was with them for a while, but I heard him go up to his room."

"The cellar? Why?"

"Apparently your uncle asked your brothers to install the outlets for cable."

No wonder they hadn't been back to the hospital. "I thought you had people coming to do that."

"I did, but your uncle said that your brothers could do it."

Her brothers were both electricians, having their Class A Master Electrician licenses. Clearly they could install outlets.

But they wouldn't want to. They were happy to come to family homes and be guys, figuring their way through auto repairs, odd plumbing noises, and other things that they didn't know a lot about. But to spend a Sunday afternoon doing what they did all the week, working on projects that hadn't been carefully thought out, never having quite the right supplies…they hated that. Once their St. Paul–based business got established, they made it clear to all their relatives—to the O'Connells, their in-laws, and their birth families—that they would work for them without a labor charge, but the jobs had to be scheduled through the business and completed during normal working hours.

So this, being put to work by an uncle they didn't respect, having only substandard tools…Colleen wished that they had refused, although if she had been in their shoes, she probably wouldn't have refused either. All three of them had been brought up to treat their elders with respect even when they couldn't actually respect said elders.

At least her father had gone to bed. As neat and precise as Sean and Finn were, they weren't dentists, they didn't need to be dentists. Having Edward B. Ridge, DDS, as their unlicensed helper tripled the amount of time any project took.

Leilah returned to her grocery list while Colleen ate. The phone rang. Leilah answered with her usual "Mrs. Ridge's residence" followed by "Are they saying how late?" and then "No, I won't wait up. There's food in the refrigerator."

Colleen stood up to put her dishes in the dishwasher. "Was that Ben?" Who else would Leilah talk to about waiting up or not? "Is Will's plane late?"

"Yes, but it should be in by eleven. Ben's going to stay at the airport until it lands."

"That's nice of him. I guess I will tell my aunt and uncle."

"Then I will do a few more things in here and go to the boathouse," Leilah said. "In case anyone needs me, you know where the intercom is, don't you?"

Colleen nodded that she did and went to find her aunt and uncle. Both the library and the sitting room were now empty, but the door to Grannor's bedroom was open and the lights were on.

"Ah, Colleen," her uncle called as soon as he saw her in the doorway. "Do you know where your grandmother keeps her checkbook?"

Laura was opening the door of the nightstand. Norton was in front of the dresser, one of its drawers only partially shut. Colleen didn't like this. "I don't know," she said.

"Leilah must know," Laura said. "Whenever Mother sends me a check now, Leilah has written it and Mother has only signed it. Go ask her, would you, Colleen?"

"Why don't we wait until tomorrow?" It was time to stop giving her aunt and uncle power that they didn't deserve. "Then we can ask Grannor herself."

"No." Norton was firm. "We need to do this tonight. It appears as if a great deal of money has been spent on this place in the last six months."

That was certainly true. "But Grannor has the resources for it, doesn't she?"

"Of course, but the opportunity for…for, well, you know…"

Were they questioning Leilah's integrity? Colleen might not like Leilah or the magazine-perfect repairs, but surely Leilah had far too much dignity to embezzle from an employer.

Norton and Laura, however, could be impossibly stubborn, and Colleen was too tired to bicker with them. "I'll go ask her where it is."

The kitchen lights were off, and Leilah was at the side door, ready to open it. Colleen stopped her. "My aunt and uncle want to know where Grannor's checkbook is."

"It's in the front room." This was a formal room across the hall from the dining room. "In the top drawer of the secretary. The bills and invoices are in the credenza. Is there a problem?"

"Oh, no. Not at all."

Everything was right where Leilah had said. The checkbook was a ledger-style notebook, and the bills were neatly sorted in an accordion file. Colleen's aunt and uncle were still in Grannor's bedroom. Norton was opening more drawers while Laura was sitting on Grannor's bed, looking at a chip in her nail polish. Colleen knew that Grannor would not like them being in there. She took the checkbook into the library. After her aunt and uncle settled themselves at the library table, she returned to Grannor's room to close the drawers and straighten out the wrinkles in the bed's coverlet.

She heard some hammering in the cellar. The sound was the high, tinny tap of a hammer against a nail head. It must be her brothers at work. She thought about going down to join them, but she wasn't going to leave Norton and Laura alone with Grannor's financial records. She went into the library.

She was already too late to save Leilah's careful organization. The bills were now spread out all over the library table; some had fallen to the floor.

Norton was shaking his head as he paged through the checkbook ledger. "Money is gushing out of here. Look at this." He thrust it in Colleen's direction, his finger pointing at an entry. "Can you explain this?"

She refused to look at it. "I don't think that it is any of my business, Uncle Norton."

"That's just like your generation. You duck responsibility. But someone has to be sure that the elderly aren't taken advantage of."

Colleen didn't trust herself to answer. Her brothers stopped hammering, and a minute later she heard the whine of a power drill.

Laura was at the table, stirring through the bills. "That woman needs to come and explain herself. Colleen, go tell her that we need to speak to her."

"She's already gone back to the boathouse."

"I don't know why Mother didn't have her sleep in the house. What did she do if she needed help in the night?"

"There's a wireless intercom, but surely this can wait until morning."

"She's the paid help, Colleen. There's no reason to be afraid of her." Laura marched into the kitchen and after a few attempts managed to work the intercom.

"Leilah, dear." Her voice was syrupy. "This is Mrs. Davenport. Mr. Ridge and I would like to speak to you. We are in the library."

Colleen cringed. Why was her aunt talking this way to a woman who was better educated, more intelligent, and more refined than she was? Colleen sat down in one of her grandfather's chairs and picked up a magazine. It was this week's issue. Leilah never let magazines pile up. The minute a new issue came, the previous one went in the recycling bin.

The drilling started and stopped. The hammering started and stopped.

"I wish those boys would stop that infernal banging," Laura fussed. "They've been at it all afternoon. They are giving me a headache."

Colleen turned the pages of the magazine. Norton fretted about the new furniture on the terrace and the cost of putting in the dock even though the dock was put in by the same people every year. Laura continued to be unhappy about the noise from the cellar and the chip in her manicure.

It was another ten minutes before Leilah appeared in the door of the library. She didn't greet anyone or sit down.

Aunt Laura had gotten more and more annoyed while they had been waiting. She started right in with the accusations. "You had the groceries delivered."

As if Leilah had willed it, the hammering stopped. She stood in the oak-framed double doorway, wreathed in silence. "Yes," she answered, her voice as cool as ever. "The big weekly trips were delivered from Staunton. Mrs. Ridge said that she always had her groceries delivered. She preferred it that way."

"Didn't she know that the delivery charge was more than triple what it was at home?"

"I believe that she did."

"And why did you pay the gardener to plant the window boxes? Why didn't you do it yourself?"

"Forget that," Norton snapped. "That's trivia. What about resurfacing the driveway? What was wrong with gravel?"

From the cellar came the vibrations of seven or eight quick hammer blows. Sean and Finn seemed to be directly under the library now. Leilah waited for the silence to return. "What precisely are you accusing me of? Padding the bills? Or are you assuming that I have some kind of kickback scheme with the local vendors?"

"More like a general lack of economy." Norton waved a stack of invoices. "Spending more money than was necessary."

Colleen had to say something. "Don't you think Leilah has run the house exactly as Grannor wanted her to? If she had done one single thing that Grannor didn't want, Grannor would have been all over her. Grannor loves to catch people in the wrong."

Maybe that wasn't the nicest way to defend her grandmother, but it was the truth. Eleanor Ridge was neither trusting nor easily manipulated.

Colleen glanced at Leilah, hoping to see the other woman acknowledge what she had said. Leilah returned her look with narrowing eyes. Clearly she did not want Colleen defending her.

Why not? What's wrong with having me on your side? I'm a good team player.

"I consider myself answerable only to Mrs. Ridge." Leilah's voice was tight and controlled. "You will also find that I did not have a contract with her."

"Well, see here, young woman," Norton blustered, "don't you be—"

Leilah held up her hand. "No." When Laura started to speak, she did it again. "No."

And then she left.

"Well, I never." Laura sniffed.

"Did she just quit?" Norton asked.

"I think so." Colleen was on her feet, halfway to the door.

"Don't dash off and try to get her to stay," Norton ordered. "Your grandmother will probably need a skilled nurse when she gets out of the hospital. There's no reason to have excess staff."

"But someone needs to run the house. This place is huge. Leilah has kept on top of everything. We aren't going to get a nurse to do that."

"For what we've been paying, of course we can."

"And we can take over managing her bills," Laura added. "We'll put our names on her accounts and set up auto-pays."

Grannor didn't trust cell phones. She would never consent to online banking. And giving Laura and Norton access to her money? That would never happen. Colleen turned to leave the room.

"Where are you going?" Laura demanded.

She didn't answer.

The lights on the second floor of the boathouse were on. Leilah came to the apartment door in answer to Colleen's knock.

"Leilah, I am so sorry. Please understand. My aunt and uncle…they aren't nice people." Words were gushing out of her. "You have to ignore them." If her aunt and uncle were her allies in a fight for Ben, then she was doing something wrong.

Leilah said nothing. Over her shoulder Colleen could see an empty cardboard box sitting by a bookcase.

"You aren't really leaving, are you? Please. Won't you reconsider?"

"I don't choose to be questioned." Leilah turned, moving back inside the apartment.

Not choose to be questioned? How could you choose that? People questioned other people all the time.

Colleen followed. She hadn't been in here since it had been refurbished for Leilah. The apartment was small, neatly furnished with soft Pottery Barn–like neutrals. It was immaculate except for a familiar green sweater draped across the back of one chair.

It was Ben's sweater. If Leilah left, would Ben go too?

Leilah was in the bedroom, lifting a neat stack of clothes out of a drawer. Two lightweight nylon duffels were on the bed. One already looked half-filled.

"You're packing already? Isn't there something I can do?"

"No." Leilah placed the garments in the duffel, added a few more things, then zipped it up. "You could carry this to my car on your way out."

"Your car? Now? You aren't leaving tonight, are you? Right now?" This was so fast. "What about Grannor? What about Ben?"

"Your grandmother and I understand each other. She would not say goodbye to me."

"But Ben?"

Leilah paused and looked down at her. Her height made Colleen feel childlike and powerless. "Relationships occupy a different place in my life than they do in yours."

What did that mean? That she was leaving without saying goodbye to Ben?

"Leilah, could you please wait until morning?"

"No. And you have no right to ask me that."

Maybe I don't. But Ben does. You have to let him have a voice in this.

Colleen didn't want to "win" like this. In fact, it wouldn't be winning. It might be losing. With this sudden departure, Leilah and her pale, drifting clothes might swirl through Ben's memory as The One Who Got Away.

Because that should be me. I should be The One.

She stood there for a moment, watching Leilah packing her clothes. Knowing that nothing she said could make any difference, Colleen went to the bookcase and started packing the books. Most were about Buddhism and other Eastern religions. Some of them were in French. Two were in Italian. The ones in French looked well-read. The Italian ones were pristine.

I could have helped you with the Italian. Colleen didn't think of herself as being able to speak Italian, but she could read it. *Why didn't you ask me?*

How unimaginable that was—Leilah asking for help. Colleen was surprised that she was even letting someone else pack her books.

Three books lay on their side; all were technical. Colleen opened the cover of one, and as she expected, it had Ben's name. She left them there. He would have taken his laptop to the airport with him, but the stack of papers in the printer was clearly his work. She put them next to his books. She supposed that he had clothes in the bedroom and toiletries in the bathroom. She was glad not to be in there. She didn't want to think about what had been happening in that bed.

The two duffels of clothes, the one box of boxes, a laptop computer bag, and a printer—that was all Leilah had. She and Colleen could easily carry it to the car. Leilah removed Grannor's keys from her key ring and handed them to Colleen.

"Do we owe you any money?" Colleen wasn't sure what else to say.

"None that I want."

"What about a forwarding address for mail and such?"

"I don't get mail here."

"But won't we need to send a W-2 or something? How will you file your income tax without one?"

Leilah waved a hand. She was not going to engage with that issue. It was too trivial.

Come next April, see if you think it is all that trivial. But Colleen stepped back, and without either of them exchanging another word, Leilah got in her car. A minute later the little car went around the bend in the driveway. Colleen could catch one more glimpse of the headlights flickering through the trees, then nothing.

The keys felt heavy and cold. Colleen put them in her pocket and looked at her watch. It was after eleven. Ben and Will should be here by midnight. As tired as she was, she had to stay up. She couldn't let Ben walk into an empty boathouse.

Chapter 6

For someone named Norton W. Ridge VI, Will Ridge wasn't such a bad fellow. While waiting for his much-delayed connecting flight to take off, he had sent Ben a text, offering to rent a car so Ben wouldn't be stuck waiting too. When he finally arrived in Charlottesville, he was gracious, telling Ben how much he appreciated having a ride. He hadn't been looking forward to trying to find his grandmother's house in the dark. Clearly, there was an advantage, when Norton W. the Fifth was your father, to growing up with a stepfather.

Will was surprised that his grandmother had asked for him. "She hardly knows me."

"You're the oldest son of the oldest son, going back however many generations. That's why you have a number at the end of your name."

"But that doesn't mean anything anymore, does it?"

"It does to some people."

Will shook his head. "Mother always told us that because we lived so far from everyone, never spending holidays with any of the Ridge family, we shouldn't expect a lot. I always felt a little guilty about the big checks Grannor sent when we graduated from high school and college."

"You're her grandsons, no matter what, and it's hardly your fault if you didn't see her when you were growing up."

"We aren't kids anymore. We could have come on our own. I did talk to my brother. He's not inclined to come, but he will if people think that he should."

"That's not for me to judge."

Ben did know one thing. If Jeff Ridge were coming, he could rent a car. Ben had driven to Charlotesville once on Friday and twice today. That was enough.

He and Will reached the lake shortly after midnight. The front of the house was dark except for the yellow globes of the exterior sconces. A faint pool of light fell on the asphalt beneath the kitchen portico. Leilah must have left the kitchen lights on. Ben led Will to the side door, the one that opened directly into the kitchen. It was the one she would have left open.

Surprisingly it was Colleen, not Leilah, who came to greet them. The kitchen light was harsh; she looked tired. Smudged shadows under her eyes made her look fragile, and he was suddenly aware of how small, even delicate, she was. At least physically.

She and Will each put out a hand, then remembering that they were first cousins, exchanged a quick, awkward embrace. She passed along the limited news about their grandmother as she began to take food out of the refrigerator.

The quinoa-chickpea salad was clearly a Leilah creation, but Leilah had not made the sandwiches. They were majestic, all-American guy sandwiches, a luxuriously thick layer of ham, two slices of cheese, lettuce, tomato, mayonnaise, mustard, and a big pickle on the side.

Colleen seemed to be having trouble making conversation with her cousin. That wasn't like her; he thought she could talk to anyone. She must be really tired. He finished his sandwich quickly and started to push his chair back, ready to suggest that they turn in. A quick tap on his leg stopped him. He looked up inquiringly.

Don't go, her eyes said. *Stay.*

Why?

Just stay.

He took another serving of the salad. He wished that Leilah didn't use so much cilantro.

He suddenly realized that her car hadn't been in its usual place by the kitchen door. Was she at the hospital with Mrs. Ridge? He couldn't imagine that either she or Mrs. Ridge would be comfortable with hospital-room intimacies. Colleen, having little sense of privacy and almost no boundaries, could provide personal care with matter-of-fact ease.

Will had been eating slowly, probably because he was tired too. Finally he was finished. Colleen stood up. "You are on the second floor," she told him. "Ben will carry your bag up for you."

"I can do it," Will answered. He had only one small carry-on.

But Colleen must have a reason for treating him like the second footman, so Ben grabbed Will's bag and obediently followed her up the back stairs, the ones that led directly off the kitchen. Colleen showed Will to the one remaining room on the second floor, the roadside room that Ben had slept in—or rather returned to—during spring break.

He listened as she told her cousin about the light switches, the bathroom, and the plans for Sunday. Back when he wasn't returning her calls, he had persuaded himself to think of her as a butterfly, flitting lightly through her life. But that had been wrong. The comparison needed to be more… what?…vegetative. That was a lousy word, but she was like a beautifully blossoming plant that had deep roots in the warm earth.

But Leilah was what he deserved: a cool, unchanging marble statue.

Colleen said good night to her cousin. She stepped into the hall, closing the bedroom's dark oak door.

"Well?" he said softly. Her father, aunt, and uncle were sleeping in the other rooms.

"Let's go downstairs."

They went down the back stairs again and sat at the kitchen table. What on earth couldn't wait until morning?

"I hate to have to tell you this, but—"

He froze. His parents…one of the grandkids? No, no, it couldn't be any of them. He had spoken to Ryan a couple of hours ago. And if it had been something with his family, Colleen would have told him right away.

"It's Leilah. My aunt and uncle were horrible to her, and she has left."

"Left? What do you mean?"

"They were accusing her, not of dishonesty, but of spending too much money. So she packed her things and left. She says that she didn't have a contract with Grannor."

"She's not at the hospital?"

"No, Ben." Colleen's voice was gentle. "She didn't want to work for people who doubted her. You can't blame her. They were awful."

"She quit?"

"She packed up her things and moved out. It all happened so fast. She's gone. For good."

Leilah was gone? Just like that? He was suddenly aware of the tabletop against his hands. He looked down. The tips of his fingers were white; he was pressing down that hard.

That would be wrong up in the air. You couldn't grip a board that tightly, and you didn't reach your hand down to grab it; you used your legs to bring the board up to you.

"I'm so sorry, Ben." Colleen's voice was almost a whisper.

"Did she say where she was going? No, no, she wouldn't have."

Snowboarding...he knew so much about the sport. But two days into his relationship with Leilah, he had become aware of how little he knew about her. Two weeks into it, he had had to accept that he would never learn any more.

"I'm sure she'll get in touch with you," Colleen was saying. "She'll let you know where she is."

He shook his head again. "No. That's what you would do. It doesn't mean that's what she would do."

* * * *

His clothes were in the boathouse's closet, his toothbrush was on the vanity; the charge cords for his phone and camera were neatly coiled on the bookshelf. Everything that was Leilah's was gone.

He had been amazed at how few belongings she had had. "Do you have stuff with family or friends?" he had asked her early on. "Or a storage unit?"

"I travel light."

"But your high school yearbook, your college diploma, your third grade class picture, haven't you saved any of that?"

"Why would I?"

From the beginning, the sex had always been about pleasing him. She would push him back against the pillows, and she would do everything, controlling the rhythm. She would bring him close, then pull back, until he exploded in near-desperate fireworks.

But each session was the same—thrilling at first, then increasingly empty. There was no shared journey, there was nothing mutual. It seemed more about her power over him than any pleasure. They left the lights on and never played music. There was no magic and, despite how unfathomable Leilah was, no mystery.

A few days ago, the night before Mrs. Ridge had collapsed, when Leilah moved to straddle him, he closed his hands over her forearms and, with a man's strength, stopped her.

She froze. Her face went blank, her pupils dilated; the muscles in her arms tensed, and her skin beneath his palms was suddenly clammy. She was having a panic attack.

He instantly pulled back, lifting his hands as if to show that he wasn't armed.

But clearly he was. He was a man. Men were the enemy.

"Leilah, were you—" *abused?* He stopped himself in time.

If Leilah had been abused, she might be compensating for how powerless she had felt as a child. A history of abuse would also explain why she was so guarded. "I didn't mean to frighten you."

"You didn't frighten me." She wasn't going to admit to anything. "What are you talking about?"

"Nothing."

But she was plenty smart. She knew that he had seen more than she wanted him to. Colleen's aunt and uncle criticizing her may have given her the excuse she needed to flee from him. But it was only an excuse.

He moved to the corner of the boathouse where the cell phone signal was the best. He sent her a text. He said nothing about her leaving, nothing about the lack of farewell. *Please let me know if you ever need anything. I will always be there for you.*

He knew that she wouldn't answer and that the next time he sent her a message, she would have changed her number. She needed a man she could control, and he hadn't been it.

* * * *

Sunday morning Colleen left for the hospital before anyone else was up. Her grandmother's bridge partner said that Grannor had had a fairly easy night. "She woke up several times and was very concerned about some pearls needing to be restrung. I asked what strand she was talking about or where it was, but I couldn't get anything more out of her."

"I assume it's the one her great-grandfather bought for her great-grandmother while they were honeymooning in Paris."

"*Her* great-grandfather bought them? Not yours? They must be very old."

"The 1880s, I think. It did take the family a while to recover from the Civil War."

Mrs. Johnson shook her head, having trouble connecting with that kind of family history. "None of my family was over here during the Civil War."

"My mother's side wasn't either," Colleen agreed.

Her brothers and Will arrived next. When Grannor woke up, Colleen spoke to each of them, using their names in case Grannor didn't recognize Will or had trouble telling Sean and Finn apart. Grannor didn't say much; she still had restringing the pearls on her mind.

The rest of the family and some of Grannor's friends were in and out all day. Among the family, the primary topic of conversation was whether or not to move Grannor to the teaching hospital in Charlottesville. It was bigger and more research-oriented, but the neurologists and cardiologists here were board-certified clinicians, experienced at monitoring people in Grannor's condition.

Norton was the one most strongly advocating not only the transfer, but also rescinding the DNR order. He played on his mother's snobbishness. Did she really want to trust a life-and-death decision to such a small-town place? Norton managed to make everyone in Staunton sound like such yokels that Grannor at least consented to revoking the order. The final decision about moving was postponed until Monday.

But, as it turned out, there was no Monday for Eleanor Ridge.

Colleen was helping the nurse rearrange the pillows when it happened. Colleen was supporting her grandmother, an arm behind her shoulders, when Grannor's face suddenly went empty, a blankness far beyond sleep.

"Mrs. Ridge...Mrs. Ridge..." The nurse, her fingers already searching Grannor's neck, tried to get her to respond. "I'm not getting a pulse." Waving Colleen aside, she swung herself onto the bed to begin chest compressions. In a moment, the room was full of people and equipment. Someone touched Colleen's arm, motioning for her to leave the room.

More people in blue scrubs were running up the corridor, hurrying to help. Behind them were her father and brothers, their steps quickening as they saw Colleen.

Finn reached her first. "What happened?"

"She crashed. She just went blank."

They could hear the sounds from the room, someone calling "clear" just as they did on television medical dramas. More equipment was brought in. They heard sharp clangs of metal on metal. Colleen knew that her grandmother would loathe the idea of being manhandled.

Because there was no DNR order, the ordeal went on and on. People would leave the room, red-faced and sweating. None of them would make eye contact with the family, and Colleen could imagine what they were thinking. *Why are you putting her through this? She's eighty-six.*

A silver-haired man in a long coat, seemingly a doctor of authority and experience, entered the room. A minute or so later, the sounds from the room stopped. The doctor reappeared and put out a comforting hand to Colleen's father. "We did all that we could."

Chapter 7

Colleen drove back to the lake with her father.

"That wasn't a tragedy," he said as they pulled out of the hospital lot.

But it was still a loss. Exacting, ruthless, and competitive, Grannor had loved being alive.

"The funeral will be back home," her father continued. "I suppose I need to go, and Genevieve has said that she will come, but you kids shouldn't feel obligated to."

"I think that we will want to." *We're still a family. We haven't figured it out, but we're still a family.*

"Suit yourself." Then, a minute later, he added that he would pay for their plane tickets. "And for Patty and Liz, if they want to come."

"They will." Her sisters-in-law would be startled by this conversation. If they had been here, they would have looked at each other, communicating in silence. How could anyone ever consider *not* going to a funeral?

I think I understand, Dad. You couldn't respect her, you couldn't approve of her, you resented the lack of nurturing, but she was still your mother.

Although Colleen had half a tank of gas, her father said that they should stop in the village "just in case." Clearly he was delaying going back to the house. While he pumped the gas, Colleen took out her phone to look at her messages. There were too many. Amanda, Cara, and a few others knew that her grandmother had been in the hospital. None of them knew she was dead. Colleen tried to compose an email to Amanda, but a call interrupted her.

It was her aunt Eileen, her mother's oldest sister, calling from St. Paul. Patty, Sean's wife, had already told her about Grannor dying. "How is your father?" Eileen asked.

Colleen looked through the car window to be sure that her father couldn't overhear her. "I think he's numb. He doesn't know how he is supposed to feel."

"That's not surprising. I suppose there will be a reception after the funeral, but what about a wake?"

"I don't know," Colleen answered. Did Episcopalians have wakes? She remembered a few gatherings before and after her grandfather's funeral, but she had been too young to pay much attention to what they were.

"I'll come if you need me, but your father has a sister, doesn't he? She'll take care of everything."

Her mother's sisters and friends had taken care of all the arrangements after Mary Pat had died. But Aunt Laura going to that much effort didn't seem likely. Back at the lake, Colleen found that Aunt Laura hadn't even washed the breakfast dishes. The kitchen was a mess. The sink was full of cereal bowls and coffee cups. The uneaten remains of the lunch sandwiches were drying up on the kitchen table. The lunch meats and cheeses had been put back into the refrigerator uncovered.

At least cleaning the kitchen gave her something to do. Her brothers were packing. They had managed to get seats on the next flight out; they would come down to Georgia for the funeral. Her uncle was on the phone in the sitting room talking to the funeral home. Her aunt, unwilling to take her cell phone to the end of the dock, was fussing because Norton was tying up the one landline. Colleen didn't know where Ben was. Had he left? Had he gone after Leilah? No, his car was still out front. She went into the sitting room and asked where he was.

"He said he could use his phone out in the boathouse," her aunt said. "So we gave him a list of people who had to be notified, mostly your grandmother's longtime friends at home."

Having to tell an old lady that once again another of her friends had died…what a crappy chore. Even when there was no actual grief, each call would be full of tedious platitudes.

"Aunt Laura, what should we do about a reception after the funeral?"

"We always did things like that at the club."

"But the club has closed. Is there a fellowship hall at the church?"

"Yes, but it isn't very nice. It's in the basement, and they haven't kept it up. We can't do it there." Laura picked up a magazine. "You'll have to think of something else, dear."

Me? Why me?

Colleen hadn't been to her father's hometown in several years. When she had been growing up, her family had always spent their spring vacations there. During its declining years, the town had had no dentist, so for that week each year her father had rented a mobile dental unit and set up a free clinic for the residents who couldn't afford to drive into the city. For many of his clients, it was the only time they ever saw a dentist. But once the chicken plant had opened, bringing so many people to town, the demand for dental care had increased. By then Mary Pat was sick, and Ned didn't want to leave her. At her suggestion, he had scrounged around for equipment and funding and had managed to get a clinic opened and staffed three days a week. Since then Colleen had only seen her grandmother at the lake.

Mrs. Sisson—Genevieve—would be happy to help Colleen plan the funeral, and she had worked hard after Mary Pat had died, but she knew even less about the town than Colleen did. They needed to talk to someone who knew the place. Sarah, her grandmother's longtime maid, had passed away, and Colleen didn't know the last name of her married daughter. Who was she going to call? This was strange. She always knew someone to call. She was the Queen of Knowing-Who-to-Call. People called her when they needed to know who to call.

But she did know. Of course, she did. Ben's mother, Marianne Healy. She was the person to call. Colleen got her phone and started for the boathouse.

Halfway there she stopped. The Healys, of course. It had been the Healys who had found her. It seemed so obvious when she thought about it. Her mother and Mrs. Healy had been good friends. Who else would have gotten in touch with a priest, especially an Irish one? They must have been the ones who had called the parishes, looking for a baby for her parents. The Healys would have been the ones who had gotten her to her true home, to the family she was destined to have.

The boathouse steps ran up the outside of the building, ending at a deck that continued parallel to the lake, extending over the water. Ben was standing at the railing, his phone at his ear. He nodded to her and shrugged, indicating that he couldn't move for fear of losing his connection.

Your family found me. God worked through them. All her memories of playing in the lake with Sean and Finn, of having her father read her bedtime stories, and of going with her mother to buy her prom dresses... all those she owed to Ben's family. *So why didn't you want me? Isn't this a sign that we should be together?*

"Yes, ma'am," he was saying, "the funeral home will know the exact time...I'm sure that the family would appreciate that...Yes, ma'am, Marianne and Tim are my parents, but Ryan's my older brother...Yes, that was me... Thank you for asking..."

Each conversation would have been like this. The simple, sad message required a twenty-minute review of family trees and hospital stays. That was what would matter to Grannor's friends.

How weary he must be. Leilah had left not even twenty-four hours ago. Colleen wished that she could comfort him. She wished that he could comfort her. *Why can't we be friends? We should be friends.*

At last he was able to end the call, shaking his head as he touched the screen of his phone. "At least that one didn't want to talk about the azaleas."

"Are you all right?" she asked. "Are you doing okay?"

"I'm fine. I only have three more people to call."

"I didn't mean that. I was asking about Leilah leaving."

His expression froze. "I'm fine. I've had relationships end before."

"But surely not like this."

"No," he admitted. "Now, what can I do for you? Do you need something? The internet?"

Clearly he was not going to talk about Leilah. "No, I need your mother's phone number. I have to figure out how to feed people after the funeral, and I have no idea where to start."

"She's the right place for that. And let me give you my sisters' numbers too, in case Mom isn't around. Do you want to go inside? The chair to the left of the table is where you can get a signal, but it's stronger out here."

She shook her head. It was good to be outside, away from the sharp light and rasping smells of the hospital. She handed him her phone and let him key in the numbers. Then he showed her the best place to stand.

"Colleen, you darling girl." Marianne Healy's voice was full of soft sympathy. "Ben told me. What can I do?"

"Don't be so nice," Colleen told her. "You will make me cry."

"Oh, dearie, it's fine to cry. You need to cry."

"Not until I get this squared away."

Mrs. Healy told her that for the kind of elegant reception that the Ridge family traditionally put on, people would need to drive halfway to Atlanta. "This may not be what you want to hear, but I think you should do it in the church. You are going to have some very elderly people coming. Why make it any harder on them?"

Colleen imagined that Aunt Laura would want people to drive halfway to Atlanta, but she no longer cared what her aunt thought. She was all in favor of making it easy on the old people, especially when that also made it easier on her.

Mrs. Healy offered to track down the name of the volunteer in charge of the church's fellowship hall. "And my advice is to do exactly what has been done at the last three funerals. Don't kill yourself or spend a lot of money to try and make it nicer. This way people can blame the church ladies, not you."

Colleen liked the sound of that.

* * * *

So, indeed, the reception was in the basement of the church. A check to the women's circle had produced country ham on slightly stale biscuits, macaroni salad, and bar cookies made from cake mixes. Colleen was too tired to care.

The church had been built for a much larger congregation, and its grand vaulted sanctuary made the mourners seem like a huddle of refugees. Some of Norton, Laura, and Ned's high school friends, men and women in their sixties, drove in from Atlanta and even Charleston, several bringing their own aging mothers. The Healys sat together, and near the back of the church was a cluster of older working people, mostly African Americans, the men buttoning their shirts at the neck in absence of suits and ties.

They were there, not for Grannor, but for Colleen's father.

"Your daddy…if anyone was in trouble with the law, he saw them first. He said prison dentists just pulled teeth. Doc Ridge, he would save your tooth."

"I was so scared, but I guess it was your mama, the one with the pretty hair, she was there, and she watched my little brothers so my mama could come back with me…"

"I bet you didn't know that my granddaughter finished her schooling, and she's a dental hygienist working in the nicest office in Macon, all due to your daddy. We're so proud of her, like to bust with it we are."

Colleen wished that she could help her father as much as he had helped these people.

Norton delivered the eulogy, talking about his mother as one who bore a standard for a different time, a time that had vanished even when she was a girl. It was formal, even labored, lacking warmth or affection. At least he had gotten his sons to come. Aunt Laura's daughter had refused.

Colleen had asked her father if he wanted them to take communion. Her Sunday school had taught her to take the Holy Eucharist only at a Roman Catholic mass, but when they were in Georgia attending this church with their grandmother, their mother had shepherded the three of them up to the altar, even participating in the ritual herself. Clearly Mary Pat thought that God was a great deal more forgiving than her mother-in-law.

Not surprisingly her father told Colleen that he didn't care what they did. So when Patty looked at Colleen questioningly, she signaled that they could stay in their seats.

But as she watched the few congregants straggle up to the altar, she suddenly asked herself why she had let her father decide. He wasn't Catholic. She should have thought about it and made her own decision. Taking communion in this church had been a bit of a sacrifice for her mother. She should have decided for herself what would honor that sacrifice.

The Healys, also Catholic, didn't take communion either. Colleen was surprised by how many of them had come. Of course, Tim and Marianne came, and Ben had flown down from Charlottesville on the same plane with her family. But his three brothers and two sisters were there as well, the married ones accompanied by their spouses. There were even some school-aged children.

The Healys and her father's former clients…their coming was far more comforting than Norton's eulogies or the priest's prayers.

Even more comforting was Colleen's increasing suspicion that Patty was pregnant.

She, Ben, her father, her aunt, and her uncle had all come down together on Wednesday. Her brothers and Genevieve had come in on Friday. Aunt Laura had insisted that they all drive twenty miles so that they could have dinner at a restaurant with proper tablecloths.

Uncle Norton ordered wine. As the salads were arriving, Colleen happened to see Sean discreetly switching his empty glass for Patty's full one. Norton soon refilled that glass. Patty picked it up twice, but set it down without having any. Later in the evening, Liz also switched glasses with her, something Colleen had noticed only because she was watching.

A young married woman not drinking alcohol often meant one happy thing, and when Patty, who had never had a princessy bone in her body, frowned at the menu and took a while to decide, Colleen felt confident that come next year sometime she would be an aunt.

A baby…how happy that would have made her mother. Grammy O'Connell was going to be thrilled. Of course, she already had fifteen— or was it sixteen?—great-grandchildren, but Sean had a special place in her heart because she had worked so hard to find the Bannings.

With Norton and Laura at the restaurant, of course Patty and Sean had said nothing. Colleen had stopped by their motel room later that night, hoping that they would tell her then. They didn't. She rationalized her disappointment. Perhaps they were waiting to tell her father and her together. And Genevieve too, of course. But at breakfast the following morning, nothing was said.

Finn and Liz knew. Liz had helped Patty hide that she wasn't drinking.

Patty and Liz had been best friends since they were five. Their families lived across the street from each other, and neither one of them had a sister. Colleen had been a bridesmaid in both of their weddings, but they had been each other's honor attendant.

Can't I be your sister too? She could understand couples keeping a pregnancy private during the first trimester, but if they were telling Finn and Liz, why not her? *We don't have secrets.* That's what her mother had always said. This was a big secret.

She felt left out. She couldn't help it, but she did.

The two-story motel had been built shortly after the chicken plant opened. While not luxurious, it was clean and had everything they needed, including free wi-fi. The rooms opened directly onto a walkway that ran around the small swimming pool. Outside each door was a pair of white plastic chairs with a low table between them. Colleen sat down in one of the chairs, opening her laptop, angling the screen so that she could read it outdoors.

She again felt overwhelmed by the number of personal messages that she had. Why did she make such an effort to keep up with so many people? She looked up when one of the room doors opened. It was Patty and Liz; Patty was carrying her laptop. Patty sat down next to her while Liz pulled up another chair. They both looked as if they had a secret…but it couldn't be about the baby. Sean would want to be a part of sharing that news.

"Have you been following this thing with Autumn Chase?" Liz asked.

"Autumn Chase? The actress?" Colleen remembered her. "The one who has all those things on the shopping channels?"

"Yes, she was in a lot of movies as a child," Patty confirmed, "and then had the sitcom for a long time."

Colleen remembered the sitcom. It was called *M.J.* and featured Autumn Chase as a relatively sane young woman surrounded by absurd friends whose antics she kept accommodating because she was too softhearted to do otherwise. It ran for years while being cute, but not a whole lot more.

The actress now had a lifestyle brand that sold a big range of fashion and home decoration products. Colleen had the impression that it was quite successful. "What's going on with her?"

"You really don't know?" Her sisters-in-law exchanged a look. After Colleen shook her head, Patty moved the laptop toward her. "Here, look."

Patty clicked on a link, and a video appeared, five women sitting on a large curved sofa. It seemed to be from a daytime talk show, and three of the women were talking at once.

"I'm sorry," Colleen apologized. "I don't think I can concentrate. Can you summarize it for me?"

"Autumn was guest-hosting on this show, and they were talking about adoption. Apparently when she was fourteen and still under contract to a Disney-like studio, she had a baby. Her parents made her give the baby up and they kept it all very hush-hush because of the film contract. She says that she totally went along with it, that she repressed all her feelings, but the baby will be twenty-eight sometime in the autumn. She always says 'autumn,' not 'fall.'"

Colleen's birthday was in October. That was in the autumn. She was twenty-seven. She would be twenty-eight next autumn.

And, yes, she was adopted.

But it didn't matter. God had put her in her family. That's what she had always grown up believing.

"So we had to wonder," Patty said, "if there was a chance that you were that baby."

"It would be so amazing," Liz gushed. She was livelier than Patty. "One of my cousins got a set of her sheets for a wedding present. I love her handbags. If she's your mother, you have to get me that blue one. I've wanted it for ages."

"You were born in the fall," Patty said. "So it is possible."

"Fall covers a lot of time," Colleen said. "A quarter of the year. I'm sure a lot of babies were put up for adoption during the fall."

"But how many of them were perfectly healthy baby girls in completely closed adoptions?" Patty asked. "Do you know any other adopted kid who knows as little as you do?"

Colleen acknowledged that the circumstances of her adoption, while once very common, had become increasingly unusual.

"But it is exciting, isn't it?" Liz exclaimed. "I used to fantasize that Princess Diana was my mother, and there are pictures of me with my parents when I was twenty minutes old. What do you think? Is there a chance?"

"I know as much as you do. Let me watch the video."

The show had three regular hosts and a weekly guest host. In addition there was also a daily guest who had an issue for the other four to discuss. Apparently on this episode, the daily guest was speaking about her experiences of having relinquished a child to be adopted by others. The other four were listening with equal sympathy. Colleen leaned forward to get a better view of the computer screen.

Autumn Chase was a lovely woman. Her thick chestnut hair fell to her shoulders in graceful waves; her eyes were shimmering green. She wasn't pretending to be a girl. There was the slightest hint of wrinkles at the edge of her eyes and on her forehead, and her face was mobile and expressive; it hadn't been frozen by a lot of plastic surgery. She seemed warm and vibrant; she had the kind of personality that made people want to buy necklaces and tea towels on the shopping channels.

"She doesn't really look like you," Patty said, "although that's probably not her natural hair color and she may be wearing tinted contacts. But she's tiny like you."

So were lots of women.

Patty ran the next few frames in slow motion. Even though Autumn wasn't in close-up, you could see her leaning forward, her eyes narrowing. The camera was moved to focus on the guest, but suddenly cut to show Autumn slumped back in her chair, her hand over her heart.

The video hiccupped. Whoever had posted it had deleted the commercials. In that interval Autumn had composed herself, and the lead host had obviously been cued to ask her about her own story.

Autumn apologized, saying that she had never considered telling her own story. "And I might not tell it very well." She had gotten pregnant while on location shooting *Cards*. She had been barely fourteen. "No, no," she said in answer to a question about who the father was, "I don't know if I am ready to say that. I wouldn't even tell my parents. But it wasn't Zachary."

Colleen paused the clip. "Who's Zachary?"

"Zachary Forbes," Liz said. "He was the kid who costarred with her in *Cards*."

Colleen pressed the play button. "But you were fourteen," the lead host was saying, "way below the age of consent. That's rape."

Autumn shook her head, her beautiful chestnut hair swinging lightly around her shoulders. "We were filming in Canada. Their laws have changed, but at the time fourteen was legal."

Autumn continued her story. To her father, she was the family cash crop. He wanted her to have an abortion, but they were Catholic. Her mother and her grandmother said she would have to endure her shame and disgrace.

"My mother said that she would not raise the baby for me, that everyone already did everything for me. I was under contract to start *Winter Splash* in Italy in December. All I remember is her yelling at me about gaining weight."

"Maybe that's why you are so short," Liz said. "You weren't properly nourished as a fetus."

A fetus? Colleen frowned. Had she once been someone's fetus? Well, obviously. Of course, some woman—some girl—had carried her for nine months.

Autumn was still speaking. "Once I knew that I couldn't keep the baby, I suppose I went into denial. I couldn't let myself care. All I thought about was how much I wanted to go to Italy and work on the new film. I suppose that makes me sound very self-centered, but I was under so much pressure. My entire family relied on me to keep working."

Her cohosts murmured sympathetically. Autumn then asked the show's guest how one went about searching for a relinquished child when she wasn't sure the name of the hospital. She wasn't even sure of the date. She just remembered it being in the autumn.

"That's really all there is," Patty said, closing her computer. "The rest is just the guest talking about how you start on a search."

A search? A search for what? For *her*? "Will you send me the link?"

Patty nodded. "Haven't you ever been curious about this before? I did ask Sean about it once. We have so much contact with the Bannings that I thought it seemed odd, but he didn't seem to think so."

"It's the way it has always been. We never questioned it."

"Being related to a celebrity could be a lot of fun. She must travel first class all the time."

"Or even on a private plane," Liz added. "Wouldn't that be amazing? Forget the purses, Colleen. Go for your own plane."

"I can't imagine myself going for anything."

Another door opened. She looked up. It was her father and Genevieve, coming out of the room next to hers. "What's going on, girls?"

Patty looked at Colleen. *Go ahead,* Colleen signaled. *We don't have secrets.*

"A famous actress"—Patty was realistic about her father-in-law not knowing who Autumn Chase was—"just announced that she gave up a baby who would be about Colleen's age. So it's hard not to wonder if it is Colleen."

"That doesn't seem very likely."

"Not on the face of it," Liz said, "but when—" She stopped, clearly not liking what she was seeing on his face. "No, maybe not."

"Would you please excuse us?" Her father's voice was formal.

"Sure...of course..." Patty and Liz scrambled out of their chairs, scooping up the laptop, disappearing into one of the rooms.

"Dad, I don't want to have secrets from them," Colleen said. "They're family too."

"Shall I leave?" Genevieve asked.

"No, no," Colleen said. "Of course not." Genevieve was her father's wife; she was as much a part of the family as Patty and Liz.

Her father remained standing, looking down at her. He sat down only after Genevieve did. "Colleen, this is a wild goose chase. It is not possible that you are connected to this actress."

"How do we know that?" *What if they're right? What if she is my birth... no, no,* mother *isn't the right word. I only have one mother.*

But her mother, her own mother, had not given birth to her. That was the way it was. Mary Pat had never pretended anything different.

How extraordinary this was. Fifteen minutes ago, she had been thinking about how many emails she had, and now she was talking about having a birth mother. A celebrity. A movie star.

"What actress is it?" Genevieve asked.

"Autumn Chase. She did a lot of movies."

"Oh, the one with all the products," Genevieve exclaimed. "I don't know much about her acting career, but she has done a very good job of branding."

"You've heard of her?" Colleen's father asked.

Genevieve nodded. "The taste level is remarkable for the price point. And she has everything made in America. That is important to her."

Colleen had not known that.

"Her name is Autumn?" Colleen's father said.

There was something stiff in his tone. Colleen could hear Grannor's sniff. *Autumn? We do not know people with names like that.*

Colleen suddenly wanted to defend the woman. *She didn't name herself. Her parents did, the parents who pushed her to make money for them. Wasn't "Autumn" the sort of name people like that might name a baby?*

"There's no point in discussing this," he said firmly. "Your mother and I promised that we would never attempt to discover anything about your origins, and I'm going to honor that promise to my grave, just as your mother did."

Wasn't that the sort of pledge that a celebrity family would demand? "But, Dad, it was her parents who insisted on the secrecy, not her. She was only fourteen."

He stared down at his hands. They were a dentist's hands, long-fingered and deft, nothing like the hands of any of his three children. "The Bannings are very good people."

Where had that come from? "Yes, they are."

"But we had to share the boys. They've even settled close to them."

No, they settled near the O'Connells, Colleen wanted to say. *They met Patty and Liz while visiting Grammy and Grampy. They like the Bannings, but they love the O'Connells.*

"We made it work," her father continued, "but it was such a relief not to have to face that with any other family for you. You felt more like ours because that's what you were—ours. That's why you and your mother were so close, that's why you and she had a special bond."

I was the only girl. That's why we were close. Mary Pat had taught Colleen to cook, garden, and sew. She had been Colleen's Girl Scout leader; she had helped her decide what to wear for homecoming and prom. They had been—they still were—mother and daughter. Nothing, *nothing,* could ever change that.

"To engage in such a search," he continued, "would be a dishonor to her memory."

"Dad, I don't know. This is all so new. I've never thought about looking before."

"We promised that we wouldn't. We wouldn't have gotten you if we hadn't made that promise."

This was the voice he had used when he had had to lay down the law with Sean or Finn. *"I do not care what your friends are doing. In this family we do not do it."*

He had never had to use this voice with Colleen. So why was he acting as if she wanted to stay out past curfew riding motorcycles? She was not a child anymore.

What was the danger? Even if she had found a birth mother, weren't she and her brothers gifts from God? What could ever change that?

Once when she had been growing up, she had suddenly been upset by the thought that she could have been raised in another home. She knew how the Bannings had called concerning their younger daughter's pregnancy after an agreement had already been reached about the baby who would become Colleen.

"Of course we wanted him," her mother had said, "but it only took us two seconds to know that we wanted you too. Even though neither of you were born yet, we wanted you both."

Two seconds? Sometimes Colleen had counted it out, *one one-thousand, two one-thousand,* to see how long two seconds was.

She never questioned that this was her true home, that this was where she belonged. If she had gone to another family, it would have been a kidnapping. She would have been a foundling, a stolen child.

But it could have happened. *One one-thousand, two one-thousand.*

"So you could have said no?" she asked her mother once.

Her mother had heard the fear in her voice. "No, no, we couldn't have. Jesus wouldn't have let that happen."

"But what if He was busy that day? What if He forgot? Daddy gets busy sometimes and forgets about things."

"Jesus is never too busy to care about us. And don't forget He had a mother. Mary was watching over us. She would have never let you go to another family."

As an adult Colleen believed in free will, that people made their own choices. But she also believed that grace and faith put goodness in your heart and gave you the strength to follow wherever that goodness led, even when it meant, as it had for her parents, having two newborns less than six months apart.

Maybe that was enough, knowing that, being so sure of it. Maybe there was no reason to be wondering about herself as a fetus. What she had was enough. Even with her father and brothers having new wives, it was enough.

On the other hand—and wasn't there always another hand?—if she believed with all her heart that her parents were her parents and nothing would ever change that, what was the harm in opening this door?

She didn't know the answer.

Chapter 8

The family was staying a second night in Carlsville because Norton thought that they should gather at the old house to have Grannor's will read. Having learned that inheritances were not considered part of community property in a divorce settlement, Norton was far less grief-stricken over his mother's death than he might have been otherwise.

After another motel-provided cold breakfast, they drove to the part of town where the trees were the tallest. The largest car that her father had been able to rent had six seat belts. Now that Genevieve, her brothers, and their wives were here, Colleen had to ride in her uncle's car, sitting in the back seat between her two cousins with Aunt Laura in the front passenger seat.

The Ridge family house was an imposing Federal structure built of red brick with white columns supporting a deep front porch. Everything about it was symmetrical. The broad steps were in the middle of the porch; the double front doors were in the middle of the façade, with two pairs of identically spaced windows on either side of it.

"What do you think that fence is worth?" Aunt Laura asked as the car pulled up to the curb.

The property was surrounded by an intricate wrought-iron fence, full of scrolls and swirls, a design that was repeated in the massive driveway gates at the side of the house.

"Close to six figures, I'd guess," Norton answered. "I'm surprised no one's tried to steal it."

Ben's father was waiting at the curb to open the car door for Aunt Laura. Still as trim as Ryan and Ben, he was wearing a classic Southern blue seersucker suit; his shirt was white; his bow tie had a navy and pink stripe.

Colleen's cousin Will got out of the car. She started to hitch her way across the seat, but in an instant, a hand was there to help her, allowing her to slide easily across the seat and pivot into standing.

But it wasn't Will. It was Ben who had his hand out. He was in a tan gabardine suit, made less formal by a silky black T-shirt. Yesterday he, like the rest of the men in his family, had worn a dark suit. He had only brought a carry-on bag down from Charlottesville with him. He must keep clothes at his parents' house. Or he had borrowed from his brother. They were close in size.

All the girl cousins on her mother's side had sisters, and they were always borrowing clothes and shoes from one another. There was no one in Colleen's family whom she could borrow from. She was too short; her shoulders were too narrow; her feet were too small.

She was adopted.

She needed a friend. She needed to talk to someone about this. She supposed that would annoy Ben, the way she needed to talk to people about things. He was so self-reliant.

Were you jealous of all my friends back then? He shouldn't have been.

She thanked him for helping her out of the car. "I wasn't expecting to see you."

"I wasn't expecting to come."

"But?"

"First Dad asked me if I was coming, then five minutes later Ryan did, so I figured that I'd better turn up."

Compared to the fence, the porch railing was simple with softly shaped white pickets supporting a continuous top cap. It was the porch where her parents had seen her for the first time.

She had heard the story over and over. If Sean had been a girl, her parents would have named the baby after the two grandmothers, "Eleanor Eileen." When he had turned out to be a boy, they had held on to the name, hoping for more children.

As soon as they had gotten the call that the second child was born, they had scooped up Sean and flown down to Georgia. A priest and a nurse were bringing the baby to Carlsville. The family didn't want the Ridges to know even what state the baby had been born in.

The message only said that the baby was healthy. Her parents had to wait, not knowing if they had an Eleanor Eileen or a Phineas Burchell. When they heard a much-awaited car stop in front of the house, both had hurried out the front door.

"Is it a boy or a girl?" her father had called out from this porch.

"You've got yourselves one fine little colleen," the priest had answered.

Any plans to name her "Eleanor Eileen" instantly vanished. She was to be Colleen.

Colleen Marie Ridge. That's who she had always been, who she was supposed to be.

But her life hadn't begun on this porch. For a day or so she had been with other people. Did that other family regret having to give her up, or had they considered her a badge of shame and disgrace?

Why would anyone ever be ashamed of me?

One end of the porch was shadowed by climbing roses supported on a white trellis. Colleen had never seen the roses in full bloom; during her family's spring visits the woody canes were sprouting new, tightly furled, light green leaves. She had heard how fragrant the roses were in the summer. "It's like you're walking through a cloud of perfume," Nancy, Grannor's longtime maid, used to say. The greenery was now covered with pink buds and small, half-opened frills of color, and as she climbed the porch steps, Colleen got a hint of a sweet spice. She wanted to go bury her face in the roses, but she heard a sharp rapping from inside one of the dining room windows. It was Aunt Laura, holding the heavy draperies aside with one hand, gesturing with the other, demanding that Colleen come inside.

Why couldn't she stay out here? The morning sun was warm on the fading white floorboards, and the porch ceiling was painted sky blue. Ben was testing the chains on the porch swing, tugging at them, then gripping them and lifting his feet off the ground. They were still solid. She could sit there and swing, learning how roses smelled in early summer.

He came back to her side. "Go on in." He motioned toward the door, but didn't touch her. His hands were dusty from the chains of the swing. "Everything will be fine."

Why had he felt that he needed to say that? What did he know? "Aren't you coming?"

"No. I'll be out here. You need to go in."

The front doors were inset with long ovals of frosted glass. Beyond them was the wide center hall with an imperial staircase. Two separate flights of stairs descended from each side of the second floor, meeting at a half-landing, then flowing majestically downward in a broadening mahogany sweep. Although Grannor had hired a caretaker to check on the place, the house had a sad, musty smell. Colleen could hear the rattle of the old window air-conditioning units that sprouted irregularly from the windows on the sides and back of the house.

The carpet was gone from the dining room, but the rest of the furniture was still there. Fourteen chairs sat around the table, six chairs on either side, one at the head of the table, one at the foot. The set was too massive to have been shipped to the lake.

"Don't get up, don't get up," Laura ordered the men who had started to rise when Colleen came in. Uncle Norton was at the head, Mr. Healy at the foot. Her family was sitting on the far side of the table. Six chairs, three couples. Once again there was no place for her.

Finn, dear Finn, her almost-twin, noticed and started to stand. She motioned for him to stay where he was. Ryan Healy was holding out the chair next to his own.

Why had she ever thought he and Ben looked alike? Ben's features were more crisp, his cheekbones more clearly defined, and his eyes were wider. Ryan was a good-looking man, but no one had ever paid him to model clothes. The camera loved Ben.

As had she.

On the walls above the chair rail were hand-painted chinoiserie silk panels, water lilies and dragonflies on a yellow background. In a niche carved into the wall between the windows there had always been a three-foot-high blue-and-white Chinese jar. In the spring the jar would be filled with freshly cut forsythia branches. The niche was now empty, and the shelf was dusty.

Tim Healy cleared his throat to speak over the sound of the air conditioner. "So, everyone is here except Miss Davenport, is that correct?"

Aunt Laura fussed, trying to excuse her daughter.

"We did not write Mrs. Ridge's will," Mr. Healy continued. "After her husband died, we had her consult with a firm in Atlanta that specializes in estates with family properties."

Colleen was only half-listening. She tilted her head back. The crystal chandelier had five branching arms hung with teardrop prisms and pendants. The electrified candles rose up from ornate bobeches, and there were swags of beads and other embellishments that Colleen didn't know the names of. She thought it was ugly, but since it was made of hand-cut Czech crystal, it was probably very valuable.

"When the estate-tax law changed, we encouraged her to rethink everything, but she refused. So, except for token bequests, everything is going directly to the six grandchildren."

"*What?*" Norton and Laura spoke at once.

Colleen was listening now.

"That's fine with me," Colleen's father said.

"So we aren't getting anything?" Laura demanded.

"Mrs. Ridge felt that you were adequately provided for by your father's will."

"But that was *years* ago." Clearly Laura had exhausted whatever resources she had inherited then. "It is going *per stirpes*, isn't it? Kim is getting one-third, isn't she?"

Colleen looked at her. That phrase had rolled right off her tongue. So Jason wasn't the only one who knew about this.

"What's *per stirpes*?" Finn asked.

Ryan Healy's explanation was similar to what Jason's had been. Basically the difference was whether Kim would get one-third of the estate and Colleen and her brothers each would get one-ninth, or whether every grandchild would get one-sixth.

"Her will is not *per stirpes*. Mr. Will, as the oldest grandson, inherits the family Bible, all the family's military decorations, and a set of sterling flatware that was buried in the apple orchard during the Civil War. The two granddaughters are the only ones with an interest in the jewelry and one silver coffee service that was also in the orchard. Other than that, Mrs. Ridge intended that her assets be divided among the six equally. The specific distribution is complex, but that is the intention."

"That's not right. It's simply not right," Laura snapped. "I'm going to challenge that. You can contest a will, can't you?"

"Of course, Mrs. Davenport, and you should consult your own counsel, but I caution you that this will was very carefully drafted."

"But—"

"Stow it, Laura," Norton ordered. The one thing that made him happy about this will was the fact that his sister was unhappy. "It is what it is. The only difference is that the one-third would have given Kim a few more years before she runs herself into the ground. And she'll be getting half the jewelry. That has to be worth a bundle."

"Why don't you let me continue?" Mr. Healy said. "Except for the jewelry, the estate is to be divided into three pots. In the first pot are this house and all the silver, china, and art specified in various inventories. Everything that came down through the families is in that pot. All of that is to be appraised and an equivalent amount of more liquid assets, the cash, stocks, and securities, is to be placed in the second pot. The remaining, the third pot, is the residual estate."

"If they are all inheriting equally," Colleen's father asked, "why this business of three pots?"

"Because"—Mr. Healy paused, looking around the table—"the beneficiaries of the first pot are William, Jeffrey, and Kimberly, and the second, which I assure you will be of equal monetary value, goes to Sean, Colleen, and Finn. The residual estate is divided equally."

Colleen was puzzled. What was in the first pot? She couldn't remember.

Mr. Healy continued, "Will, Jeff, and Kim will receive the real property and tangible personal property that Mr. and Mrs. Ridge inherited from the Ridge and Burchell families while Sean, Finn, and Colleen will get a monetary equivalent."

Everything inherited from the families? This house, the silver, the china, the crystal…were she and her brothers to get none of that? She must not be understanding this right.

"Is that what the business with group A and group B are about?" she asked. "What's the difference between groups and pots?"

"It is a little confusing," Mr. Healy said, "and 'pot' is my term. The articles in the Group A inventory, the family heirlooms, are the first pot along with this house. They are all to be appraised and divided among Will, Jeff, and Kim. The second pot will have the liquid equivalent of appraisal, and you and your brothers will split that. Then the items in the Group B inventory and any remaining money will become a part of the residual estate which all six of you will share."

So Group A had been all the items Ben and Leilah had put on the dining room table. There had been platters and bowls, pitchers and tea urns, most of it sterling, swirling with Victorian embellishments or elegant with Federal lines. Group B had been more contemporary and had had many, many fewer items.

And Group A was going to the "real" grandchildren, the ones who never visited, who never sent birthday cards.

*Tap…tap…*a dull ringing, metal against wood, broke the silence. It was her father, tapping his gold pen on the table. Her brothers used to say that when Dad started tapping his pen, they were in trouble.

"Let me get this straight." He spoke more slowly than Colleen had ever heard him. "My children are not inheriting the family property?"

"That is correct about the real and personal property, but not about financial instruments, the stocks, the securities, and the bank accounts. Your children will receive considerably more of those assets than their cousins will. Their inheritance will have equal value."

"Equal *cash* value."

"Yes."

"I'm sorry, but I don't understand," Will said. "Why the distinction? Yes, there are three of them, but this doesn't fix the *per-stir-whatever* issue."

"My children are adopted." Colleen's father let his pen drop to the table. "And apparently this disqualifies them to be considered true family." He looked back at Ben's father. "What about the jewelry? Is it all going to Kim, who, I'd like to point out, is not here, and none of it to my Colleen, who was at her grandmother's bedside around the clock?"

"Miss Davenport does inherit the family jewelry. It is to be appraised, and Miss Ridge will receive an equivalent amount from the brokerage accounts."

Miss Ridge? Why was he calling her that?

How could this be happening? Kim was getting the beautiful sapphire earrings and the pearls that needed to be restrung, the three diamond engagement rings and the garnets...everything that had been in the heavy jewelry box on her grandmother's mahogany dressing table. Grannor had let her try them on when she had come to Georgia each spring.

Why, Grannor, why? You called me a treasure. You were proud of me. You trusted me. Why?

The fox-head brooch was ugly; the topaz choker was heavy and designed for a woman much taller than Colleen; the cloisonné bangles were too big for her wrist. And wasn't she perfectly happy with her fake pearls and her department-store earrings? Of course, she wanted a diamond someday, but she didn't need it to be big or expensive, not as long as it came from a man who loved her.

Didn't you love me, Grannor?

He loves me, he loves me not, he loves me...that was the chant when girls plucked the petals off a daisy. Had her grandmother been thinking like that when she had made up those lists? The real grandchildren, the real grandchildren, the not-real grandchildren, the real grandchildren...

"After all this compensation," Norton demanded, "is there going to be anything left? Or are my boys and Kim going to be stuck with a house that they can't maintain?"

"We can't know that until the executor arranges for the appraisals," Mr. Healy replied.

"I assume that I am the executor."

"Actually, she named Dr. Ridge."

"Ned? She named Ned? Why would she have done that? I was executor of Father's will."

Mr. Healy didn't answer.

"I'm the executor?" Colleen's father sounded disgusted. "She does this to my children and then expects me to serve as executor? She is crazy if she expects me to execute a will that disinherits my three."

"It seems to me," Laura said, "your children are going to come out of here just fine. They are going to waltz out of here with straight cash, especially Colleen. The jewelry has to be worth a fortune."

"Is that all that this means to you? The cash? This is our family history. Or it used to be mine. I'm done." Colleen's father pushed back from the table so fiercely that the legs of his chair must have clawed a mark in the wood floor. Before anyone could say anything, he was out of the room.

Colleen, closer to the door and quicker out of her chair, caught up with him under the curve of the staircase. "Dad, please, don't be upset. There's nothing we can do. She didn't leave us out altogether. She didn't do that."

He paid no attention. "All those years I came down here to help people because the name Ridge used to mean something. Yes, my ancestors were snobs and racist. They owned slaves, for God's sake, but they helped the community. They fed people during the Depression; they never bought their supplies in Atlanta; they kept their business in town. I grew up, believing that I had something to uphold. So I came back. Chicago has plenty of people who could use free dental care, and believe me, that would have been a hell of lot easier for me, but no, I came here because we were Ridges… and now I find out that my children, my own children, are not real Ridges. Maybe you should be proud of that, Colleen, because whatever blood you have in your veins has to be better than what's in mine."

"Oh, Dad…"

"I am going upstairs and getting whatever is mine from my room, and then I am never setting foot in this house again."

"Ned."

It was Genevieve, standing behind Colleen's shoulder.

"Ned, you've always known what your mother was like."

"But this…" His voice trailed off.

"…is awful," she agreed. "It is contemptible, but not unbelievable. Even Mary Pat said that your mother didn't know how to love."

"This is such a slap in the face."

"Of course it is, and you're entitled to be angry, but you've been entitled to that for years. That she didn't disinherit them altogether was probably a big concession for her. She may have thought that she was being very open-minded to treat your three as equally as she did. Let's go get the things you want and see if we can get an earlier flight home."

Colleen watched as the two of them climbed the stairs. At first her father was moving heavily as if he were fighting a downward-rushing river. Genevieve had her hand on his back. As they turned the landing, he put his arm around her shoulders.

Colleen had been pleading with him. *Please don't be mad, Daddy. It scares me when you're angry.*

She was a daughter. Genevieve was a wife. *Yes, you're angry, but you've been mad at her before. Accept it.*

Her father had needed a wife.

"Ah...Colleen?"

She turned. Her cousins Will and Jeff were standing awkwardly a few steps from the door to the dining room. Her brothers and their wives had to step around them. Patty looked as if she didn't feel well; Sean had his arm around her protectively. Finn paused, silently asking Colleen if she needed him. She shook her head. They went out to the front porch—Patty clearly needed to get some air—while Colleen waited with her cousins.

"We aren't sure what to say," Will said.

"It's not your doing." She hardly knew what she was saying. "You have nothing to feel guilty about."

"This is strange for us, the whole Ridge family legacy thing. We always called Frank 'Dad.' He wanted to adopt us, but Norton wouldn't sign off on it. I suppose this is why."

Norton was their blood link to the family, and yet they called him by first name. He might be their father, but he wasn't their dad.

I thought I was family. Surely by every standard except for one I am more family than either of you.

But apparently that one standard was what mattered to Grannor.

"Norton is all full of doom and gloom at the moment, wondering how we are going to be able to afford to even insure everything, but it is our heritage, our family history, and Grannor trusted us with it."

"I suppose you'll have to deal with Kim on that."

"The lawyer said something about some silver buried in an orchard?" Jeff asked. "Do you know what that was about?"

Of course she knew. *I know the family stories. You don't.* "General Sherman came here on his way to Atlanta. His army looted the house and burned the orchard, but our something-great-grandmother Ravenel had buried the valuables. She did it herself because the family slaves all had the sense to run off. It was the first time she had ever done any manual labor, but she picked up a shovel and did it."

Grannor had told that story with such pride. The Ravenels had gotten back on their feet during the Reconstruction by selling a lot of what this once-pampered lady had buried.

Why had Grannor thought that Will, Jeff, and Kim were fit custodians of the family legacy? They knew nothing about the Ridges and the Burchells, the Ravenels, Sinclairs, Haywoods, and Singletons. Colleen would have gone without lunch for two months if that's what it took to get the pearls restrung. She could imagine what would happen when Kim got them. She would never get around to having the work done. Then one day the pearls would go with the outfit she was wearing, so she would put them on, and they would break. She would be in a club or a taxi, and they wouldn't all be found. She would dump the rest in an envelope, and God only knew what would happen to them then.

Is that what you wanted, Grannor?

Her cousins went back in the dining room. She went outside.

The sun was higher in the sky, and the porch was less bright than it had been. Patty and Liz were on the porch swing by the rose trellis; they started to move to make room for her. She stopped them. She didn't want to sit.

"How's your father?" Liz asked.

"Genevieve knew what to say."

"We've been talking," Sean said, "and we know you're hurt and Dad's furious, but Colleen, we're fine with this—"

We? We? His word rang through her head. *Why aren't I a part of this 'we'?* While she had been inside talking to the cousins, they had put their heads together and decided that they were "fine."

"—I've never felt much connection with this house, and God knows Patty and Liz don't want to spend their lives polishing silver. We know you care, but I think I can safely speak for Finn—we're going to be quite happy with stocks, securities, and other investments, thank you."

"And," Finn went on, "we are damn lucky. If we aren't 'real' grandchildren, she could have disinherited us altogether."

"But doesn't this…surprise you?" *Hurt you, injure, wound you?* That's what she meant.

"It's hard to figure anyone thinking Kim deserves more than you, but it is what it is, Colleen. Grannor was who she was."

"I suppose."

She crossed the porch to where Ben was leaning against the railing. As she approached, he pushed himself away to stand properly.

That's what you did in the South. A gentleman didn't lounge in front of a lady.

But you're a snowboarder, an ex-snowboarder, a cheating, faithless ex-snowboarder.

What was wrong with her? How could she say he had "cheated" on her with Leilah?

She kept her back to the others and spoke softly. "How much of this had you figured out?"

"It did occur to me that the reason you couldn't do the inventories was not because you were inheriting, but because you weren't."

"Why didn't you tell us? Why didn't you warn us?" *A real friend would have.*

He frowned. "I couldn't. It wasn't my place. Plus it was all speculation. Everything I knew, you knew. And I was wrong about a lot. My guess was that everything from the family was going to Will. It never occurred to me that you all being adopted made such a difference to her."

"It never occurred to me either. So some warning would have been nice." *If you weren't a faithless cheat.*

"I couldn't. You must see that."

Well, she didn't. "If you were on a mountain and you saw a crevasse or something dangerous, would you turn around and warn the others?"

"That's different."

"Why?" It was a struggle to keep her voice low. "Because that's physical and this is emotional? Because that was a competition and this is jewelry?"

"That's not fair, Colleen."

"Unlike Grannor's will? What's fair about the foundlings not getting the heirlooms? Does the money make it fair?"

She was so sick of this. Her father got to be angry; her cousins got to feel awkward, her brothers relieved. What about her? Why couldn't she stand up and say how she felt?

Because she was a nice girl, and nice girls weren't Drama Queens. Nice girls didn't tell their summer tenants to find another place to live. Nice girls didn't leave their grandmothers alone in the hospital. Nice girls let Holy Communion be an etiquette problem.

As a teacher she could be firm; she could exert her authority. She didn't need her students to like her—although they did—she needed them to learn. But in the rest of her life, she was nice.

And where had all that niceness gotten her? Alone. Disinherited and alone. Her father had Genevieve. Her brothers had each other and their wives.

Ben. She ought to have Ben. That must have been why his father and brother had wanted him to come, so he could be here for her. Little did they know. Ben's specialty was leaving her, wasn't it? She couldn't trust him. Why hadn't she learned that four years ago?

Apparently nice girls were also big idiots.

All her thoughts about his watch and their mothers being friends meaning something...they didn't, of course they didn't. They didn't mean a thing. Wanting them to was nonsense, sentimental nonsense.

She wanted to leave, but she was going to have to wait for her uncle. She would have to sit in the back seat of his car and listen to her aunt complain.

Never again. She was never going to allow herself to be the afterthought, the one always in the middle seat. *Oh, Colleen's legs are short; she doesn't mind being in the middle.* Everyone would fuss if she started renting her own car. *Oh, Colleen, we'll take you...there's plenty of room....*

Well, too bad. They could fuss all they wanted. She would rent a car. She was an adult. Let them sit in the back seat of her car.

The door opened, and Ryan Healy came out. Reluctantly Colleen turned around to face the others. She suddenly felt exhausted. She didn't want to be an adult. She wanted to be a little girl. She wanted to sit on her mother's lap and have her mother kiss the hurt away.

Sean spoke to Ryan. "I know that this isn't our problem, but are Will, Jeff, and Kim going to keep this place going without a ton of capital?"

Ryan shrugged. "We aren't going to know that until all the appraisals come in, but it certainly is a concern. This heritage mattered to your grandmother, but ultimately it may not have mattered enough. The best way to preserve it would have been to leave everything to Will."

"No," said Finn. "The best way to have preserved it would have been to leave everything to Colleen."

Chapter 9

He and Colleen were the only ones going back to Virginia. Ben had to ask his brothers if one of them could take them to the airport, but his parents insisted on doing it.

His father had an agenda.

"Colleen," his father said once they were out of town, "you should get your father to agree to serve as executor."

Colleen was sitting in the back seat with his mother. "He doesn't want to."

"I know, but it is in your interest. I can say this because it is in the estate's interest too. There are two ways to appraise the house. The usual thing would be to call a local appraiser who will value it as a piece of real estate, and viewed that way, it is a white elephant. There is almost no market for such a house around here. But if you get in a high-end architectural salvage firm to appraise the fence, the chandeliers, the paneling, all of those, separately, that would make a big difference. There's a very active market in Atlanta and other cities for such things, especially when the history can be so well-documented."

"That sounds like a lot more work," she said.

And a lot more money for her and her brothers. "Maybe Dr. Ridge's wife is the person to talk to about this," Ben suggested.

His father nodded. As deeply fond as his parents had been of Colleen's mother, they had had a very good impression of Dr. Ridge's second wife, too.

"As long as we are overloading you with advice"—his mother had an agenda too—"there is another thing. Ben told us that your grandmother's housekeeper quit."

Needless to say, Ben had only mentioned Leilah to his parents in the context of being Mrs. Ridge's housekeeper.

"With the house having so many valuables," his mother continued, "we don't think you should be living there alone. We hope you'll agree to let Ben stay until things get sorted out."

"But—"

He interrupted her. "It's fine. I don't mind." His parents had already talked to him about this.

He hadn't liked the idea. "Mom, I'm really not the right person for this. What about Tommy?" His younger brother was a cop. "He's licensed to carry. He goes to target practice. He's going to be a lot more useful than me."

"We're actually more concerned about someone being there to support her emotionally. She has had quite a blow."

Support her emotionally? How could his parents possibly think that he would be any good at that?

Colleen was listening politely and then, when his mother finished, murmured something noncommittal, not promising one way or the other. Instead she asked if the lake house was a part of the residual estate. His dad confirmed that it was and that she and her brothers would indeed own half of it once the estate had been settled.

"But it could be sold to raise the money to pay my brothers and me?"

"That's another matter for the executor, but if you have other questions, try me and see if I can answer them."

Colleen was quiet for a moment, then said, "I have a question about my adoption. You know how my mother's mother found my brothers' birth family? I was wondering who found me. Did you all?"

Ben had to force himself not to swivel and stare at her over the car's headrest. Where had that come from?

Her grandmother's will, he supposed. That must have made her think more about her adoption.

"It was probably my idea," his mother admitted. "I was just getting to know Mary Pat then. She was so happy with Sean, and of course, she wanted a bigger family, but she felt that her mother had called in every chit that she had. I thought it would be nice if we tried down here. But I didn't do it. I was in the trenches with all those babies, so my mother-in-law, Ben's grandmother, took it on."

Ben had not known any of this. Of course he had been one of the babies keeping his mom in the trenches.

"But neither of us knew anything," his father said. "My father told me when contact had been made with a family, but he felt it was best to keep everything confidential even though I was technically his partner.

If you're curious, I believe that in Illinois adoptees are now entitled to see their original birth certificate."

"Even though my birth certificate is from Georgia?"

"It is? Really?"

Ben glanced across the car. His father was frowning.

"That's unusual," his father said. "I would have thought that since your parents were Illinois residents, that the legal work would have been done there."

"Some of the papers were signed by Judge Rutherford. Ben said that he was a family friend of yours."

"Yes," his dad agreed. "My father did say that Judge Rutherford always did what was 100 percent right, but what was sometimes only 89 percent legal. If he and Dad took a shortcut, they must have been very confident that the adoption would never be challenged. Has anyone ever reached out to you?"

"No."

That was all she said, but Ben knew the rest of her answer. *Why would they? I was where I belonged.*

* * * *

The flights between from Atlanta to Charlottesville were on small regional jets. A single cabin had four seats across, and those seats were even smaller and narrower than usual airline seats. On the way down, Colleen had sat with her father. Now she and Ben were side by side.

Once they were airborne and the view from the little window beyond Colleen's shoulder was of flat gray clouds, the flight attendant dimmed the lights. The blue-gray upholstery of the high seatbacks seemed to be a wall creating a little room for just the two of them in this narrow, pressurized world.

"Ben."

He turned to face her, but she was looking at the blue-gray wall in front of her.

"I know that you promised your parents that you would stay with me, and I also know that you say that you don't mind—"

Her tone was very controlled. She had rehearsed this.

"—but I don't want you to stay. This isn't me being nice. This isn't me talking in 'nice code' like you always said that I did. This is about me. I don't want you there."

He had never before heard her be so definite about what she wanted. "Can I ask why? This isn't because I didn't tell you about the will, is it?"

"No, I made too big a deal of that. I must have needed to make a big deal out of something just then."

Oh, shit. Was this where the emotional support business came in?

"A lot has happened in the past two days," she continued, "and I need to think. I can't do that with you around."

"I'll keep out of your way. You know I will."

"That won't be enough. Grannor trying to fix us up over spring break was embarrassing and confusing. I didn't know if that was what I wanted, and just when—I might as well admit this—just when I was thinking that maybe it was, you'd taken up with Leilah."

What she had wanted? What could he say to that? "Colleen, I'm really—"

She held up a hand, stopping him. "No. Stop. You don't need to say anything about that. It wouldn't make any difference. I feel confused right now. I am having trouble making sense of things, and it is too hard to be around you. Right now I am not strong enough."

"Strong enough for what?" He had no idea what she was talking about.

"Strong enough to resist trusting you. I trust people, Ben. That's my default. But I can't let myself trust you. It would be crazy, given everything that has happened. I need to be on my guard with you. That's new and strange for me, and I have enough on my plate." She reached forward and pulled the airline's in-flight magazine out of the seatback pocket in front of her. "If you stay, I'll get all friendly and trusting because that's what I do, and that seems really stupid right now." She started flipping through the pages of the magazine. She was done talking to him.

He watched her as she pretended to be reading. How ironic was this? The real reason he had stopped calling her after their summer together was that he had felt so crappy about himself, but he had also had his list of complaints about her. At the top had been the way she cared so much about everyone else's feelings, what they wanted to do, where they wanted to eat. She never seemed to speak up for herself, say what she wanted.

She seemed to have found her voice now. And how was she using it? To send him away.

If there had been a return flight to Atlanta that night, he might have gotten right back on it, but the Charlottesville airport was too small for that. He also didn't think anyone had thought to stop the mail or the newspapers at her grandmother's house. The newspapers were left at the end of the driveway. Anyone driving by would know that the house was empty. The cable installers had also been working while they were gone. His parents had a point. He should not let Colleen go back to the house alone.

"I hope you will let me go back with you tonight," he said as they were landing. "I do need to get my stuff."

"I guess you do." She spoke without looking at him.

He had turned in his rental car when they had flown to Atlanta, but if he tried to rent another one—especially since the counters seemed to be closed—she would get back to the lake and the empty house long before he did, which would defeat the purpose of his going. He offered to drive her car, and she accepted his offer. She was probably too tired to realize that he would then have no way to get back to the airport.

She fell asleep, waking up only when he stopped at the end of the driveway to get the mail and scoop up the Sunday paper. It was the only one there. As he drove up the long, curving drive, the car's headlights swept across the open meadow, picking up the line of disturbed earth where the cable had been buried. The rest of the newspapers were tucked neatly next to a planter. One of the workmen must have done that.

He walked through the house ahead of Colleen, turning on lights, checking the doors and windows for any sign of a forced entry. Nothing had been disturbed.

"Do you want me to stay in the house?" he asked.

"All the beds have been slept in."

"I was a snowboarder. We are not a fastidious lot."

She smiled in a vague way and told him to go on out to the boathouse.

He stopped in the library and poured himself a drink. He dropped his bag in front of the boathouse door and sat down in one of the deck chairs, balancing the drink on its wide wooden arm.

It was late enough that the moon, having risen in the east, was now over the lake, sending a glittering white ribbon across the dark waters. The light at the end of Mrs. Ridge's dock was a dim mustard-gold. Some nights it glittered a bright white, but it was solar-powered. The skies must have been overcast the last few days.

He was going to miss this place, the early morning silence, the fire-kissed colors of the sunsets, the wildflowers that were beginning to blossom in the front meadow, the deep green thickets running along the property lines down to the lake.

But he wasn't going to miss Leilah.

At first he had thought that this was the ideal relationship for him. He never had to talk about his feelings, and she hadn't wanted him to listen to her talking about hers because—he eventually realized—she really and truly didn't give a crap about him. The relationship he thought was so perfect was actually empty.

That was what he had hurt Colleen over. What a prince he had been, but the thought of Mrs. Ridge fixing him up with her had swamped him with guilt and regret. Guilt for what he had done to her; regret over what he had thrown away.

Is she a Colleen? That's what the guys had always asked when someone started dating a new woman. Colleen was the standard by which every other girlfriend was judged. Maybe he had been doing that. Even when he was consciously enumerating her faults—she had too many friends, she wanted to chat too much, she was too other-oriented, she didn't respect other people's boundaries—maybe unconsciously he too had been thinking that there had been something magical about her that he would never see again. Maybe he had been avoiding serious relationships because he secretly didn't believe that anyone could measure up to her.

But that didn't mean they were right for each other.

He got up and pulled the chair to the corner of the porch where the cell signal was strongest. He balanced his phone on the chair's arm and went inside. Then he shoved the little dining table closer to the front wall and took his computer out of his suitcase.

What a pain communications were. They were about to get better—the boathouse was getting its own network—just in time for him leaving. He waited while his computer found the signal coming from his phone. He scanned his most recent messages. Seth had sent him a rough cut of his latest snowboarding video, a promotion for Seth's family's company, Street Boards. Ben flagged it to open later. Downloading the file through this crappy connection would take too long.

What would Seth and Nate say if he told them about Colleen? They knew that he was staying in the boathouse of one of his father's rich clients. What if he told them that the old lady had been Colleen's grandmother? They wouldn't ask him if she was a "new Colleen." She was the real thing.

There was no point in telling them now. He was leaving tomorrow.

He was deleting email after email when he heard a soft knock on the door. He switched on the outside light. It was Colleen, still in the clothes she had been traveling in. In the harsh light, she looked fragile and pale.

"I was hoping you were still up," she said.

How beautiful she looked. Her skin had such a fine grain; her eyes were so soft.

"What do you need? Why didn't you use the intercom? I could have come to you." There had been no reason for her to walk over here in the dark.

"Actually I was hoping to use the internet for a few minutes. Mrs. Si—Genevieve called and said that there was something I should see."

"Of course." Without sitting down, he exited out of his programs, then pulled out the chair for her. He went into the bedroom to unpack, wanting to give her privacy even though privacy was one thing she never seemed to need.

As he was shoving his suitcase under the bed, it occurred to him if he was leaving in the morning, he probably shouldn't have unpacked. He was wondering if he should reverse the procedure when he heard Colleen gasp.

She was staring at the computer screen, her hand over her mouth.

"What is it? What's wrong?" Clearly something was. He pulled the other chair close to her. "Tell me. If it's bad, we'll deal with it."

What could be worse than her grandmother's will?

"My birthday is in October, October nineteenth."

Ben hoped that he had once known that. "And?"

"She's looked at her old call sheets and calendars and thinks from the notes there that my birthday would have been sometime between October fifteenth and twenty-second, sometime during that week."

"Colleen, what are you talking about?"

She turned the computer toward him. It was open to the site for the actress Autumn Chase.

"You know who she is, don't you?" Colleen asked.

He nodded. A couple of years ago, after the competition season was over, he had spent a week in Portland with Nate, who had—as usual—been in the rehab facility, recovering from one of his many injuries. Nate's mom had asked him to keep Nate from overdoing the exercises. It was a hopeless mission—snowboarders overdid everything, the good, the bad, and the incredibly stupid—but Ben had gone anyway.

During the mornings the TV in the exercise room had been set to reruns of *M.J.,* Autumn Chase's sitcom. The main character, a warmhearted, engaging young woman, had reminded him of Colleen in her inability to say no to other people. He supposed that was true of many women, but at that moment he'd had Colleen on his mind. Even though they had split six months before, he still had been thinking about her a lot.

He clicked on the link. Autumn Chase's site opened with a lovely wash of fall colors, cinnamon, honey, bronze, amber, and hunter green swirling into a vortex, then crystallizing into a kaleidoscope of autumn leaves that melted into letters forming Autumn's name. Pictures of her came forward, then dissolved. *Click here to get to know me.* Ben did so.

Can you help me find Ariel?

"What's this about?"

"She says 'Ariel' is the name she would have given the baby. She wanted the two of them to have the same initial. There's a tab."

The baby? What baby? Ben glanced at the tabs along the top of the page. They were the usual, *Home, Bio, Appearances,* etc. There was a tab for *Autumn's Lifestyle Collection*—whatever that might be—and farthest to the right was one labeled *Finding Ariel.* It led to another interestingly designed page. It seemed to be a letter on stationery with feathery edges. The script was mocha-colored, but still readable.

He scanned the letter. *Teenage...movie contract...forced to give her away...Florida, October...would have called her Ariel...*He was good at absorbing printed information quickly.

"At first she only remembered it as being in the fall," Colleen was saying, "but now she's figured out that it must have been October."

This was huge. "When did you find out about this?"

"Ah...yesterday, just yesterday. My sisters-in-law told me. One of my high school friends had texted me about it, but I didn't see that message until today."

"So are you thinking you might be Ariel?" he asked. No wonder she had looked so pale. This was a lot to take in.

"Those dates in October do increase the chances, but I don't look anything like her."

Ben went back to the bio page to look at a picture. He couldn't see a resemblance.

"Plus the baby was born in Florida." She was clearly trying to come up with reasons why this wouldn't be her. "If your family helped find me, wouldn't it have been in Georgia?"

"My MeeMaw"—that was his father's mother—"had cousins in Florida. If she was helping, she might have called their priests."

"Oh." She hadn't been expecting that answer. "Do you know where in Florida?"

"Not close enough to Disney World for us kids' tastes, that's all I know, but I can find out."

Underneath the letter was a link to a message board. It included an introductory message warning about respecting other people's privacy. Its language suggested that it had been written by the lawyers.

The first thread was from people encouraging Autumn to search for her relinquished child. The messages were smiley-face positive, unable to imagine anything except the rosiest of outcomes.

But the later threads took on a darker tone. Those writers were birth mothers themselves, some of whom belonged to an online support organization. They were bitter; they felt that their children had been stolen from them. Adoptive families were the enemy. Their position had a strong undercurrent of class warfare. Adoptive parents used their financial, educational, and social privileges to scoop up babies from the less privileged, believing that their status entitled them to have however many children they wanted, whenever they wanted them.

Their solution to everything was a reunion between birth mother and child. According to them, no one searching for a birth mother or a relinquished child needed to worry about what might be found. All troubles, whether substance abuse, legal problems, financial catastrophes, an inability to form healthy relationships, anything, were caused by the psychic trauma of the separation. After a reunion, healing would inevitably occur.

Therefore, the most bitter women asserted, no one involved in the "adoption triad"—child, birth mother, adoptive mother—should claim a right of privacy, the right not to be reunited. Reunions had a healing power that no one could predict in advance. The person you were looking for would be grateful when you found them…even if they thought that they wouldn't be.

One day, wrote a woman who had been kept from stalking her underage birth child by a restraining order, *my child will hate his second family for what they are doing.*

"Do you see that?" Colleen had been reading along with him. "Second family? Is that who my parents and brothers are? My second family?"

"Not to you, they aren't. Do you really need to be reading this?"

"Yes."

One-word answers weren't her usual mode of communication. So he sat with her while she read every post on every thread. As anger-filled as the rants were, Ben did feel a twinge of compassion. Some people had such difficult lives. When Colleen was finally finished, he reached over and closed the computer so that she wouldn't start over. "Let me walk you back to the house."

She protested that that was crazy, she could walk herself, but he went with her anyway.

* * * *

Shit.

Ben had to struggle to kick aside the covers and swing his feet to the floor. That had been a dream, hadn't it?

Of course, it had been. He had been out on the slopes, riding his favorite board. He had been launching off the wall of the pipe. It was a blur. He somehow turned into Nate, soaring through Big Air jumps, and then Seth, stunning even himself with an Olympic medal.

He had only dreamed about snowboarding once before. It had been a week into the software boot camp when he had realized that he was only okay at systems design. He wasn't gifted, not like some of the other people there. They were so quick to see patterns and solutions. They couldn't explain how they did it; they just could. That's how he had been at coaching snowboarders. He had no idea how his eye went to the one tiny thing a rider was doing wrong, but it did. That had been his gift, not this.

But first software engineering and now cyber-security was what he had chosen for himself, and he could make peace with being B-plus at it. He just needed to finish his degree and find a job. Then he'd been fine. He could adjust to anything.

He looked out one of the back windows. The morning sun hadn't risen above the tree line yet, but there were lights on in the big house. He found Colleen in her grandmother's bedroom. She must have already been working for a couple of hours. The bed was stripped, and she was going through her grandmother's clothes, folding a blouse into a shopping bag. A big black trash bag was nearby, and garments on hangers, some still in dry-cleaning bags, were piled on the bare mattress.

This must be one of the things that his mother was worried about, Colleen getting all frenetic to mask her grief and confusion—and his mother hadn't known anything about Autumn Chase. What stress that was adding. Someone needed to be here for her.

He wasn't the right person for the job. But he was the only one here.

"Are you donating all that?" he asked. "Shall I start carrying it out to the car?"

"That would be nice. The hospital in Staunton has a thrift shop. I thought I'd take things there."

Mrs. Ridge's car was much bigger than Colleen's. Ben got the keys from the kitchen and brought it to the front door. He left the passenger seat open for a while in case Colleen wanted to come with him. But the cable installers arrived, and Colleen needed to stay at the house. So he piled more bags onto the passenger seat and wedged shoeboxes on the floor.

He had to sweet-talk the volunteers into accepting donations on a Monday, but that was the sort of thing he usually had a fair amount of luck at because of the Irish cheekbones, the Southern manners, and all that. The cable truck was gone when he returned to the lake. Colleen was in the library, her computer open. She had set up the household network herself, something his sisters usually asked him to do.

She looked up at him. "Someone's opened a new website. FindAriel. com. People are to put forth possible candidates for Ariel."

"They aren't naming names, are they?"

"Oh, yes."

How stupid could people be? "Has anyone named you?"

"No one has even gotten close. This one"—she tapped her finger against the screen—"worried me because I went to Girl Scout camp, but that camp was in Colorado, and our council had our own camps. I never went out of state."

Ben looked at the post. The writer had gone to Girl Scout camp with a girl who had been adopted and had a birthday sometime in the fall. She couldn't remember the girl's name, but she would drive up to her mother's over the weekend and go through the boxes in the storage unit, see if she could find something from camp. She was that eager to help Autumn find Ariel.

"Now look at the one about collecting evidence," Colleen said.

That post started with an acknowledgment that it was important to obey the law, especially when dealing with a minor child…although Ben, proud brother of a police officer, quickly concluded that the writer wasn't talking about obeying the law; she was talking about what illegalities would be tolerated by an overstressed justice system. As long as you did not use any words that might be considered a physical threat, she wrote, you could ring a person's doorbell or speak to her in public multiple times. Even if the person called the authorities, a police officer might ask you to move along, but your behavior would not be actionable. Working in teams would help you avoid a pattern of established harassment.

It was, they claimed, entirely lawful to collect "abandoned DNA." You could retrieve something from a public trash can; a drink can, a toothbrush, or a used tissue could be a source of DNA.

Ben shook his head. Snowboarders had crazy courage, but looking at this website, Ben was seeing all kinds of reasons to be alarmed. Dumpster-diving for used Kleenex? If someone would do that, what wouldn't they do? Pull out a hunk of hair by the roots?

There must be thousands and thousands of people who had been involved in an adoption and who were sane and happy, birth mothers who were content in the belief that by giving up their child they had done the right thing, and adopted kids who, like Colleen, believed that they had grown up in the right family. It was only the most troubled who got involved in these message boards, but there were enough of them to be dangerous.

However secure Colleen had felt last week, her grandmother's will must have made her feel like she was standing on quicksand. "Are you tempted to go forward?" he asked carefully.

"I think Autumn is really unhappy, Ben. This matters to her. I hate to think of someone struggling if I can help."

That was a typical Colleen remark. "But what about you? Is coming forward right for you?"

"If you were me, wouldn't you want to know?"

He couldn't answer that. He was having enough trouble figuring out who he was if he wasn't snowboarding, but if he had been born to a different family...he had no idea.

"Your whole life," she went on, "people have been saying that you look like Ryan, haven't they?"

"Yes." Actually ever since his snowboarding career had taken off, people were more likely to say that Ryan looked like him.

"I've never had that. No one has ever said that I look like anyone. Your bio says that both your parents were gymnasts in high school. It's no surprise that you're so flexible. But me? I'm really good at languages, but neither of my parents is. My dad says that my teeth are amazing, perfectly straight, very strong. No one else in the family has teeth like that."

"I guess it's easy for me to say that none of that is important," he admitted. "I've always had it. I don't know anything else."

"I wish I knew what to do. My dad doesn't want me to look."

"Oh?" That made any decision easier. "He knows about this?"

She nodded. "He says that he and Mother promised that they would never look, that they wouldn't have gotten me if they hadn't made that promise, but this is different. We're not looking. She is."

It sounded as if she was trying to persuade herself that it was all right to do this. "Don't do anything impulsive, Colleen. Please."

She suddenly straightened. "Is that what you think of me? That I am all impulse? That I don't have a rational bone in me?"

Oh, crap. He had been thinking that way. Colleen was capable of flinging herself into this mess heart-first. As she had said, she trusted everyone.

She would turn over her DNA, her Social Security number, and her last dollar to anyone who could make a good case for needing them.

"I think," he said carefully, "you are the most kind, the most thoughtful, the most helpful person that I have ever met, and in that way you are like your mother. You're like that because of the way she raised you."

Chapter 10

The cable guys had pulled a line out to the boathouse. Ben set up that network and set about learning more about Autumn Chase.

She was a very attractive woman, but now only occasionally appeared in movies. There probably weren't many parts for women in their forties. She kept herself in the public eye through her Lifestyle Collection, a line of products sold on a television shopping channel. She had purses, jewelry, kitchen accessories, bath mats, wallpaper, and organizers of every description. She offered items in a range of price points, and even the lowest-end items were made in the United States.

On her blog, she offered little tidbits of advice about "living beautifully." None of her advice involved spending money on anything, including Autumn's own products. She didn't tell her fans to exercise self-care by booking a massage; she told them how to moisturize their own feet with whatever product they happened to have. The advice she was offering was realistic about what a woman without much disposable income could do. She was respectful of the challenges such women faced. She was forgiving about the shortcuts they needed to take. A woman wasn't a failure if her kitchen drawers were a mess.

He liked that.

He watched a clip of an appearance on the shopping channel. Her manner was warm and appealing; she seemed authentic. Viewers must feel as if they were getting to know the real her. No wonder her fans were so devoted to her.

He went back to the message board that was on her site. A new banner was up, announcing that the site was now being moderated. Each post would have to be approved by an administrator. That was good. He scrolled through the threads. The angriest comments had been removed. That was even better.

The other site, the unauthorized FindAriel.com, wasn't moderated. People could post anything, and they were. Ariel was being selfish, one thread argued, by refusing to reveal herself. Didn't she owe it to Autumn to come forward? Another thread countered that perhaps Ariel needed to be rescued. Perhaps she was too afraid of her "second family" to come forward.

Whoever Ariel might be, she sure as hell should be afraid. Didn't people know how dangerous the internet could be?

He might not be any good at the emotional-support thing. But this was something he could handle. He could crash the site. All it would take was a DDoS—Distributive Denial of Service. You hammered the site with so much traffic that it shut down. A message board like this wouldn't have the infrastructure to repel such an attack.

Sure, the organizers could set up another site, but the crashed-site alert about third-party applications or unwanted website visits was enough to unnerve most amateurs, especially if it happened a second time.

He found Colleen in the library; she was on her computer again reading the FindAriel.com board.

"This can't be a good way for Autumn to go about finding Ariel," he said.

"There are a lot of weird people posting," she admitted.

"Worse than weird, I'd say. I am thinking about crashing the site."

"What do you mean? Crashing it? Like taking it down? Is that legal?"

"It's not as if I would be stealing passwords or people's data."

"But is it legal?"

He shrugged.

"No, Ben, really." She pushed her computer away. "I know that you have had to learn how the hackers do all the bad things that they do, but surely you all are supposed to be like doctors—'first, do no harm' and all. Doesn't your school have a code of ethics?"

It did, and when he had tried to contact Leilah last week, he had adhered to it. He had done a deeper search than your average Joe could do, but he had not crossed any lines. "I would not call this doing harm. They are the ones causing damage."

"If you want to work for the government, aren't they going to ask you if you've ever done anything like this?"

She had a point. The security clearance you needed for the best government jobs could be denied for pretty minor infractions. "There are lots of other places that only care what you promise to do in the future."

"Haven't you already done this to yourself once before?" Colleen demanded, her voice a little sharp.

Where was that tone coming from? She was sitting up very straight and looking at him directly, her eyebrows raised, her head slightly tilted. Apparently he had not been turning in his French homework on time. "Once before? What are you talking about?"

"Once before," she continued, "you ruined your professional opportunities. You can't work for any of the major snowboarding programs. Are you trying to make sure that you can't work for the government either?"

Wow. He hadn't see this coming. "That was different. I don't want to coach in a program that I don't think is safe enough or fair to the parents."

"Then this is even more stupid because you wouldn't have any high-falutin' reason for doing it."

Protecting innocent people from being harassed seemed plenty "high-falutin'" to him. "You're making too big a deal of this. I don't know for sure what jobs require a security clearance and whether something as nickel-and-dime as this would matter."

"I don't care if it is a half-a-cent matter." She was very definite. "I won't having you mess up this career on my account. If you don't want to be in cyber-security, face that. Don't back-door your way out of it. Whatever self-destructive urges you've got, you need to own up to them."

Self-destructive urges? Not want to be in cyber-security? She was really going overboard. Sure, a felony conviction wouldn't look great on a résumé, but no prosecutor would ever go after him for shutting down an amateur message board when there had been no monetary damages.

He could hair-split this until the cows came home, but he had asked her opinion. He probably hadn't expected her to give one, but she had. He couldn't go out and do it now.

At least he could leverage this noble behavior. "If I leave the message board up, I need you to agree to my staying here."

"Why?" She suddenly looked a lot less schoolmarm-ish. Apparently her students didn't try to make deals, or they weren't as good at it as he was. "Are you afraid that I will do something stupid?"

He didn't answer.

"Are you about to say that if I don't agree, you will call my father?"

That had never occurred to him, but it wasn't a bad idea, not because Dr. Ridge was her daddy, someone with patriarchal authority over her, but because he had been named executor. The executor was really the only one to authorize who could stay at the house.

"The estate doesn't have an executor yet," he answered. "When it does, I will ask permission. In the meantime, I hope you and I could discuss this as adults."

"Oh, fine." She sounded annoyed. "As long as you promise me that you won't get all wizardy with this site."

"I promise."

* * * *

He came to regret that promise as the week went along. By Tuesday morning the Find Ariel people had found a likely candidate, a graphic artist in San Francisco. She was adopted. She was the right age. She had an October birthday. She was petite and delicately beautiful just as everyone was imagining Ariel to be. Tuesday night the website published her name and the addresses of her apartment, her office, and her parents' home. By Wednesday Autumn's fans were waiting outside her apartment, trying to get her DNA, refusing to leave her alone. By Friday her parents had hired a lawyer and had released a copy of her adoption papers, both the translation and the original Korean. She was petite and delicately beautiful because, as anyone looking at her picture should have known, she was by birth Asian.

What a nightmare for that family. Surely they would have wished that Ben had risked a future security clearance and shut down the site.

Feeling a little like a stalker, he checked Colleen's Charlottesville address on Google Earth. She lived in a slightly funky old Victorian house that appeared to have been cut up into apartments. The street was residential. People could easily gather on the sidewalk. He looked at a map of her school. Its campus had several buildings and was connected by sidewalks to the grounds of a large church. A public road lay between the school's main campus and its sports fields. She would be vulnerable there too. At least here at the lake there was only the one unmarked driveway. Colleen was probably safer here than anyplace else.

At least physically safer. Emotionally she didn't seem to be doing so well. Once she finished her grandmother's room, she pulled everything out of the downstairs coat closet and the closets in the attic bedrooms. By Thursday she was unfolding tablecloths, measuring each one, guessing the fiber content, assessing the stains, noting all this on a card, and refolding the cloth. Ben couldn't imagine why it was important to do this.

He did not know what to do. He asked her if any of her friends were planning on visiting. That would be good. Maybe they could help her more than he could.

She said that, yes, Amanda and Jason were coming the Fourth of July; they might be bringing some other people. No, they couldn't come any earlier. Amanda was working in the school's summer athletic camp. The Fourth of July was the only time she could take more than one day off.

He felt helpless. One of the picture books that his older sister used to read to the rest of them had had a picture of a knight standing at the base of a stone tower. A beautiful princess was imprisoned in the top of the tower behind its one lone window. The knight had had a horse, armor, and a lance or whatever it was that knights had. None of those were going to help him reach the princess. Ben couldn't remember which story it was or how it ended, but he supposed one or the other of them had figured something out.

Which was more than he could do. He longed to help Colleen…although it wasn't clear that she wanted help from him. This Rapunzel was not going to let down her long hair, not when she didn't trust the knight waiting below.

They had known each other forever. Their mothers had been such good friends. Why wasn't that helping him reach her?

There was one other thing. It seemed like a very odd idea, but he couldn't think of anything else. At lunch on Saturday, he suggested it. "I'm going to the five-thirty mass in the village tonight. Would you like to come with me?"

He had decided that he needed to phrase this as being about him wanting to go. This might result in him being stuck going to mass by himself, which would truly be a unique moment in ecclesiastical history, but at least it wouldn't keep him from getting a security clearance.

She looked for a moment as if she might refuse, but then thought about it. "Actually, that would be nice. I mean, good," she added quickly. "Good."

The church in the village was small and built of rough-hewn stone; dim light came through the small stained-glass windows. Colleen paused inside the door to light a candle. After they took places in one of the wooden pews, she clasped her hands and bent her head. The window near them showed the Adoration of the Magi, and a ray of blue light, filtered by the Virgin's dress, touched Colleen's cheek.

He had always liked this about church, the peace. Mass had been the one time each week that the noisy Healys were quiet for an hour. His liking that silence had led his mother to think he should become a priest when, in truth, he hadn't been paying any more attention to the service than his brothers.

The service opened with words that were deeply familiar. There were few other worshipers, so he and Colleen didn't have to share a hymnal.

He was sorry about that. As soon as Ryan and Kate had been old enough to keep order among the rest of them, his parents would sit side by side during church, holding hands. Then when they would stand for the hymns, they would be so close together that his mother's curling red hair would flatten against the sleeve of his father's dark suit.

Maybe that was part of why his dad liked going to mass.

He had made a dinner reservation at the historic inn that proudly displayed the bullet holes and scorch marks made during a Civil War skirmish. The hostess escorted them to one of the original rooms, small and away from the noisy family groups.

At each place setting, the utensils were rolled inside the napkins. Colleen unrolled hers and carefully placed the fork on the left and the knife and spoon on the right. She flipped the knife over so that the straight edge was next to the spoon. She was still adjusting the handles, making them line up perfectly, when she spoke. "I wish I had gone to confession. I am not proud of how I have been this week."

He wasn't sure that was a mortal sin. "You've been dealing with a lot."

"I'm so full of resentment." Now she was looking around the room. "I feel like Grannor was treating me like the paid help. All through Christmas I unpacked the crystal and silver. She told me the history of the pieces, but not once did she indicate that I wasn't her 'real' granddaughter."

"She probably thought that she was being generous including you in the will at all."

"Like I said, paid help. She left her former maid money too. And it's not just her. It's all of them. My father is too angry to care about what is happening to me. He's still refusing to be executor of the will. And my brothers. They work together; Patty and Liz are best friends. I felt left out. My whole family is falling apart. We weren't like this when Mother died. I remember at her funeral feeling like we were all so close, that we would go on being a family even without her, but now…"

"Does that make Autumn Chase seem like a tempting option?"

"Well, sure, sometimes. If they don't want me, I'll find someone who will. But also no. All that stuff about second families. That's not me. I just want my own family not to make me feel like an afterthought."

"Have you told your father how you feel?"

"I don't want to hurt him."

"Colleen!" This was what was so frustrating about her. "I know this is going to sound super-critical"—he really did suck at emotional support—"but there is a consequence to spending so much time keeping from hurting other people's feelings. They may not have any idea that they have hurt yours."

"I'm not a victim, Ben," she spoke firmly. "I don't let people push me around. But I don't want to make my problems a big deal for everyone else."

She started to sound a little defensive. She wasn't used to being criticizing. People didn't criticize her, not because she was some kind of Queen Bee bitch whom people were afraid of, but because she really didn't do much that was wrong. Her mistakes came when she acted from a quick impulse of her heart—which was what was worrying him about this search for Ariel.

He felt like he was stumbling through a jungle without a map. "Okay, but it ends up with people not understanding you. Or even resenting you."

"Resenting *me*? Why would anyone ever resent me?"

"Leilah did."

Oh, shit. He really should have called AAA for a TripTik before starting on this conversation. At some point he knew he needed to talk to Colleen about Leilah, to try to explain a little of what had happened. But now? What kind of timing was this?

She was waiting for him to say something. Finally she spoke again. "You have to say something, Ben. You can't get away with the strong, but silent act, not after saying that."

He nodded, acknowledging that she was right. "Because you don't want to make a deal over your problems, you make it seem like you don't have any, like everything comes easily to you. You're always so pleasant; everyone always likes you. It seems as if you are sailing through life."

The waiter arrived with their salads, and Colleen could only glower at him through the freshly-ground-pepper routine.

"You know that's not true," she said as soon as she could.

"I'm saying that's the appearance you give." There must be a lot of vinegar in the salad dressing. Ben could smell it without having picked up his fork.

"Okay, but why would Leilah care one way or the other about me and my life?"

"Honestly, I don't know enough about her to be able to tell you why, but you saw how she acted like you were too spoiled to ever help with anything."

"That drove me nuts, and it wasn't like that at all when I was there at Christmas. I helped her with everything then. Wait." She suddenly sat back from the table. "The two of you didn't talk about me, did you? Oh my God, I do not want to hear about those conversations."

"No. Never." At least he had clear road here. "We didn't talk about much, but certainly never you. I don't mean to excuse myself here—"

"You don't have to make any excuses. You didn't owe me anything at that point."

He ignored that. "The first moves were hers. It was a surprise, let me tell you. Your grandmother must have told her that you and I had been together, and she wanted to take away something that you might want."

"Maybe." Colleen didn't sound convinced. "But, Ben, you are a very good-looking man. Maybe she just wanted you for yourself."

He never knew how to respond to comments about his looks. He'd made a lot of money off of them, but the other guys were earning because of their success in the sport. He would have rather had that kind of money.

"It was more than that. Even though we never talked about you, I think the relationship was a whole lot about you."

She stared at him, then slowly shook her head. "That makes me very uncomfortable."

She looked as if she wanted to grab her purse and run. Some women did things like that. But she wouldn't. She was a whole lot tougher than most people gave her credit for.

"Let me finish. You nailed it the other day, taking about my self-destructive tendencies, making sure that something good isn't going to happen. I was as drawn to you as I was four years ago, but this time I knew that it wouldn't be 'something good,' not in the long run. Your grandmother tried to fix us up without having a clue if I could make you happy. I don't think that I could. We would end up just as before, and it would hurt more this time."

Colleen looked at him with another one of her schoolteacher looks. That was something else that was different about her, everything she had learned from being a teacher. She picked up her fork. "Not thinking you can do something is pretty much a guarantee that you can't, isn't it?"

* * * *

Colleen had not liked hearing that anyone thought things came too easily for her. Okay, she didn't have student loans, and maintaining a healthy weight wasn't the nightmare that it was for some women, but still…especially now with her mother dead and her grandmother having disowned her, what was easy about that?

She hoped that Ben remembered what he had always said about his friend Seth, that no one worked harder or practiced more to make his tricks look effortless.

And Ben…was he correct about them not being right for each other? It was an awful thought, but they were both so quick to criticize the other, she accusing him of self-destructiveness, he accusing her of not having any backbone. Neither one of them was critical by nature. They weren't bringing out the best in each other.

On their way to mass, they had picked up the mail and the newspaper from the end of the driveway. Colleen put the junk mail in the recycling bin and took the bills to the front room, where Leilah had kept Grannor's checkbook.

They weren't the first bills that had come in, and something was going to have to be done about them. The utility bills were coming due, and the semi-annual payment for the insurance on the house had to be paid by June. So far no medical bills had come; they must have first gone to Medicare and Grannor's supplementary insurance, but eventually some percentage of them would need to be paid. Colleen had learned from the internet that Grannor's estate would pay for all of this; the executor would have to set up a new checking account. But at the moment there wasn't an executor.

Ben was definitely right about this—she needed to call her father and try to make him understand. Her father was entitled to be angry. Genevieve had been right about that. But if he let the anger block out everything else, he would cause more pain than he would ever allow a patient in his dental chair to feel.

She and Ben had gotten back from dinner at a little after eight. It was only seven o'clock in Chicago. There was no excuse not to call.

She got straight to the point. She wasn't going to let this be just about the practicalities of paying the bills. "Dad, I know what is in your heart, but your actions are saying that you aren't looking out for the three of us."

"Have you been talking to Genevieve?"

"No, of course not."

"She's been saying that my refusing to be my mother's executor may seem like I am abandoning you three."

In her uneasiness about her father's remarriage, she sometimes forgot that Genevieve Sisson had been her mother's best friend. Genevieve probably knew more about Colleen and her brothers than anyone except their parents. "Yes, Dad. Yes, it does."

"And she says that maybe this isn't the best time to be neglectful of you."

Genevieve must have been talking about Autumn Chase. "I know that you love me, Dad."

"That isn't something that should be ever called into question. I'll call Tim Healy on Monday and tell him that I will handle the estate."

He must have told his siblings first because Sunday morning Colleen got a call from Aunt Laura. "Colleen, dear, you do know, don't you, that much of the jewelry is actually mine? Mother gave it to me on various occasions. She was just holding it because I travel so much."

"I don't know anything about that."

"Why would you? But there's no reason to go to the expense of appraising the things that belong to me. I'll send you a list. If you send those pieces straight to me, they won't have to go through probate and any nonsense about ownership and taxes."

"We all have to do what the executor and the lawyers say."

"What do they know about what my own mother said to me? I have pictures of myself wearing the pearls. There are three little rings in a small tin box, Mother gave them to me, and—"

Colleen stopped listening. Laura was lying. First of all, the stones in those rings were not little. Moreover, Grannor had said that she might give two of the rings to Will and Jeff. She had not given them to Laura.

A few hours later Colleen got a carefully worded message from Genevieve. Genevieve had offered to help Colleen's father with the estate. There were a few things that had to be done at the lake. Would Colleen be agreeable to the two of them working together?

Colleen didn't mind in the least. Genevieve was an interior designer with a successful business. Colleen's mother had always said that Genevieve was the best person to be on a committee with. She always did what she said she was going to do and never complained about the way you did your share.

Colleen called her and told her that.

"What a nice thing to remember. I loved working with her too."

The most urgent thing was to get the jewelry to a safe deposit box. Genevieve would work on finding one as soon as the banks opened on Monday, if Colleen would take the jewelry in.

"What about the house in Georgia?" Colleen asked. "Mr. Healy said something about having the fence and the chandeliers appraised separately."

"I thought that the minute I saw the house. I am already getting some names together."

Colleen decided to go look at the jewelry. Grannor's triple-drawer walnut jewelry case was locked, but the key was in a small china dish on the other side of her dressing table. Colleen began unloading it, wanting to make a list of what was there. The pearls were in their own dark green padded velvet folder. Stamped in gold on the outside of the case were the name of a jewelry store and a street address in Paris. Colleen took the pearls over to the window and looked at them in the light. The silk thread had stretched enough that there were little spaces between a number of the pearls and the hand-tied knots. In some spots the thread was clearly fraying.

Just as she was putting them away, her phone rang. She didn't recognize the number, but of course she answered anyway.

"Hi, it's Kim. My mother gave me your number."

Kim? Oh, Cousin Kim. Colleen couldn't remember when they had last seen each other.

"She wanted me to talk to you about the jewelry, but as I see it, she's trying to cheat both of us. She doesn't want me to have it or for you to get paid for it."

What a family. "I can only do what my father and Mr. Healy tell me to."

"That's good. I may not want any of that stuff, but I don't want my mother getting it."

"Grannor was very proud of the collection." Colleen didn't try to keep the reproof out of her voice. "Some of the pieces are beautiful."

"Oh, God, I suppose I must sound awful, don't I?" Kim apparently had some sense of decency. "But it was a surprise, my getting all this. For years Mother has been fussing that you might get more than your share because Grannor liked you so much. Every time she'd hear about you visiting her, she'd call me and say that you were sucking up, and that I needed to get in there too."

Sucking up? All the time that Colleen was doing things that a daughter, that Laura herself, ought to be doing, and it was called sucking up?

"That's why Mother made such a big deal out of me joining the DAR and the Daughters of the Confederacy because you couldn't."

Colleen had never given joining either organization a minute's thought. "Why couldn't I? Don't adopted children count?"

"Apparently not. You have to have the blood. Mother always said that that was the one thing I had going for me in all this. I have Ridge blood. You don't."

If this was what Ridge blood amounted to, then her father might have been right. Colleen was lucky not to have it. "Kim, I hope you remember that the pearls absolutely have to be restrung."

"What does that mean? Do you have to take them in to a jewelry store or something?"

"You should probably find a specialist. Seriously, Kim, that was one of the last things Grannor talked about."

"Okay, sure. I'll do it."

Colleen didn't believe her.

She felt uneasy. What if Laura tried to go to court to prove some of the jewelry was hers? How messy would that be? What Colleen needed to do was protect herself. She didn't want there to be any question about what she was taking to the safe-deposit box.

Her grandmother had subscribed to the area newspaper. It wasn't much of a paper. Some days she and Ben forgot to go to end of the driveway to pick it up. But it did have a Sunday edition. Colleen locked the jewelry back up and went outside to get it. She spread out the front page on Grannor's bed and carefully photographed each piece of jewelry, making sure that the date was in the picture.

As she was taking a picture of the fox-head brooch, Ben knocked lightly on the frame of the open door. He looked at what she was doing. "I don't know much about these things," he said, "but isn't that kind of ugly?"

"It's hideous, but the eyes are diamonds."

"Can you pry the diamonds out and sell them?"

"You'll have to ask Kim about that. It's hers."

"Why are you photographing it on top of the newspaper?" he asked. "Wouldn't it show up better on a blank background?"

"I'm establishing the date that I took the picture. People always talk about how time stamps on digital files can be altered."

"That's true, but all you're doing is establishing that you didn't take it yesterday. You could reproduce that shot any time from now on."

He had a point. She slipped the brooch back into its little bag. "You know what, Ben? I don't care. I agree that this might not make any sense, and I don't really know why I am doing it, but I don't think my relatives are very nice people. I'm circling the wagons."

She didn't usually worry about much. She used the same password on everything from her online banking to a junky cosmetics website. Circle the wagons? Pioneer Colleen would have gone out to greet the Indians with a potted plant and a tin of homemade cookies.

"Then print up a second copy of the pictures," Ben suggested, "put them in an envelope, we'll both sign our names across the flap. Mail it to yourself and then don't open it. The postmark will set the date."

"Would that work?"

He shrugged. "It can't hurt."

She sighed. She was being stupid. "This doesn't make any sense, does it? I'm wasting time, aren't I?"

"I think it's good you are seeing the importance of protecting yourself."

She recognized that tone. "This is about Autumn, isn't it? Protecting myself against the perils of the internet?"

He didn't deny it. "Have you seen the latest announcement on the website?"

She shook her head. "That was one of the things I promised myself during mass, that I would stop checking every five seconds. What's the news?"

"Why don't you finish up and we can sit down?"

"No. I can put away jewelry and listen at the same time. My auditory skills are actually quite good."

She wasn't usually this snippy, but between her awful relatives and Ben acting like she was six, some snippiness seemed in order.

"There's going to be a television show," he said, "a cable thing called *Are You Ariel?*"

"What?" A string of lapis lazuli beads slid out of her hand. "A television show? What are you talking about?"

Apparently one of the entertainment-oriented cable television channels was going to air a live special for the purpose of identifying Ariel. Any young woman who thought that she might be Autumn Chase's relinquished daughter could submit an application. If she seemed to be a likely candidate, she would send a DNA sample. The samples would be tested beforehand, and the results would be revealed during the show while Autumn Chase herself sat in an off-stage room.

Colleen was sitting on the bed, looking up at him bewildered. "Like those shows where men find out if they are the dad or not the dad and end up throwing chairs? Like that?"

"They say it will be very tasteful. But I am surprised Autumn agreed. Her public persona has always been well managed until now."

"Maybe some things are more important than public persona."

"But she's not just an actress anymore. She is a businesswoman. There are probably a lot of people whose livelihoods depend on the sales of her products. She must be feeling urgent to be taking this risk."

Urgent? What did he know about the loss, the uncertainty, that Autumn might be feeling?

He waited for her to say something. When she didn't, he came to sit down next to her. He had to pick up the beads. "Don't you see that this is good for you? If one of them does prove to be Ariel, then you are out of it without any fuss or publicity."

"So are you saying that my not being Ariel would be a good thing?"

"No, I am saying that a lot of publicity that we can't control isn't great, especially if it is pointless. And these women turning over their DNA? That's risky. The producers say that they are promising confidentiality, but there's too much at stake."

"I don't have anything to hide."

"You don't know that. Who knows what tests they will run? This isn't supposed to happen, but you could have some marker that could someday make you uninsurable."

She didn't want to listen to him anymore. He was probably right, but she was a little tired of him being right. At least right about her life. He wasn't doing such a perfect job of managing his own.

She pulled the beads out of his hand and jerked open one of the drawers of the jewelry box. She shoved the rest of the pieces back in, and locked it. She needed to find out about this TV show herself.

But as she waited for her computer to boot up, she knew that, however desperate she was to be doing something, she couldn't fill out an application. It didn't have to do with having a marker for strange, incurable diseases. It was her father.

He might not have the right to tell her not to contact Autumn, but Colleen certainly owed him the respect not to do it on national television.

She looked through the application on the website. They wanted a lot of information, birth certificate, height, weight, two pages of health history, a form that would allow them to access even more health records, previous addresses, Social Security number, and job history. If the DNA was going to give a thumbs-up or a thumbs-down, why did they need all this? What if the actual Ariel hated filling out forms?

She didn't want to blame Autumn. Autumn was warm and generous, she was kind, she was funny. Autumn wouldn't have had anything to do with designing this application. It had to be other people, not Autumn, never Autumn.

Chapter 11

Genevieve apologized for how much needed to be done before Grannor's estate could be settled. The sorting, packing, and shipping would take Colleen the whole summer, but the estate would pay her.

Pay? No, she refused the money. Nice girls weren't paid for helping their families.

And she was grateful to have the project. It kept her from thinking about Autumn and Ariel.

The big second floor bedroom was so full that it felt like an attic. Colleen found three large flat white boxes, each labeled with a woman's first name and a date. She opened the one from 1927. Beneath layers of brittle tissue paper was an ivory satin wedding gown. She lifted it out. Gorgeous in its simplicity, the dress was made of the glowingly liquid fabric that cascaded into a scallop-edged hem. The front of the dress below the waist was badly snagged; the bride must have caught her bouquet on it. Colleen held it up to herself. The bride must have been tiny. The dress was so narrow through the waist and hips that even Colleen wouldn't have been able to wear it. The gown from 1905 had froths of beautiful lace, trimming the skirt and the lower part of the sleeves. The dress had been cleaned but was still stained under the armholes, and the fabric had rotten beneath the stains. Colleen looked at the date again. Yes, the wedding had been in the summer. This bride had gotten hot. The third one had an overdress of beaded chiffon, and the heavy beads had pulled and shredded the light fabric.

The dresses must have been beautiful once. What a shame to put them back in the boxes. Surely a talented seamstress could have created something new from them. The first one could be made into a baptismal gown for a baby. The lace of the second was exquisite and attached to the dress by tiny hand stitches. It was as if someone had expected that the lace could be used again. Perhaps the beading on the third could be used as a trim.

But these gowns weren't hers. They were heirlooms and belonged to her cousins. She got fresh tissue paper and refolded the dresses.

In a brass-studded, leather trunk, she found the military decorations that were to go to Will. The trunk also contained packets of nineteenth-century letters, each bundle tied with a narrow ribbon. Some of the handwriting was spidery, some of it cramped; all the ink was fading. Grannor had told her about these letters. Colleen eased a few out of their envelopes. She learned about the weather and how many jars of plum jelly the writer's cook was putting up. Grannor had told her that there were some written from Johnson's Island, the POW camp in Michigan for captured Confederate officers. They needed to be scanned, and the originals donated to a museum.

Would Will, Jeff, or Kim ever bother to do that? Why would they? They didn't care about the family legacy.

What would Grannor have done if Will and Jeff had been adopted by their stepfather? Would she have left the family Bible to someone whose last name was Gunderson? Would Kim then be her only *real* grandchild?

Two weeks ago she would have felt obligated to—she would have wanted to—look through the family trees and find more information about those brides. She would have written down their maiden names and their married names, noting the year that they died and where they were buried. But Grannor's will told her that these women and their graves had nothing to do with her.

Then who am I? She had always been the girl everyone liked; she had never lacked confidence. Now she felt like a stranger to herself.

What if I am Ariel?

Ariel was the name of the character in Disney's *The Little Mermaid.* Except for the villainous sea witch and the leglessness-thing, it would be okay to be that Ariel. She was charming, spunky, and curious.

But at the moment Colleen was a more of a Cinderella, wasn't she? The unpaid, but oh-so-nice spinster packing up other people's heirlooms.

She might not know how she felt about being Autumn's child, but she certainly did not want to be Cinderella.

She called her father. "You and Genevieve were right. This is too much work. I need to be paid for it."

Her father was relieved, and when she told Ben, he was impressed. "You asked for money?"

"They offered. At first I said no. But I could feel myself getting even more negative about everything, so why not at least get a really great trip out of it?"

"Good for you."

As she had predicted, seeing Ben so often in such an easy way—she cooked, he did the dishes and the grocery shopping—left her treating him like someone she had grown up with, like a friend.

Every afternoon he would come looking for her, offering to move heavy trunks or load up the car for a trip to the village dump. She could have done those things. She instead needed him to help her make decisions about what to throw away. Every check her grandfather had ever written? Six handmade, now-shredded, lace baby bonnets?

"Why do people save stuff?" she asked him that evening. "Letters, I can understand. They add to the historical record. But I am saving the dress my mother wore to all three of our baptisms. It's beautiful and it's real silk. But it's emerald. I look horrible in such bright colors, and of course it is way too big. A seamstress said it would ruin the lines if I had it cut down."

"Are you hoping that you might have a daughter who would wear it? My mom saved her wedding dress for Kate and Nina. My sisters weren't interested so now she says she's saving it for the little girls."

"At least there's a chance that your mother's granddaughters could wear her dress. How likely is it that I will have a five-foot-nine red-haired daughter? And why does the DAR care about biological connections?" Colleen didn't know if she was exasperated with herself, her grandparents, or a lineage-based service organization. "Can't you be proud of the country and the Revolution even if you've only been here for five minutes?"

"I would think so, but that is a different question than saving physical artifacts."

"We—the Ridge family, that is—has a set of flatware and a tea service that a former slave owner hid from the Union Army. Does knowing that make them more interesting or valuable? Grannor couldn't find the piece of paper that said who had owned some engagement rings. Why does that make the rings feel like orphans? Part of me wants to find out about the brides who wore the dresses so that people know who they were. Why does that matter? The past is past. Saving a dress no one can wear isn't going to bring it any closer. So why?"

"I have no idea, but—" He broke off and started to put his utensils on his plate as if he was going to clear the table.

"You were about to say something, weren't you?" Colleen could feel her shoulders go up and her neck tighten. This still happened to her, the tensing, the anxiety that he was about to criticize her. "You started; you might as well finish."

He wasn't her friend. He wasn't the boy next door. He was a man, a dangerous man, with broad shoulders and a long lean torso, with deep-set green eyes and knife-edge cheekbones.

"I was just going to suggest"—his voice was mild, slowly and softly Southern, the voice she had known her whole life—"that if it would make you feel better, why don't we look up the information about those brides and attach it to the dresses?"

That wasn't a dangerous answer. That was a friend's answer. Why couldn't he stay one or the other, her friend or her peril? "You don't think that is a waste of time?"

"Not if it would mean something to you."

* * * *

Colleen was dreading the Fourth of July holiday. She wished her friends weren't coming. She knew that there were people who had to give up on their own families, who created families from their friends, celebrating holidays together, planning each other's funerals, but that wasn't her. However focused they were on their wives, she would never give up on her brothers. She would move to Minnesota and risk freezing to death rather than live without family.

Autumn's *Are You Ariel?* show would be on over the holiday. It would be strange watching it with her friends. None of them seemed to know that she was adopted.

"I didn't think you ever hid that," Ben said when she told him. The moments when he seemed to be her friend were coming more and more often.

"No, not deliberately. I guess it never came up. It turns out that a lot of my college friends don't know either. It's never seemed very important before."

"Wouldn't it be easier on you if they knew? You don't like secrets, do you?"

That was certainly true. "I also don't want to have to tell Amanda how little I've done on our grant application. I don't like disappointing people."

"You probably don't do it very often. Tell me more about the grant. What would the money be for?"

"Partly so we would have time next summer. Developing a detailed curriculum is a lot of work, and we've always had to have summer jobs."

Ben looked at her, his head tilted, his eyes glinting. "It sounds like you don't completely realize how much money you're going to have when the estate settles."

That was true. She wasn't thinking of herself as an heiress. The terms of Grannor's will still hurt. If Colleen had been inheriting half of the jewelry and a sixth of the silver and china, she would be thinking about what she wanted. She would have tried on the pearls. She would have compared the cake forks in the different sets of sterling. But the money? Thinking about the trips she would be able to take, all the things she would be able to buy, made her feel as if she hadn't really mattered.

"This curriculum is something I care about," she said. "Even if we can do it without the grant, we would still have to do this preliminary work. It isn't a waste of time."

Ben knew a lot about how athletic kids learned. "There are kids whose teachers think that they are as dumb as a post because verbal instructions mean so little to them, but their motor memories and kinetic awareness are off the charts. They are whip smart, just not in the ways the classroom cares about."

He went on to say that sometimes you simply had to grab hold of a kid's shoulders or hips and have them feel what they needed to do. Words, even pictures, didn't help them, but once they felt it, they never forgot it. "Of course, it's a bitch because you can't touch the kids anymore. That's right. Of course, it is, but it disadvantages some of them so much."

This was the real Ben, not the overly controlled, overly polite man of the last few months; this was the Ben she had once loved so dearly. Why wasn't he trying to get back into coaching? He cared so much about how these kids learned. This was what he was supposed to be doing. That was the only way he would ever truly be himself.

* * * *

The Fourth was on a Friday. Two other of Colleen's friends, Cara Hernandez and Libby Tyson, were coming to the lake with Jason and Amanda. They were arriving Thursday evening. From the kitchen window Colleen saw Jason's car come up the drive. She called to Ben, and they went out the front door to greet the others.

Colleen introduced Cara and Libby to Ben. Cara almost closed her finger in the car door, and Libby tilted the plate of cookies she was carrying. Ben's reaction time was so quick that he steadied the plate before any of the cookies fell. This didn't add to Libby's composure.

Amanda sent a teasing glance to Colleen. *I didn't warn them what he looks like.*

In the dusky shadow cast by the sprawling house, Ben's hair looked black, its flashes of copper needing the sun, but the perfect symmetry of his features, the easy grace of his carriage, dazzled with its own light.

It was a moment before Libby was sure enough of herself to speak. "I hope no one minds what I spent." She loved to cook so she had taken over planning the menus and had brought a lot of the groceries with her. "Divided six ways it won't be that bad."

Now it was Ben's turn to send Colleen a look, this one pleading. He did not want to go Dutch when four of the others were teachers.

She gave her head a slight shake. Her friends had come expecting to pay their own way.

Was this what it would be like when Grannor's estate was settled? Her friends would still have to budget for every little indulgence while she could easily treat them. Wouldn't that be awkward? Would they start to expect her to pay? Would that make her feel taken advantage of?

She supposed that there were worse problems to have.

"Amanda told us that you got the internet a few weeks ago," Cara said as they were carrying the groceries in. "What about cable TV? I hate to sound like the low-brow ditz that I am, but I am interested in watching Autumn Chase's show."

This would have been a good time to tell everyone, that there was a chance, such a slight chance that it was hardly worth mentioning, that she might be Ariel. Everyone would be shocked. All the bustle of putting away the groceries would stop. They would want her to tell the whole story. They were smart, they would figure out that there was a whole lot more than just a slight chance that she was Ariel. They would want to know if she had had her DNA done, why she hadn't said anything, she always told everyone everything, and on and on. She couldn't face it.

So only Ben would know.

* * * *

The Fourth was everything that the holiday should be. Ben wheeled around the old Weber grill, and they grilled hot dogs and hamburgers over the charcoal. At dusk, they crowded into the rowboat and watched the village fireworks from the lake. People with homes along the shore had turned off their lights, and the music from the open-air dock in the village carried over the water.

Saturday morning Colleen sat down with Amanda to talk about the grant application. "I'm sorry. I got new ideas, some of them thanks to Ben, but I haven't gotten much writing done. I've been helping my father organize my grandmother's estate."

"Jason and I are finding it strange to be here without her. It must be a nightmare for you. Do you still expect her to sweep in the room and tell you what you are doing wrong?"

"Actually, no."

In the first few days after Grannor had died, before they had gone down to Georgia, Colleen had felt that her grandmother was still in the house, but once she and Ben had returned, she hadn't. She used paper napkins and set the ketchup and mustard out in their original containers without feeling that Grannor was watching her. Her shock over the will must have stifled her grief. That probably wasn't healthy.

"Her will caused a lot of hurt feelings," she said to Amanda.

"Oh?"

Amanda was an English teacher; she liked stories. She would have liked to hear this one. But how could Colleen explain the will? Amanda didn't even know that she was adopted, and with Autumn's show coming on tonight, it was too complicated.

Amanda was also a good friend, so when Colleen murmured something about her aunt and uncle being angry, Amanda didn't push her. "Then can we talk about Ben?" Amanda asked.

"What's to say? We aren't a couple. We are trying to be friends, but there is a lot of baggage."

"You haven't been tempted to jump his bones?"

"I certainly haven't done it."

* * * *

Cara and Libby were not the sort who indulged in holiday flings. They were only interested in something serious, and Colleen felt sure that Amanda had warned them that there was something complicated between Ben and herself, no matter how often she had tried to tell Amanda otherwise.

"We're thinking of him as a museum piece," Libby said when the four women were alone Saturday afternoon. "Look, but do not touch."

"His mother did want him to become a priest," Colleen said.

"A priest? A *Catholic* priest? As in a poverty, chastity, and obedience kind of priest?"

"Yes," Colleen answered. "But I don't think he would be good at any of those."

"I'd certainly start going to mass a lot more," said Cara. "My mother would be very pleased."

"Especially if she started going with you," Amanda added.

Ben as a priest...going through his day, dressed in black with a touch of white at his throat, the white calling attention to the Irish beauty of his face; celebrating mass, wearing the white vestment, lifting the chalice overhead as he consecrated the Host, his robe rippling down from his broad shoulders.

Colleen might well be in the pews too, but for all the wrong reasons.

* * * *

Finally it was eight o'clock on Saturday night. Ben and Jason moved the furniture a little so that they could all gather around the TV. In groups Colleen usually took a seat in the middle of a sofa. She was small; she didn't feel cramped by having people on either side of her. And she liked being in the middle of things. Tonight she sat in a wing chair.

What were the next ninety minutes going to be like? Would it be like a beauty pageant? Would confetti cascade from the ceiling when the winner was announced? Would there be a tiara and flowers?

Whatever happened, it wouldn't be Colleen who was crowned.

She knew that either she was Ariel or she wasn't. Nothing that happened Saturday night was going to change that. But she couldn't help feeling that by not submitting an application she had lost her chance, that someone else was going to step in the place that was rightfully hers.

People she had grown up with had been in touch with her since the search for Ariel had begun. She had always said that her father had said that it was impossible. That was the truth—he had *said* that—which was fortunate because she was no good at lying, but he had said it because he wanted it to be so, not because he had any evidence.

A commercial began telling them about a weight loss pill that they could order directly from the manufacturer at a one-time special savings. The next commercial was again direct-marketing, this one for a set of inspirational songs from various country artists.

"I would have expected better ads." Jason said. "At least ones for her products."

"This could backfire on her brand," Ben said. "The people in charge of the merch may have dug foxholes for themselves."

The cable channel's logo came on the screen followed by a blandly handsome young man. "Welcome to *Are You Ariel?*" he said dramatically. "I am Brian Raines, and we are *live!*"

"Okay, Colleen, you have an October birthday," Amanda said, "this is your last chance to pretend to be adopted."

"What are you talking about?" Cara asked. "Are you adopted, Colleen?"

Colleen could feel Ben looking at her. *No, I didn't tell them.*

So he rescued her. "I think Amanda said 'pretend.'" His voice was deep.

"I was born in October," she said, "but I don't think my dad would like me to emerge as the poster child for adoption." That was certainly true.

"We are here tonight," the host continued, "in hopes that we can find the lost daughter of the beloved Autumn Chase. Autumn is backstage in a separate room." The screen switched to a shot of her. Brian complimented her on how lovely she looked and asked her how she was feeling.

"I'm nervous, I'm hopeful," she said, her hand brushing against her chest as if she were touching her heart. With her was Bethany Ares, a "celebrity journalist."

"What's a celebrity journalist?" Jason asked. "Does she write about celebrities, or is she a celebrity herself?"

No one in the room knew. None of them had ever heard of her.

Bethany took over the interview. At fourteen, Autumn explained, she had been the sole support of her extended family. Her parents, grandmother, and great-grandmother all lived in houses owned by the trust in which child-labor laws required her earnings to be placed. Her parents' only source of income was the fees that they took for managing her career.

"The fees were not inappropriate, but if I wasn't earning, they weren't either."

Her multi-picture contract was with a division of a squeaky-clean film corporation. The parents of her young fans would not have considered a pregnant teen to be an acceptable role model for their daughters.

"Why didn't you have an abortion?" Bethany asked.

"My father expected me to. I couldn't believe it." Autumn blinked and tilted her head back as if even now she couldn't believe it. "We were Catholics. I had grown up hearing that an abortion might sever my relationship with God. My father didn't care about that, only about my career."

Her mother's continued refusal to take her in for an abortion had been the breaking point in her parents' already difficult marriage.

"Did you want to keep the baby?" Bethany asked.

"Of course. Of course." She leaned forward, making a despairing little gesture, her hand near her chin, her fingers flicking open, her palm turning outward. It was a familiar gesture; Colleen recognized it as characteristic of Autumn's TV character, M.J. "But my mother wouldn't hear of it. She told me that neither she nor my grandmother would do a thing to help me raise it, and I would need to come up with a plan not only to take care of my child, but how I was going to replace the income that I would be losing."

"That's a lot of pressure to put on a young girl."

"That's why adoption felt like the only choice. Now I need to know where Ariel is and how she is doing. I need to know if I did the right thing. I want her to understand why I did what I did; I need to know if she forgives me."

The interviewer asked her what the search for Ariel had uncovered so far.

"Not a great deal. I was apparently admitted to the hospital under a false name and my mother destroyed all our paperwork. My grandmother was the one who contacted her parish priest, asking him to find a good Catholic family, but both of them are dead and they left no records. Even the most experienced investigators haven't found a trace of what happened to her."

The investigators had also examined all the registries where adoptees could express their interest in reuniting with birth families, but there had been no trace of Ariel on any of them.

"The mother searching for her child," Amanda said, "that's the Demeter myth, Persephone being kidnapped and taken into the underworld, and her mother plunging the world into winter while she went looking for her."

Colleen spoke. "I don't think adopting families would like to be compared to the underworld."

After a commercial break, the host came back onscreen to explain the format of the show. "The production staff has screened dozens of applications—"

"Dozens?" Jason interrupted. "That's not very impressive."

The others shushed him.

"—and every person who had the slightest possibility of being Ariel has been investigated. Since the secrecy about Ariel's birth was so important, we had to allow for the possibility that identifying information, including the birth date, may have been falsified. We accepted anyone with a birthday from September through January. In one case we have even been willing to entertain the possibility that Autumn was misled about the gender of the child."

He then introduced the first candidate. She was a lovely young woman with an astonishing resemblance to Autumn Chase. She was petite with the same thick chestnut hair, the same high cheekbones and balanced jaw, the same little nose.

"She has to be Ariel," Libby said.

"No." Amanda was confident. "They will save the most likely candidates for last. This one has to be a total non-starter."

Back on the screen, the candidate and Brian had moved to sit down in a pair of leather chairs. "You certainly look as if you could be Ariel."

"Yes, as long as I can remember, people have been telling me that I look like Autumn Chase."

"Do you think that you are Ariel?"

"No. I'm not adopted. I know I'm not. My looking like her is a fluke… although I deliberately wear my hair like she does. I figured that if it looked good on her, it would look good on me."

"Even so," Brian said, "the resemblance is extraordinary. Is it possible that you were switched at birth, that your parents brought the wrong baby home from the hospital?"

"Ever since this started, people have been asking me that, but I was born in December in Akron, Ohio. No one in my family has ever been near Florida."

"If you are so confident that you are not Ariel, why did you come on the show?"

"It was a free trip to LA," she admitted honestly. "And I've never been to California. But also, my family's been getting so many questions, people accusing them of lying about my not being adopted. Someone even suggested that my parents were lying because they had taken money to pass off Autumn's baby as theirs. My mother was really hurt. It's been horrible having people say these things about us. Coming on the show seemed like the best way to let everyone know for sure."

The second hopeful was a slender, young man in a remarkably tight version of an Oxford-cloth shirt. He had been a fan of Autumn Chase since he had been able to turn on the television himself. He had been adopted, and the dates weren't too far off. He felt sure that the attraction he had always felt for Autumn must be genetic. She must be his mother.

"You do know that Autumn's mother and grandmother have said that they each saw a baby girl?" Brian asked.

"Yes, but the hospital could have shown them the wrong baby. Or they could be lying. They've lied so many times. Why should we believe them about this?"

"You do have a point. How would your life change if you found out that you were Ariel?"

The young man spun out a fantasy about going places with Autumn, traveling with her. He had always been interested in fashion, and although he had had no formal training, he prided himself on his innate taste, taste that had been inherited from her, no doubt. Of course, she had professional stylists, but he could see himself supervising them.

"Can you imagine what the professionals would think about that?" Amanda asked.

The third hopeful was a ten-year-old girl whose adoptive parents had decided that she might be Autumn's granddaughter. Her birth mother, the actual potential "Ariel," had been sixteen. The family didn't have her name, but knew that she liked to read books and sing in her church choir. She had a family history of elevated blood pressure similar to that of the Chases'.

"That proves nothing," Ben said. "Every decent Southern family has hypertension all over the family tree. We live on fried food and cream gravies."

Until the little girl turned eighteen, the parents would not be able to find out anything more about the birth mother, and admittedly, they had no reason to think that she had been adopted herself. But the father went on and on about how exceptionally talented his daughter was. If she was allowed to sing, everyone would know that she must be carrying Autumn's DNA.

The host started to ask the girl a question. She interrupted him, not letting him finish.

"What a brat," Libby said as soon as the commercial came on. "We have kids in the lower school like that. You always want to slap them."

"These three do seem like long shots, don't they?" Cara said.

"Does it matter?" Jason asked. "Isn't this all about the publicity? Wouldn't every forty-something actress kill for this publicity?"

"Don't be so cynical, Jason," Cara admonished. "We're supposed to care about this."

"The Nats are playing the Dodgers," he answered. "The game's out west. It might still be on. That's what I care about."

As Amanda had predicted, the producers had been saving the two most likely candidates for the end. Both were within a few months of being the right age and had been adopted by Catholic families. The first one had been raised in Alaska, one of the few states that allowed adoptees easy access to their original birth certificates once they turned eighteen. The shows' producers helped her get hers. It had been issued in Alaska. Her mother was "Jane Doe," her father was unknown. This level of secrecy might have been promising if the original certificate had been issued in Florida, but this candidate seemed to have been born in Alaska.

This candidate herself was the exact opposite of the annoying little girl. She was pathologically shy. She whispered monosyllabic answers and never looked at the camera or the host. It was painful to watch her. Fortunately the host treated her gently and got her off-camera quickly.

The final woman was one tough cookie. Her spiky hair was dyed a flat, lifeless black; dense, dark tattoos spiraled up her arms. Her lip was pierced, and she had a ring through her eyebrow. Colleen's mother would have sighed and called her "hard."

"She isn't someone the shopping channel is going to want to be associated with," Ben said. "From a marketing standpoint, this would be one bad outcome."

This candidate had, indeed, been adopted by a Catholic couple—"a fine pair of Christians they were," she scoffed—but when she was five, they had gone to court to dissolve the adoption. She had spent the rest of her childhood being moved among foster homes, finally ending up in an institutional environment.

She was so angry with her adoptive parents that she had never thought about her birth family. Now all she wanted from Autumn Chase was money. "She owes me. She abandoned me to them. You heard her. She dumped her baby to save her movie contract. It was all about money for her. I was the one who allowed her to go on making money. She owes me."

"You are confident that you are Ariel?"

"I don't give a rat's ass about any Ariel. I just know that someone owes me."

"You have indeed had a difficult life," the host said and after a few more platitudes, he cut to a commercial break.

"There's your underworld, Amanda," Jason said. "That girl has been in hell for most of her life, but I don't see how much a rescue can do."

"I guess we have to root for the one from Alaska," Cara said.

"I don't agree," Ben said. "At least that last one had her anger to sustain her. Can you imagine what would happen to Miss Alaska if she got caught up in the celebrity machine? She would be roadkill."

"Then we have to root for the guy. He wants to be caught up in the celebrity machine."

Colleen hadn't said anything. So this was what it meant to be on national television. Perfectly nice people like Cara and Ben felt that they had the right to call you a brat or roadkill. What would people have said about her if she had been on the show? That she was boring, overprivileged, stuck up, too eager to please? That she needed to lose ten pounds or gain five? That her earrings were all wrong? They could say anything.

The commercials ended. The first three candidates came onstage one by one. The lookalike who hadn't been adopted, the young man, and the annoying little girl were each told that they were not Ariel.

The final two hopefuls, the shy one from Alaska and the angry one, were brought out together, standing side by side. It was indeed as if this were a beauty pageant and the two women were waiting to see which one would be first runner-up and which one the queen. When Miss Alaska was told that she was not Ariel, a look of relief flashed across her face, followed by an expression that was weary. She had failed yet again.

The tattooed one was looking grimly smug. The host repeated some of her story, dwelling on how rare, but how tragic it was when an adoption failed. "And you are...*not* Ariel."

Not...Had he really said 'not'? Colleen wasn't sure that she had heard right, but the woman's expression was hardening into unreadable sullenness. No confetti fell; Autumn wasn't rushing onto the stage.

So it wasn't over. She could still be Ariel.

"Yuck," Libby said. "I feel as if I need to take a shower. That was horrible. Why did we watch that?"

The camera cut to Autumn. "Of course I am disappointed, and I feel so badly for some of those people." She made the little M.J. gesture again. "But this only makes me feel more urgent about finding Ariel. What if she, too, ended up in institutional care?"

This doesn't mean that it's me. The real Ariel could be in the Peace Corps, serving in a village cut off from American celebrity gossip. She could not know that she was adopted. She could be dead.

Onscreen a woman from one of the radical birth-mother organizations joined Autumn and Mia, and the journalist began to question her about what else could be done to find Ariel.

"Why isn't anyone asking about the father?" Jason said. "No one has mentioned him. Doesn't he have a role in this?"

"Autumn won't name him," Cara said. "She said that he never knew that she was pregnant and that his family has a right to privacy."

"And Ariel and her family don't?" Ben asked.

Chapter 12

Libby wanted a nine-by-thirteen pan for breakfast in the morning. Colleen got one out. Jason asked if he could look in Grannor's room for another lamp to use at the jigsaw puzzle. She told him that he could.

When Libby had everything she needed and the other three were settled at the jigsaw puzzle, Colleen went through the French doors and across the patio. She didn't try to make up an excuse. Let people think what they wanted.

The door to the boathouse was ajar. Ben was sitting at the table with his computer open. Next to him were a bottle of wine and two glasses.

You knew.

Genevieve, Patty, and Liz had been very helpful during the search for Ariel, Genevieve reassuring Colleen's father, Patty and Liz keeping track of everything being said in magazines and on social media. But she hadn't talked to them about how she felt, how confusing and bewildering this had been.

Ben had understood, and he knew that she would need to talk to someone. He had been waiting with a bottle of wine and two glasses because he got it. Quietly observant, he understood what she was going through better than anyone else.

While she was waiting for him to open the wine, she saw that he had paused his screen on an image of a snowboarder. "Is that Seth?" She knew that he was still making promotional videos for his family's company.

"Lord, no." Ben grimaced and reached forward to close the computer. "Seth's form is a million times better. It's one of the newer kids. He needs help."

"Are you going to give it to him?"

"You know I'm not." He handed her a glass. "But that's not why you are here."

He was right about that. "After the show tonight, don't you think that it's even more likely that I'm Ariel?"

There she had said it. *I am Ariel.* Or almost said it.

"A lot of other doors are closing. And I understand that you must be wanting to come forward, but with the publicity from—"

She knew where he was going with this. She stopped him. "There will always be a reason to wait. I am done waiting."

"What about your father?"

"He and Mother promised that *they* wouldn't look, and I'm not looking. Autumn started it. I'm doing this. I'm going forward. I don't need your permission or my father's. I just wanted you to know."

"How are you going to do it?"

She paused. He wasn't arguing. He was asking her questions. Her girlfriends shared her feelings; they were sad when she was sad, outraged when she was...but she didn't need Ben to be her girlfriend. She needed him to do this even if she didn't always like it. "What do you mean, how?"

"You can't apply through the TV show anymore. Are you going to go through the message boards?"

She hadn't thought through this. "In the long run it probably doesn't matter how I do it."

"It sure as hell does. Post on either one of the message boards tonight and there will be people going through our garbage tomorrow morning. You don't have to go crawling to her like everyone was doing when this first started. You have leverage now. That show tonight has to change some things. It's bound to have hurt her brand."

"Maybe she doesn't care about her brand." Autumn might be her birth mother. Who would want to think that their birth mother cared so much about money? "Maybe this is more important to her than sales."

"You can't know that."

He was right; of course he was. Autumn was a celebrity, a personality. What people saw onscreen wasn't necessarily what she was like. She was an actress. She could be playing a part.

"Colleen, you need to stay at arm's length at first if you are going ahead with this. Do you want to be harassed like that woman in San Francisco? Will you please let me handle it? If not me, then my brother or my father."

"Why? What could any of you do that I can't?"

"Keep your name out of it. Insist that you control the DNA comparison, not them."

"How's anyone going to do that? Autumn has all these people, agents and publicists."

"So do I," he said bluntly. "My agent hasn't heard from me in ages, but she's still making money off residuals. She'll be able to find out who Autumn's agent and manager are. She can work with them for a while without anyone knowing my name, much less yours."

Oh, right. With the two of them so isolated here at the lake, it was easy to forget that Ben had been a public figure. He had access to a world that she didn't. Once again he was right. He needed to take the lead on this.

She didn't love that. It made her feel like a child, naïve and helpless, when she wasn't. It wasn't like he was making such perfect choices about his own life.

But there was another difference between Cinderella and Disney's Ariel. Cinderella sat around waiting for Prince Charming to rescue her; Ariel had saved Prince Eric from drowning. Ben Healy could use a little rescuing.

"I will accept your help on one condition." Hadn't he made a deal with her when she told him not to crash the Find Ariel site? That's why he was still here—because he had said he wouldn't crash the site if she would let him stay at the lake.

"Name it," he said.

"While you're working on this, I will find you a coaching gig for next winter even if it is just for a week."

He drew back. "Colleen, what does that have to do with approaching Autumn?"

"Everything. You always seem to think you know what's best for me. Maybe you need to accept that I might know what is best for you."

He was shaking his head. "The politics are more complicated than you understand."

"I think you are letting them be that complicated. Here's what I do understand—whenever you get close to something great, you go out of your way to screw it up. That's what I meant when I talked about your self-destructive impulses. You screwed up with me four years ago, you screwed up your coaching opportunities, and last spring the minute you saw me again, you made sure nothing could happen by running off with someone else."

"I won't dispute that pattern, but I still believe everything I said, the high-powered programs are taking advantage of kids and their parents."

"Then we won't go to a high-powered program. I'll find one where the kids are just having fun on weekends. That's how all three of you started, by having fun. You don't mind working with little kids, do you?"

He shook his head. "I take the nieces and nephews out. But why do this right now? It's July. You're talking about something months away. Why not wait?'

Where had she heard "please wait" before? "Because—to quote you— right now I have leverage with you, and I am going to use it."

"Do you know what you're doing?"

"Not right now, but I will soon. Finding the right people and connecting with them, I'm good at that."

"I don't want you to call Nate or Seth. I am not putting them in an awkward position by asking for favors."

Colleen thought that was nuts. She had no problem asking people for favors. If someone asked for something reasonable, she tried very hard to do what they had asked. Wasn't it arrogant to assume that other people weren't equally generous? But she agreed not to ask his friends for help.

"And I can't sign anything without clearing it with my agent."

"Give me her name." Colleen felt confident that his agent would love to hear that he was getting back into coaching, even if it was only for a week. "Do you agree that if I trust that you want the best for me, you will agree to trust that I want the best for you?"

He nodded.

"So we have a deal?" She put out her hand.

He took it. His grip was warm and firm. "We have a deal."

* * * *

Colleen was sure—completely, 100 percent, down-to-her-bones sure— that this was going to be easy; Ben had to be wrong about his reputation in the snowboarding community. It had been more than two years since his flame-out. Surely he was being typically Ben, always expecting the worst to come walking through the door, even to the point of extending a helping hand to help the worst cross the threshold.

Sunday morning she made up an excuse to get Amanda alone. Without mentioning that it had been a two-sided deal, she explained that Ben was going to let her find him a foothold back into coaching.

"Just what were you doing when you got him to agree to that?" Amanda wanted to know.

"I had my clothes on, if that's what you're asking."

"Of course it was," Amanda said cheerfully. "But are you really that sure about Ben being wrong? He doesn't seem like he'd misjudge something like that."

"He makes plenty of mistakes, believe me. I am actually more concerned about selling him short, that I will get him a week at a dinky little resort when one of the big sports academies would have hired him for the whole season."

"Doesn't he have people who would do this and do it much better than we ever could?"

That was a good point. Colleen had to take a moment to think. "He probably agreed because he thinks we can't do it."

Like Ben and his friends, Amanda was a competitive athlete; she took that as a challenge.

Together they made a plan. The sports academies were residential schools where talented young athletes went to get intensive training in their sport as well as a scholastic education. Colleen and Amanda knew from their research that the foreign language instruction was limited to teaching English to the speakers of other languages. Nonetheless they had already thought that it would be useful to talk to those teachers because all their students would be extremely active kids.

Amanda was going to make some calls. She would start with the tennis academies, as they would be in session. Once she got comfortable with the conversations, she would get in touch with the winter sports places. When she was talking to the administrators, she would work Ben's name into the conversation.

"How are you going to do that?" Colleen asked.

"I'm a better liar than you. I know that's a pretty low hurdle, but I take my wins where I can get them."

Amanda promised to start on this Monday, but it would take her some time. The calls would have to be made during business hours. With her job in their school's summer sports camp, she didn't have a lot of free time during the day.

If they didn't get the grant for next summer, Colleen could probably fund the development of the curriculum herself. Ben was right about that. But how would she go about doing it? Write Amanda a check every pay period?

It was raining in Charlottesville. Amanda was able to turn over the indoor drills to her assistants. She had more time than expected. By Wednesday she had set up weekend calls with the ESL teachers at the tennis academies to discuss their teaching techniques. By Friday she had spoken to a few of the winter sports academies.

"I wish I had better news," she told Colleen. "He cost some of those places a lot of money. They defend themselves—it's a risky sport, there will be injuries, and they aren't going to tell the parents of a hard-working, motivated kid to stop investing in the kid's training even if the coaches aren't sure of the kid's basic ability. The bottom line is, while they say nice things about Ben's abilities, they feel betrayed. He benefited from this system. He shouldn't have criticized it."

Colleen had not expected this, not at all. "So he was right?"

"It isn't as bad as he thinks it is; it isn't as good as you think."

Colleen sighed. "He and I do sometimes live at the opposite extremes."

"Then you need to find a middle. He could try apologizing, coming out publicly and saying that he was wrong."

"He won't do that. He doesn't think he was wrong."

Colleen was not going to give up. If the academies weren't an option, she would try the resorts. She spent the weekend researching them. She ruled out the high-powered ones where big-time coaches held expensive weeklong sessions. She looked instead at the family-oriented resorts. It surprised her that the group lessons for skiers started at a much younger age than those for snowboarders. She did a little more research. Apparently skiing was easier to learn than snowboarding. Little kids had trouble getting the hang of standing sideways until they were around five, and their center of gravity was in their heads, not their core. Group snowboarding lessons often didn't start until children were eight.

But Ben and his friends had all started much younger than that. Nate's mom had said that Nate had started before he was reliably potty-trained. Of course the three of them had each had one-on-one instruction from an uncle or a family friend. So why not approach a resort and suggest that Ben offer individual lessons to the younger kids?

It sounded like a good plan to her...but that didn't mean much. It was fine to let her natural optimism inspire her, but at some point, caution needed to be a guide. That was part of what Amanda meant when she said that she and Ben needed to meet in the middle.

Monday morning she called his agent. The agent's assistant, Chloe, returned her call. Chloe was new to the agency, so she'd never met Ben, but she was interested enough in proving herself to her new boss that she was willing to take on the long shots.

"A coordinated little one can start young if they have individual instruction," Chloe agreed. "But anyone crazy enough to pay for private lessons for a four-year-old is going to go for skiing. The short-term return on the investment would be better."

Colleen was teaching in a nice Catholic school with, for the most part, nice Catholic parents, but she had friends at the elite prep schools, and she had a pretty good idea of just how crazy parents could be.

"Does he want to go back to Endless Snow?" Chloe asked. "Or Almost Heaven is just across the mountains from where you are now."

Neither of those was an option. Colleen had promised that she wouldn't trade on Ben's friendships. Endless Snow was Nate's family's resort, and Nate himself was currently affiliated with Almost Heaven in West Virginia.

"Then let's try Mountain Ash," the agent suggested. "It's even closer to you, and they are having to up their game because of losing business to Almost Heaven."

Clearly Chloe was intending to make the call. Colleen supposed that made sense.

On Tuesday Chloe reported that Mountain Ash had not dismissed the idea. "But they know that we are coming to them because of the big black mark by his name. They are going to try to get him cheap."

"He doesn't care about the money."

"Good, because they may only agree to pay him when he actually has a client, and they aren't going to invest in any promotion. He may only have one or two kids a day, and he might have to spend the whole session trying to get them to keep their hats and gloves on. Some little kids hate hats."

A few days later Chloe said that the contract was ready. "You're really sure that he will sign this? It's not the kind of deal he used to get."

"He'll sign it. He gave me his word."

"I hope so. It was amateurish of me to do this without actually talking to him. I see that now."

Genevieve had had Colleen get an inexpensive fax machine for dealing with estate business, so when Ben came back from his workout in the little gym in the basement of the historic inn, she tapped on the kitchen window, encouraging him to come in the main house before going back to the boathouse.

"What's up?" he asked.

"You need to re-up your CPR." She handed him the contract. "I got you the gig, one week of teaching little kids, although their not liking their hats might be an issue."

"You're kidding." He took the papers. "Does Kristen know about this?"

Kristen was his agent. "She knows about it, but her new assistant did the work. There's an agency clause in the contract, but no one's going to be making much money."

"That's not a surprise." He was skimming through the contract.

She wanted him to be more excited. She wanted him to lift her off her feet, spinning her around, singing "She's a Jolly Good Fellow." She wanted him to think that she had Saved The Day.

But as long as he was going to give it an honest try, as long as he wasn't assuming that it would end terribly, that could be enough.

The contract was long. He was still reading. She was starting to feel uneasy. "Do you think it is demeaning?" He might not have been a household name throughout America, but at the peak of his career everybody in snowboarding knew who he was. So to be teaching five-year-olds in a small resort did seem like a big come-down.

"Of course it is demeaning, but I don't care about that. If no one signs up, I will ask my parents to bring up some of the grandkids so we can say it is mostly a family thing." He set the contract on the counter, open to the page where he would need to sign. "Now is it my turn?"

"Go for it."

Except for asking her what her schedule was, he had said nothing about the progress he had been making on their deal. It turned out that he had a complete plan in place.

He had learned that Autumn's longtime advisors, both the people who had guided her career so well and those who were involved with her lifestyle merchandise, had smelled a disaster in the very public search for Ariel. They had advised against it. She had hired new people. They had been the ones to set up the television show. Now everyone was in damage-control mode. The shopping channel had cut back on her appearances; sales were already dropping. It was a problem. The layoffs had already started. Autumn's search for her child was costing people their jobs.

Her new advisors had agreed to release her DNA to a lab of Ben's choosing, but only after a face-to-face meeting first.

"Why do they want that?"

"I suspect that they, not Autumn, would rather not find Ariel at all than have Ariel be unacceptable."

"So if I am unacceptable, they won't release the DNA?"

"I didn't pursue that. It is inconceivable that anyone would find you unacceptable."

Colleen had to agree with that. "So when's the meeting? Do we need to go to California?"

"No. As I said before, we have leverage. They're coming to DC when we take the jewelry in to be appraised next week. It's going to be completely private. Just Autumn and one PR person. She always travels with a hairdresser and a stylist, but they won't be in the room, and they won't know what's going on."

Next week. Colleen had almost stopped listening as soon as she heard that. They were going to DC next Tuesday. Today was Friday.

So this was going to happen. It was actually going to happen. "I wonder if she and I will know, looking at each other. Do you think we will?"

"You need to be careful about that," Ben advised. "You might think you know when it is only something that you want. I have the DNA kit here if you want to send in your sample. I did a fair amount of research. The lab is as secure as can be."

"That's fine." She sat down on one of the kitchen chair and tilted her head back like a baby bird. Ben deftly swept the inside of her cheek with swabs that retracted into sealed containers.

"This won't hold up in court," he said as he put them in a small cardboard shipping box. "If you want it to be legal, the sample has to be collected by professionals, but I didn't think we cared about that."

He said that he would run in to the village so the box would get sent out before the weekend. "Oh, and for all this, my name is Gary Vogel."

"Gary Vogel? Why? Are you trying to pass as German?"

He smiled in that way he had. His lips didn't move, but you still knew that he was smiling. "Actually the first time I was him, I was trying to pass as twenty-one. Ryan had a fake ID, and that was the name on it. Since it was his picture and we look so much alike, he passed it along to me when he turned twenty-one."

Another advantage of having siblings who were from the same gene pool as you. "Did Tommy and Mark use it?"

"Tommy couldn't. He doesn't look like us. You know him, he has that whole 'map of Ireland' face. Mark used it a couple of times, but by then Gary was getting a little long in the tooth. Why are you looking like that? Didn't you ever have a fake ID made?"

"Of course not," she answered self-righteously. She hadn't needed to. Her features were sufficiently indistinctive that she could easily borrow an ID if she needed one. Pam Sellers, one of her older sorority sisters, had had mono and couldn't go out much. Colleen had been Pam a lot. She had also been Reena Schone and Rachel Perdue.

And now she would find out if she was also Ariel.

Chapter 13

On Monday Colleen picked up the jewelry from the safe-deposit box. She had initially brought it in Grannor's big walnut case. There had not been room for the case in the safe-deposit box, and she had taken it back to the lake, but she hadn't thought to bring it with her this time. She had to ask one of the tellers for a shopping bag.

She supposed that Ben was right. Even if she did feel a connection with Autumn, she shouldn't trust it. Of course, Autumn would feel familiar. When Colleen had to rest her ankle after hurting it in dance class, her mother had let her watch Autumn's Disney movies. Reruns of *M.J.* had been aired often enough that Colleen supposed that she had seen all the episodes.

What if the meeting was awful? She had heard that meeting a celebrity could be disappointing. They didn't make eye contact; you felt invisible. You might try to start a conversation, but any question you could ask, they had answered a million times. They weren't going to ask you about yourself; they didn't care about you.

But surely Autumn would care about Ariel.

Leilah hadn't cleared out the basement, so Colleen hid the jewelry behind a pile of dirty Venetian blinds. She came upstairs, washed her hands, and started making dinner even though it was barely noon.

What was she going to wear on Tuesday? It would be nice to wear something of her mother's. Why hadn't she had the emerald suit altered to fit her? Yes, the color would make the rest of her look like an unbaked oatmeal cookie. The buttonholes would be too widely spaced when the jacket was cut down, and the yoke of the skirt would hit her at the widest part of her hips. But so what? It was her mother's. She wouldn't have to tell Autumn, but she would know herself.

But she hadn't done it. She was going to have to wear her boring "back to school night" black pantsuit.

She could have at least gotten her hair cut, but she hadn't. This always happened to her. Her hair was fine one day, fine the next, fine the day after that, and then suddenly it was awful, a scraggly nightmare. Why didn't she schedule regular appointments?

Because she was a foreign language teacher at a parochial school. She wanted to get every last second out of a haircut. She supposed that if she did indeed get money from Grannor, she could get better haircuts. At least that wouldn't be as complicated as having more money than your friends.

* * * *

It would take at least three-and-a-half hours to drive to DC. They were taking Grannor's big Lincoln as it was more comfortable than Colleen's little tin can of a car. Ben suggested that she pack a small overnight bag in case they wanted to stay over.

They were first going to drop off the jewelry at a place on Connecticut Avenue. Ben would call ahead. Someone would come out and escort Colleen and the jewelry inside while he parked the car. Then a limousine service would take them from the jeweler's to the small hotel where Autumn was staying. It was in Georgetown, and Ben said that he didn't want to have to find parking. It didn't seem like him to worry about something like that, but she had agreed to let him do things his way.

Colleen insisted that they leave extra-early. It was a good thing as rain slowed the traffic on I-81. The rain let up as they headed east, but there was roadwork on I-66 and a stalled vehicle in the middle of Connecticut Avenue. They were going to arrive at the jeweler's thirty minutes after they had hoped to.

Colleen started to fret. Ben assured her that they still had plenty of time, and even if they were a little behind schedule, the jeweler's would be open all day, and Autumn wasn't going to leave.

"I hate being late," she said.

They finally pulled up to the front of the jewelry store. Waiting outside were a burly security guard and a middle-aged man in a neat pin-striped suit. The man introduced himself as Seth Robbins, the grandson of the founder and the company's senior gemologist. He accepted the jewelry as unblinkingly as if clients always carried their jewels in a Forever Twenty-

One shopping bag. He then directed Colleen through the carpeted retail space and into a back room, half of which was divided into three glass-walled cubicles with the rest given over to a conference table. Coffee and pastries were set up on a sideboard. Colleen accepted a cup of coffee and sat down at the table. Mr. Robbins began to unpack the jewelry, careful to keep his hands visible to her at all times. Two young apprentice gemologists took the pieces from him one at a time, going to glass-walled cubicles to examine the jewelry under a microscope, careful not to turn their backs or hide their hands. They were doing a preliminary examination of each piece, Mr. Robbins explained. Preparing the appraisals and lab certificates was much more time-consuming.

He didn't say it, but they were probably checking to be sure that she hadn't brought in any fakes. For all she knew, all the pieces might be fake. That would be an interesting twist.

She watched blankly as the gemologists worked. Shouldn't she be feeling something more? She might never see any of this jewelry again. When she was a little girl, she had been dazzled by the five-strand topaz choker with its pave diamond bars. Now she knew that she would have to be at least six inches taller to dream of wearing it. And even if she were taller, where would she have worn it? The last charity gala that she had attended had been a pancake supper at the elementary school.

She looked at her watch. They were to meet Autumn in sixty-seven minutes.

Mr. Robbins told her that the pearls needed to be restrung. She said that she knew that.

Sixty-six minutes.

"Mr. Robbins, could you please come here?" It was one of the apprentices, speaking from the entry to her cubicle.

Mr. Robbins signaled to the security guard to come stand closer to the shopping bag. With another gesture, he encouraged Colleen to come to the cubicle with him. It seemed rude not to go. The breath-mint tin was open on the apprentice's worktable. Two rings were still in it; the third was under the microscope.

He bent over the microscope. Colleen looked at her watch again. Fifty-nine minutes.

"Oh, my," Mr. Robbins said. "This is unusually fine."

Apparently the diamonds in all three rings were not only large, but had remarkable clarity and unusual cut. The gemologists exclaimed over them to one another. Mr. Robbins asked her what she knew of their history. "Do you know when they were purchased?"

"No." Their history was lost.

Another three minutes had passed.

The sapphire earrings were taken out...the garnet bracelet...forty-eight minutes...a single ruby earring, its mate long missing...two gold pocket watches...the cameo brooch...the cloisonné bracelets...finally, finally they were done. Mr. Robbins signed a receipt, which Colleen put in her purse without looking at it. The security guard told her that the car was out front.

Ben was waiting for her near the retail counters. "Any surprises?" he asked, slipping his phone in his pocket.

"Are we going to be late? Do we have enough time?"

"We'll be fine."

The car waiting for them was black and quietly luxurious. The back seat was more spacious than the front, and there were, as in airplanes, drop-down trays that could be used as desks. The windows were tinted. Colleen could see out, but it was hard for other people to see in.

Colleen noticed Ben looking at his phone. "What's wrong? I thought you said we were okay."

"We aren't going to be late," he assured her. "The publicist was supposed to text me the suite number, and he hasn't."

"Is that a problem? Should we do something?"

"If we don't hear by the time we get there, we'll ask at the front desk." He was calm.

Colleen looked at the window. She had no idea where they were. The street was wide; there were businesses on both sides, small boutiques and chic-looking bistros. They came to a traffic circle, then a stoplight. The driver had to stop. Colleen leaned forward and looked ahead. There seemed to be a stoplight at every single intersection.

They were never going to get there.

The driver turned off the wide street onto a narrow one, then again onto one that was narrower still. The street was lined with brick row houses. The street must have once been residential, but the houses now had small brass plates or discreet signs identifying places of business.

"The hotel is up ahead," the driver said. "I'm going to have to pull up ahead of the entrance."

Colleen looked around. She didn't see anything that looked like a hotel, but on Ben's side of the car, one building had a maroon awning covering the passage to the curb. A cluster of people were standing under the awning as if to escape the rain.

But it hadn't rained here. The pavement was dry.

She reached into her purse, wanting to check her phone to be sure that the ringer was turned off. The purse tilted, spilling out half of what was inside. Her lipstick fell to the floor. As she bent forward to retrieve it, she heard Ben opening the car door. The lipstick had rolled farther than she had thought, and she had to undo her seat belt in order to reach it. She was putting it back in her purse and sliding across the seat when suddenly Ben was back in the car, shouldering her aside. He slammed the door.

"Go, go," he yelled at the driver. The car shot ahead, then stopped so quickly that Colleen jerked forward, falling against the back of the front seat.

The car's horn blared. Someone was pounding on the car. Ben had his hand on her, pressing her down. She turned her head so she could see out the side window. Someone was trying to look in. It was a woman. She had her face close to the window, her hands forming a tunnel as she tried to block out the glare of the sun.

Colleen tried to sit up. Ben used his forearm to force her to lie on the seat. "Stay down," he ordered, then he twisted in his seat, doing something, and an instant later she was swaddled in darkness. He had thrown his blazer over her head.

She tried to throw it off. "Don't," he said. "We can't let them get your picture."

"What on earth is going on? You have to tell me."

"I can't move," she heard the driver say. "Someone's right in front of the car." He started honking the horn again, over and over, a fast, rhythmless tattoo.

Colleen lifted the edge of Ben's jacket. Spurts of light, sharp little bullets, were flashing in the car window. They were from cameras. People were trying to get a picture of her. She heard a clicking near the door handle. They were trying to get in.

Ben's cell phone rang. Colleen felt his weight shift as he pulled it out of his pocket.

"I'm not saying one word," he snapped, "until you get these people off of us...no...no...I don't want to hear it until the car can move...I'm turning off my phone."

The driver had stopped using the horn. Colleen could hear the pounding on the car and the voices... "Ariel, Ariel. Ariel, *please.* Roll down the window."

"How many are there?" she asked.

"Not sure." Ben was trying to keep out of view too. "Eight...ten...but two people are in front of the car, and one in back. We can't move."

"Jesus," the driver swore, "someone's climbing up over the hood. What's wrong with these people?"

"How good are their pictures going to be?" Ben asked.

"Awful. We can't have a lot of tint on our windows here, but there's enough that they're only going to get their own reflection, especially the idiots who don't know how to turn the flash off on their cell phones."

"That seems to be most of them."

"No, there's at least one professional," the driver said. "There's also a guy with a sound boom. This was planned."

"You're with a big outfit, aren't you?" Ben asked him.

"Biggest in DC."

"Then call your boss and tell him to tell the hotel that if they don't get some staff out here, you'll never pick up anyone at this hotel ever again. And you'll get the other services to blackball them too."

Colleen lifted up the edge of the jacket again. "Shouldn't we call the police?"

"No, ma'am. Not yet," the driver said. "We'll be here all afternoon if we have to explain ourselves to the cops."

"And they'll only care about your safety," Ben added, "not your privacy. First thing they'll have us all get out of the car."

And then everyone would take her picture. They would want to get close to her, they would want to…actually, Colleen had no idea what they could possibly want.

The driver was still on the phone, not using his horn, so there was nothing to block out the pounding and the voices. "Ariel…Ariel, please…" It was like being in some horrible zombie-attack movie.

In a market in Egypt…or had it been Cambodia?…she had once been surrounded by a swarm of beggars' children, but a tiny bit of money had gotten her out of that.

"Please, Ariel…come out…" The voices, the pounding continued.

"I think I can back up," the driver said. Colleen felt the car move a foot or so, then stop. "Nope. Damn these people. They're crazy. They deserve to be run over."

At least they were in the car. It was protecting them from this frenzied little mob. What if they had been on foot, walking from wherever Ben had parked?

"Okay," the driver said in another minute. "Got a text from my boss. Some publicist is going to come out with the hotel people."

"Then get away as fast as you can."

"Do you want me to go around to the delivery entrance? Hotel security could meet us there."

"No."

"The suits are coming out of the hotel now. I'm putting the car in gear."

The pounding on the car instantly lessened, and a moment later the car shot forward. Colleen felt a pressure on her covered head; it was Ben's hand, still keeping her down. She felt the car turn, then turn again, and she sat up, pulling his jacket off her, running her hands through her hair.

"Are you okay?" Ben asked.

"I'm fine."

"So where to?" the driver asked.

Ben gave him the address of the parking garage.

"Wait a minute," she said. "We need to talk about this. Are we giving up? What about the delivery entrance?"

"We are not giving up," Ben snapped. "This is not giving up. This is us not putting up with their lying bullshit. Do you honestly believe that we can get out of the car, up the elevator, and into her suite without being besieged again? Or that there will only be two people in the suite? They weren't going to tell anyone about this, and yet all those people were there. How do you think that happened?"

"I don't know." Colleen hated the idea that Autumn hadn't kept her word. "Maybe the publicist—"

He interrupted her. "It doesn't matter to us how it happened. It happened. We can't trust them."

"Let's at least give them a chance to explain and see if we've got other options. Call the publicist, and put your phone on speaker. I want to hear."

"Okay. As long as you don't grab the phone and say, 'Hi, this is Colleen.'"

As soon as he turned the phone, it began ringing.

"Yes?" he said curtly.

"Oh, Gary, thank you." It was a man's voice. "Let me try and explain what happened out there. I didn't know until yesterday that some of Autumn's new supporters were coming, and I apologize for that. She feels a tremendous obligation to them. Apparently she felt that she couldn't tell them not to come."

"What about the professional camera crew? Don't tell me that wasn't your deal."

"I will take responsibility for that, Gary, and I apologize. It may have seemed like poor judgment to you, but once you understand how many people will care about the meeting between Autumn and Ariel, people who truly wish them both well, you will be able to see it from our point of view."

"I wouldn't count on it."

"Gary, if your friend is indeed Ariel, she will have some very exciting opportunities open to her. Why don't you and I sit down, just you and me, and talk about this. We've never discussed any compensation for all your efforts, but there is room—"

Ben turned off his phone.

The man had offered Ben money. That had been the worst possible thing to say.

So it had been Autumn who had told all those people about the meeting. Telling her fans was more important than keeping her word.

Maybe she didn't understand. Colleen wanted to find an excuse for her. She had been a celebrity for so long that it must feel normal to have cameras stuck in her face, to have to do her hair and makeup every time she left her house. She must not realize how uncomfortable that would make normal people. Perhaps breaking her promise on this was no big deal, like bringing chicken sausage when you said that you would bring turkey sausage.

Except how could anyone think that?

Colleen felt betrayed.

"It doesn't make sense," she said. "She always seems so sincere about everything."

"She did, but she's an actress. She could make us believe that she was sincere."

The driver pulled into an underground parking garage, and Ben directed him to Grannor's car. The driver got out to help put their overnight bags in the truck.

"That's what famous people have to deal with, isn't it?" she said as soon as Ben got in the Lincoln. The late Diana, Princess of Wales, had spent the last moments of her life waiting outside an elevator in an underground garage. She hadn't been able to eat in restaurants, try on clothes in stores, or even walk in front doors. Why would anyone want to live like that?

"What's our plan now?" she asked. "Go back to the lake?"

"If that's okay with you."

She said that it was.

I don't need her. I've never needed her. I have a family. I have a great family. She's the needy one, not me.

And Autumn was the one who had screwed this up. Colleen had played by the rules. Colleen always played by the rules, and she didn't like people who didn't.

There wasn't much to say. After they were out of traffic, Ben turned on the radio, but Grannor's car didn't have a satellite hookup or a Bluetooth connection, so after a while he turned it off.

They were still on I-66 when Colleen thought to ask about their hotel. "Do we need to cancel the reservation?"

"Good point, but I'm going to need to turn on my phone to get the info."

There was a big semi passing on their left. Ben glanced in the rearview mirror and passed his phone to her. "Too much traffic. You'll have to do it."

She turned the phone on. The screen showed that the publicist had called him again and again. She ignored the messages and looked for the email from the hotel. It had buttons for confirming or cancelling a reservation so she could cancel without having to call. As she was confirming that cancelling was really what she meant to do, the phone rang again.

"It's the publicist. Do you want me to turn it off?"

"He'll keep after me until I answer. Put it on speaker."

Colleen did so and held up the phone between them.

"What is it?" Ben snapped.

"Gary, thank you for answering. I need to apologize again on Autumn's behalf. She is so distraught about what happened after you left."

"*After?*" Ben looked across the car. Colleen shrugged. She didn't know what happened after they had left Georgetown any more than he did. "Well, you'd have to be pretty damn distraught to have done that," he improvised… without knowing what "that" was.

"Her heart is broken, Gary. Truly broken. She didn't intend to say your name—"

"*What?*"

"She says it just slipped out. She wanted so badly to get in touch with you, and she thought if her fans knew…They have been so helpful in the past."

"Her fans are looking for me? Are you fucking kidding?"

"She admits that she might have been too impulsive. She really does want to apologize as well. I'm sure that she will make you understand. She's not available just at the moment. Can we call you in an hour or so?"

"No, you can't."

"But, Gary, we truly want—"

"Whatever you truly want had better not involve talking to me." Ben started lowering his window. "Because the next thing you hear is this phone going into the Shenandoah River."

He grabbed the phone from Colleen's hand and as the car passed over the bridge, he flung the phone out the window. Colleen twisted in her seat to watch its flight.

"That might not have been so smart," she said mildly. "You could have simply turned it off."

"You have a point there."

"And it didn't go in the river. It landed in the road."

"Oh, crap…we need to go back and get it. I don't want someone else using it."

"You don't need to worry. A chicken truck crunched it."

"I guess that's a good thing," he groaned.

Chapter 14

The rain started up again as soon as they turned down I-81. They stopped for gas and something to eat. Neither was hungry, so Colleen had two white Styrofoam leftover containers, which she put in the refrigerator once they got back to the lake.

"Do you mind if I use your computer?" Ben asked. The rain was coming down hard now; it didn't make sense for him to go to the boathouse.

"It's in the library, and no"—she knew what he would ask next—"there's not a password."

He frowned. "You do talk to your students about digital security, don't you?"

"All the time."

She followed him into the library and sat down next to him. "I thought you were being paranoid, using a fake name, but I can see why you did. Can anyone connect you with Gary Vogel?"

"My family, but Ryan knows everything. I ran all my plans by him to see if they made sense."

The beautiful color wash of Autumn's home page quickly melted into a still image from a new video. It looked well-lit and professional without the shadows and jerkiness of most people's cell phone videos. The professional crew must have taken it.

Autumn was standing in front of some tall palm fronds so the background was green and natural. She looked lovely. Her chestnut hair swept back from her face in soft wings and fell gracefully below her shoulders. Her eyes were clear and bright.

When Colleen was "truly distraught," her eyes got squinty and her face turned blotchy.

Ben hit the play arrow.

"My beautiful Ariel was supposed to meet me today." Autumn's voice was low; she seemed close to tears. "We were to be reunited at last, but someone is keeping her from me. Ariel, my darling Ariel, if you are being held against your will, I can protect you. If you can't get to law enforcement, signal to a waitress or a gas station attendant or the other ladies in the restroom. They will help you. They are—"

Colleen stopped the video. In the quiet she could hear the rain hammering against the porch furniture. "She is so unhappy."

"Fixing that isn't your responsibility."

She didn't need to be lectured. "Obviously I know that, or I'd have done something weeks ago."

"She shouldn't be saying that she was meeting Ariel until she knew for sure," Ben said. "It would be a big embarrassment if the DNA doesn't match. Her business is already suffering. She needs to be thinking about that." He started the video again.

"And, Mr. Vogel, please, I know that there was a misunderstanding," Autumn pleaded from the screen, "but surely that is not enough to keep me from my Ariel. I love her so much. Gary, please, don't keep her from me."

Ben stopped the video again, backed it up, and replayed the last few seconds. And then did it again.

"What is it?" Colleen asked.

He sat back. "Did you hear how she started with 'Mr. Vogel,' then switched to 'Gary'? She got the whole name in without making a big point of it."

"It might not have been deliberate," Colleen countered. "When my mother was sick, Genevieve asked me to call her by her first name, but 'Mrs. Sisson' was automatic. I might well have used both in one sentence." Colleen didn't want to believe that Autumn was as manipulative as Ben was suggesting.

She knew that her memories were turning her mother—Mary Pat—into a saint when she hadn't been. She had a bit of a temper. Even Colleen thought that she hovered too much sometimes; the boys thought that she did all the time. Because her children were adopted, Mary Pat thought that she had to be the Perfect Catholic Mother, and that was a big burden for any family.

If Colleen wasn't going to let herself idolize the mother who had raised her, she really shouldn't do that for anyone else.

"Let's see if people are actually looking for Gary Vogel." Ben switched to the Find Ariel message board. Even though Autumn had mentioned the name only a few hours ago, there was a new page for Gary Vogel, and people were checking in with all the Gary Vogels that they knew. Princessbee3 posted that her father was named Gary Vogel. He was a fifty-seven-year-old auto mechanic in Louisville, but her mother said that he had definitely been in his shop all day. Cheerleadergal said that her boyfriend was also Gary Vogel. She had seen him in homeroom that morning, but he had been taking a makeup math test during lunch period so she hadn't seen him then. He was supposed to be at football practice now. She would run over to the field and be sure he was there.

"They live in Montana," Colleen said. "Does she really think he might have left homeroom, gotten himself to DC, picking up Ariel on the way?"

Other people mentioned a classical musician in California and a man who had worked in a Kentucky sandwich shop two years ago, but no one knew exactly where they had been earlier in the day. One of the moderators had posted the whitepages.com listings for all the Gary Vogels in the United States.

"This really sucks for these guys." Ben was shaking his head. "I feel like I should apologize to them."

Yes. Colleen could understand that. "Hopefully it won't be as bad for them as it was for the Ariel in San Francisco whose parents had to hire a lawyer."

"Maybe, but this is crazy-making. I screw up things for myself, but not for other people." He slammed the computer shut. "This really pisses me off. These lying idiots. I can't stand dealing with liars."

No, Ben, it isn't anger. You have lost control of this situation, and you don't like that. You wanted to make it easy for me, and you couldn't. You hate that.

He was staring out the window. With the rain darkening the sky, the lamps in the library turned the mullioned glass into a mirror. His eyebrows were low over his eyes; his soft lower lip had narrowed.

She said his name. He didn't answer.

Isolation and withdrawal might work for him, but it didn't for her. Today had been about her too, actually more about her, and she had the right to do what would help her.

"I was supposed to marry Tommy or Mark."

"What?" That made him turn. "My brothers?"

"Our mothers planned it. I don't know if Sean and Finn were supposed to marry Kate and Nina, but I was destined for your brothers."

"Why them? Why not me?"

She stepped forward and put a hand on one of his arms. She needed this too, the comfort of touch. "You were supposed to be a priest, remember?"

"Oh, right. That didn't work out so well. But why are we talking about it?"

"Because I'm glad you aren't a priest." She started moving her hand, just an inch or so at first, up and down; with each motion, the stroke became more sweeping.

His eyes were down. He was watching her hand. "I'm glad too…but, Colleen…"

How good it had been between them that summer. They had been so in love.

She reached up and laced her fingers through the warmth of his thick hair to pull him down. His face was rough with the day's stubble.

"Is this what I think?" he asked.

"I want it. Don't you?"

His arms closed around her, tight and hard. On his shirt she could smell the exhaust from the city streets and the fumes from the gasoline pump. The hard pressure of his arms reminded her of his blazer, how smothering it had felt. She ran her hands along his back, hoping to forget the smells and feel of the city. *You care about him. You used to love him. Think of that.*

He was erect against her. The tempo of his kiss became hard and urgent. All his frustrations of the day spilled out, seeking a release. His hands were strong, raging against the powerlessness of being trapped in that car. He was gripped with a raw need to act, to be doing something, anything, even if it was as stupid as throwing his cell phone out the window. He gripped her hips, lifting her up to the library table, thrusting his body between her legs.

Why was she wearing pants? Why wasn't she in a skirt? This would have been so much easier in a skirt. His hands were at her waist fumbling with the waistband, but there was a set of double hooks on the front, a button on the inside.

She put her hand on his chest, moving him aside, and hopped off the table. She had to undo the two hooks, then the button, then the zipper. She slipped her thumbs inside the waistband, making sure that she caught her panties as she pulled the pants down her legs. She kicked her feet free and, putting her hands on the edge of the table, hoisted herself back.

She couldn't look at him. She had started this. She hadn't said no. But it was all too matter-of-fact…almost professional. *My pants are now off; you have permission to enter.*

Did he feel the same way? She didn't want to know. She caught his belt, pulling him to her.

This wouldn't have happened with Leilah. Leilah never wore pants.

Ben's hands were hot on her shoulders, her back, now her inner thighs, but the outside of her legs, her feet, wherever he wasn't touching her, were cold.

With Leilah he would have been in a bed.

He paused and whispered her name questioningly. "We don't have to—"

No, no, she wasn't going to stop this. This wasn't going to be one more thing that didn't happen. She slipped her hands around him, feeling the warmth of his skin. The light fabric of his pants was low on his hips. She slipped her hands beneath his belt, feeling the strength of his muscles and urged him to her.

She gasped at the first pressure. He quickened and she tried to let her breathing match his, hoping to concentrate, trying to mirror what he was feeling, trying to feel something, anything, besides the cold against her legs and the thought of Leilah.

She felt more distant from him than ever. She was standing on the shore, and the water's dark current was carrying him into a darkness, a cell phone striking the rain-slick pavement, the heavy tires meeting it, flattening it. At this moment of most complete physical intimacy, all she felt was the edge of the table biting against the back of her thighs.

He gasped and shuddered, and for an instant the weight of his body sagged against hers. She wasn't sure that she could hold him. Or that she wanted to.

He regained his balance. "Did you...?"

"Oh, yes. Yes. Almost at once."

It was a lie. She who hated to lie had lied. But how tedious it would be if she had told the truth. He was a gentleman, he would feel that he had to...It would be a nightmare. So she lied.

She felt desperately unclean, not only the stickiness between her legs, but the dirt of the city, of being smothered under his jacket, of those people pounding on the car. She wanted to throw herself in the lake, feeling the dark natural waters. She would keep her blouse on and let the water plaster it against her skin.

What a failure this had been. Trying to reach out to him, trying to soothe herself, left her feeling more alone than ever.

"Well, I guess I need to go take a shower," she said as if that's what she always said, as if having bad sex, horrible horrible sex, was routine for her.

She couldn't walk through the house wearing only her blouse and bra, not this house, not her grandmother's house. But there was no easy way for her to cover herself. He was still wearing his shirt, sweat having glued it to his legs. She had to stand up and untangle her panties from the leg of the pants. He was fastening his trousers, straightening his shirt. She forced herself to walk out of the room slowly with dignity. *Is this what it means to be a Ridge, Grannor? Would you approve of this?*

What a mistake this had been. He had been angry; she should have accepted it, but she had felt desperate…and of course it hadn't made any difference. The sex—no one could ever call it "lovemaking"—had been full of his anger and her blank desperation.

Her overnight bag was still in his car. She had forgotten about it. She had to take a toothbrush from the little basket of toiletries that Leilah had provided.

Leilah…he had said that he had known he could never love Leilah. *What about me? Could you love me?*

Even if he could, it would do no good, not as long as neither one of them believed that that love would be enough.

It wasn't even six o'clock when she finished showering, but she dreaded going downstairs. She couldn't imagine facing him. What would she say? She had no experience with having had bad sex with someone. She supposed that most people could simply avoid seeing each other again, but that wasn't going to work for them.

She couldn't stay in the attic until morning. She hadn't had enough to eat during the day. Her attic room was at the front of the house, facing the sunrise. She went across the hall to one of the rooms that faced the lake. The boathouse lights glistened through the rain. He had already gone there.

Gingerly she went downstairs, listening, dreading that he might have returned. She heard nothing. When she opened the refrigerator, she saw that he had taken one of the leftover containers. He was going to eat at the boathouse. He didn't want to see her either.

* * * *

She lay awake that night, planning what she was going to say. *We're friends. Let's talk about this as friends, a pair of friends who made a mistake…a sordid, nasty mistake.* She would put out her hand. Handshakes were a sign of trust and goodwill, weren't they?

The house was quiet when she went downstairs the next morning, and on the kitchen counter was a note.

A note? She glanced out the kitchen window. Grannor's car was gone.

Oh, no, Ben Healy, you don't get to walk away leaving just a note. A note is what a coward does. You can't be a coward, and you can't be Leilah. You can't whisk yourself away as if none of this mattered.

Except what would she do if he had?

The note was folded. She took a breath and opened it. *Took your grandmother's car to Staunton to get a new phone. Text me with a grocery list.*

So he hadn't left. This afternoon he would come home with a package of deboned chicken breasts and a bag of kale salad. What was wrong with her, assuming that he had? That was the way he thought, not her. It was like they were trading personalities, she becoming the worst-case pessimist.

She went to work on the grocery list. They needed everything. Before she had made much progress, the landline rang. "Colleen, this is Ryan Healy."

"Oh, Ryan, hi. I'm sorry Ben's not here, and he had an accident with his phone. That's why he didn't answer."

"I did try him, but it's you I wanted to speak to."

"Me? What about? Did Ben tell you about what happened yesterday? Us trying to meet Autumn and then the thing with Gary Vogel?"

"I'm calling about Autumn naming Ariel's father."

"Ariel's father?" Father? Dear Lord in heaven. Ariel had a father? It had been hard enough to think about one other person being involved in bringing her to life. But two? This was too much.

But, of course, a man had been involved...although since Autumn had only been fourteen, hopefully it had been a boy. "I haven't been online this morning. What did she say?"

"Actually, believe it or not, she said it was Gideon Forbes."

Ryan had said that as if accompanied by a trumpet fanfare. "I'm sorry," Colleen apologized. "That doesn't mean anything to me."

"It doesn't? Really? You don't know who Gideon Forbes is? I guess you were living up north and were a little kid when he died."

"*Died?* He is dead?"

"Let me start over," Ryan said. Gideon Forbes had been a singer-songwriter in the Southern rock tradition. His younger brother Zachary had been Autumn's costar on *Cards,* the movie she had been making when she got pregnant. Gideon was very talented and very successful, but troubled. He had died of a drug overdose.

"Oh, great. So he's dead and a drug addict."

"But so gifted. The Allman Brothers, Lynyrd Skynyrd, all those guys, said that he was a better songwriter than anyone except for Tom Petty."

"That's something," Colleen murmured.

"His estate is probably still generating a bit of money, but if you are involved, your adoption terminates any inheritance rights."

Had he honestly thought that he needed to say that? "I don't want to hear anything about inheritances ever again. I don't want anyone's money."

"We know that. But this changes everything about the search for Ariel. Gideon's fans are a cult. They are obsessed."

"More than Autumn's?" How was that possible?

"In a different way. Autumn's fans are nice people who maybe don't have enough to do. Gideon's fans are seriously weird."

"So what do we do now?"

"Hold tight. Let's see what happens. I'll talk to Ben and we'll figure something out."

"I need to be a part of this figuring," she said.

"Of course, of course. That goes without saying."

In Colleen's experience, when people said that something went without saying, it usually needed to be drafted into a treatise and nailed to the door of a church somewhere.

But getting annoyed with Ryan Healy would accomplish nothing. She agreed that she would call him or his father if she needed anything. She said goodbye politely and hung up.

A druggie and a child molester. Colleen didn't care what the age of consent had been in Canada then. Many of her students were fourteen. They needed to be protected against older men. She was repelled by the thought.

But she still didn't know for sure, did she? She might not be Ariel. For the first time that uncertainty was a comfort.

She went to the computer and opened a search engine. She started to enter Gideon Forbes's name, but she hadn't even finished with the "Gideon" when his name popped up in the auto-fill box right under "Gideon v. Wainwright." Apparently Gideon Forbes was searched for almost as often as a landmark Supreme Court decision.

She clicked on the images tab. A grid of pictures appeared. She enlarged one. It was of a skinny blond man, his head bent over his guitar, his arms curved around it. She couldn't see his face. She clicked on the next one.

He was looking straight at the camera, a wary expression on his face. He looked gaunt. His cheeks were sunken, and he had heavy bags under his eyes.

She couldn't see any resemblance. His light hair was straight, much straighter than hers. She clicked through more pictures. He had nice teeth, but that could have been orthodontics. She tried covering different parts of his face, putting her thumb over his eyes, then his nose, then his mouth, but she still saw nothing.

When the search for Ariel had started, her sisters-in-law had looked at pictures of Autumn's family, checking for resemblances there. So Colleen entered "+*Gideon Forbes* +*family.*" Another grid popped up. Again she clicked on the first picture, but it was a group of motley-dressed young people in front of a bus. It must have been his touring ensemble. The next three pictures were similar. "+*Gideon Forbes* +*mother*" yielded nothing.

What was his younger brother's name? Zachary. *"+Zachary Forbes +mother"*. A few thumbnail pictures appeared. She clicked on the first.

A teenage boy was standing between three petite women, two of them more or less his age, one clearly older. They were lined up in front of a Christmas tree. *"Zachary Forbes,"* the caption read, *"with mother Donna, sisters Becca and Mary."*

Colleen enlarged the picture as much as she could.

She didn't need to cover anything. It was so clear. There were her eyes, the shape of her forehead, her nose, her hairline, sometimes in one of the women, sometimes in two. All three seemed to have her lips.

She had never looked like anyone before. Never. "Colleen looks just like herself," her mother had always said. Her mother had been wrong. Colleen looked like these women.

She was Ariel. Now that she didn't want to be, she was.

She went back to the pictures of Gideon. His eyes were distant and blank. *Are you my father?*

No, God, no. Edward B. Ridge, DDS, was her father.

It was hard enough to have been thinking about a birth mother, but suddenly a "bio dad"? That's what some of the websites called the man who had produced the sperm, the "bio dad." The term sounded dismissive as if he didn't matter as much as the "first mother."

But in terms of genetic makeup, the sperm and the egg were equally important.

She started reading about this man whose mother and sisters she resembled. She first did the math. He would have been twenty-two, six years older than Autumn. Then she looked at a list of his songs. She actually had heard a number of them; they had been covered by other artists and had been used in the soundtracks for movies. She hadn't known that they had been written by the same person.

There was a hopelessness about the songs that Colleen couldn't imagine connecting with. Gideon Forbes might have spoken to many people, but she was not one of them.

She read more. He had posed as the voice of the Southern underclass. He sang about people trapped in marginal jobs, driving rusty cars, longing for a country life but being forced to live in the outskirts of big cities.

Some of his fans were indeed strange. There were persistent rumors that he was still alive despite a detailed coroner's report. Over the years a number of people had claimed to be his offspring. One or two had based their claim on the spiritual connection that they felt with Gideon, just like the connection the young man on the TV show said that he had felt with Autumn. The rest of the claimants seemed to be after money.

There wasn't much about his family on the sites associated with him. She learned more when searching on Zachary. Gideon had been the oldest of five children. Despite his songs about working people, the family was comfortably middle-class, living in Charlotte, North Carolina, the father owning an insurance agency, the mother giving piano lessons. They had been a musical family; even Gideon had sung in the church choir until he began to rebel.

Zachary, the youngest brother, had quit acting after only a few films. He had settled in Hollywood and become a sound editor. He had been nominated for several Academy Awards and had won once. There was a third brother, Jonathan, the middle one. He was a professor of linguistics at Duke University in Durham, North Carolina, specializing in anthropological linguistics.

Music…sound editing…linguistics…this was a family who could hear. This was where her gift for learning languages had come from.

Were the parents still alive? Yes, apparently they were. What about the sisters? She couldn't find much. They must have married and changed their names.

Colleen kept trying one set of search terms after another. "+*Jonathan Forbes + linguistics +Duke*". As long as she was searching, she didn't have to think. "+*Jonathan Forbes +anthropological linguistics*".

Wouldn't the offspring of Autumn Chase and Gideon Forbes be glitteringly special, bursting with talent, a shooting star across the genetic sky? That wasn't her. "+*Zachary Forbes +actor +choir*". She was an ordinary person. She taught French and Latin at a Catholic school.

Four years ago, she had marveled at the drive and ambition Ben and his friends had. She didn't have that. "+*Gideon Forbes +estate*". Yes, she wanted to be a good person and make the world a better place; she wanted her students to learn and to love learning, but she didn't want to be famous or reach the top rung of some success ladder. "+*Gideon Forbes + estate*

+*intestate"*. Surely the offspring of Autumn Chase and Gideon Forbes would want to be a star. "+*Gideon Forbes +estate + lawyer"*.

It didn't feel right. "+*Donna Forbes +Charlotte +church"*.

Finally she had to admit that there wasn't much else to learn about the family. Apparently they managed to protect their privacy despite Gideon's rabid fans. Then suddenly a new entry appeared in the search results.

It was a new article, published seven minutes before. "Forbes Family Denies Autumn Chase Claim."

A reporter for an online site had attempted to call Gideon's family. A lawyer had issued a statement for them. *To the best of their knowledge... died without issue...claimants...disproven...respect privacy...difficult time...serve no purpose...*

The message was clear. The Forbes family wanted nothing to do with her. They didn't know her, they didn't know anything about her, and they were already rejecting her.

Chapter 15

She needed to talk to her father, her real father. She looked at the time on her computer screen. It was quarter to one already, quarter to twelve back in Chicago. This was the time each day her dad set aside for emergencies. If he didn't have a patient, he would be at his desk, doing paperwork.

She was connected to his line immediately. "Dad, it's me."

Sean and Finn sounded so much alike on the phone that they had to identify themselves even to their parents. Only one female on earth called Dr. Edward Ridge "Dad," and it was her.

"Colleen, is everything all right?"

"Yes, it's fine." But his voice was so full of warmth and concern that she started to cry.

Dentists made your pain go away. They made it easier for you to eat. They made your smile prettier. They fixed things; they made things better.

So did dads. At least the good ones did, and her father had been a good one.

"Are you calling about the jewelry?" he asked. "Believe or not, I heard from someone this morning." The appraisals had barely been started, but Seth Robbins had wanted to alert the estate executor how valuable some of the pieces were. "You should start thinking if there are some pieces you want."

"But Grannor wanted Kim to have it all."

"My sense is that Kim may sell a lot of it. If there is something you think you would wear, it would keep us from having to raise the cash. But only if it's something you want. Don't take something because you think it will help your cousins."

Colleen couldn't think about jewelry right now. "Actually, Dad, I was calling about the other thing."

He cleared his throat. He knew what the "other thing" was. "Genevieve tells me that the actress hasn't found her daughter yet."

"She released the name of the father, and Dad"—this was going to be hard for him to hear—"his mother and sisters, they look a whole lot like me."

"Oh."

Even in that single syllable Colleen could hear his most professional voice. *I strongly advise an immediate consult with an oral oncologist.* Dentists couldn't fix everything.

"He sounds awful, Dad." She knew her father would be able to hear the tears in her voice. "He's dead, a drug overdose. He was years older than Autumn, an adult when she was a girl. I don't want to be connected to him, and his family, they don't want to have anything to do with me. They think I'm after their money."

"Oh, Colleen, my girl...my dear, dear girl." This wasn't his professional voice. This was a father, a daddy, aching for his little girl. "You don't have to have anything to do with these people. You have us. We love you. Your mother, Genevieve, your brothers, Patty and Liz, we all love you."

"I know." Now Colleen didn't try to hide her sobs. "We tried to meet Autumn yesterday, Dad, and it was so horrible. We couldn't even get out of the car. There was a mob of her fans. We were trapped."

"Trapped by a mob?" He did not like the sound of that. "I think you should come home. You'll be safer here."

Home. Home was the big white house in Kenilworth. The yard had been fenced in, and it had a swing set and Colleen's little princess playhouse. She would go there if she could, if her mother with her flaming red hair and flashing Irish smile would be waiting there, asking Colleen if she wanted to have a tea party in the playhouse. But to her father and Genevieve, home was a beautifully renovated, hundred-year-old row house on the north side.

Her father would stand up for her. But she knew what the Find Ariel website would say about him. He would be demonized as a baby buyer, a heartless thief who believed himself entitled to three perfect babies because he was white and rich.

If he found himself in the middle of a gang of amateur paparazzi, he would come across as stiff and authoritarian. It was hard to think of him as a Baby Boomer. Because he had grown up in such a formal home and had gone to college in the South, he seemed more like a member of the Greatest Generation. He had gone to fraternity mixers in a navy blazer while others even older than him had been burning their draft cards and going to Woodstock.

He would make a perfect villain, and he wasn't a villain at all. He did not deserve that. She needed to protect him—a thought that he would hate.

"I'm not alone, Dad. Ben Healy is still here, and he is being cautious about everything. He's been talking to Ryan, and their dad knows what's going on. So it's not just me."

"That's good."

After she hung up, she had no idea what to do with herself. She wasn't going to keep searching on the Forbes family. Her in-box and social media accounts were full of messages from friends, chatter about their summers, pictures of their cats, pictures of other people's cats, pictures of the meals they were about to eat, reposts of what they had been doing this time last year, and on and on. Why did she think that she had to keep up with every person she had ever met?

The phone rang. It was the landline again. How strange. In Charlottesville she didn't even have a landline. No one did.

"It's me. I mean, Ben."

"I know who you are." She recognized voices. If she heard a voice once; she remembered it. That was one of the abilities she had gotten from the Forbes family. "Did you hear about Gideon Forbes?"

"Yes, but there's not time to talk about it. I need you to take the battery out of your cell phone and disconnect the modems in the house and the boathouse. Not just unplug them, but unscrew the input line."

"What? Why?"

"I honestly don't have time to explain. Just please do it and meet me in the village at the place with the computers. Can you do all that?"

"The arcade? Sure. I can be there."

"Good. I will see you soon. I'm leaving the hospital now."

"The hospital? Why—"

He had already hung up.

She hated not knowing what was going on, but she—unlike some other people—always did what she promised. She had to find a little screwdriver to open up her phone, and it took some tugging to get the battery out. She hoped she hadn't broken it. The modem for the house was in the corner of the library. Unscrewing the cable was easy. Then she got the key to the boathouse and went across the lawn and took care of that.

The summer season was at its peak. All the parking spots on the village streets were full. She parked at the school and cut through the soccer field. It wasn't raining, but the day was gray enough that the arcade was crowded. Little kids were shoving each other to get to the Whack-A-Mole; preteen girls were clustered around the dance machine. The driving simulators burst out with the sounds of shrieking tires and car crashes. The old pinball machines played tinny music, and the familiar "SPINNN TO WINNN" blared over everything.

No one was at either of the two computers. Colleen went to the counter to pay for some time. Some children were selecting which prizes to redeem with the tickets they had won. It was taking them long enough that the mom gestured to Colleen to step in ahead of them.

"If you go sit in front of the library, you can get wi-fi," the kid behind the counter told her. "It's free. The password is 'guest.' You don't need to pay us. No one does anymore."

"I'm meeting someone here," was all Colleen said. She didn't need to explain herself to everyone all the time.

As he had been driving from Staunton, Ben wouldn't be here for a while. She turned on the computer, and because she hadn't done so yet today, she entered the URL for Autumn's site.

Suddenly the screen was completely filled with an image of an erect penis going in…

Horrified she tried to exit the site. That only brought up a worse image. She pressed the power button on the computer so hard that her finger turned white.

What had happened? She was no prude, but still…She hoped that none of the children had seen the screen. Or any of the grown-ups. Someone would probably call the police, and this was the sort of site that teachers lost their jobs over.

She moved to the other computer. Gingerly she turned it on and typed in the address for the Norwegian newspaper that she read a few times a week. That seemed safe.

Things were good in Norway. Greenhouse emissions were decreasing, thanks to more and more electric cars. Princess Ingrid Alexandria was turning into a very pretty young lady. The sailing team…

A shadow fell across the screen. It was Ben. The arcade was too noisy for her to have heard him approach.

"What on earth is going on?" She hoped he would know something. "Autumn's site is coming up as porn."

"It's been hacked." He pulled over the chair from the other computer and sat down. "And my identity's been compromised. Look at this." He pulled some folded papers out of his pocket. "The ladies at the hospital thrift shop remembered me and let me use their computer and printer. This is my credit card statement."

Ladies did remember him. Colleen took the paper. Marked with a yellow highlighter were four charges made this morning. They were all small. The first one, $2.19, was the largest; the other three were under a dollar each. "I don't get it," she said.

"Two one nine…those numbers are my Social Security number."

"Good Lord." Someone was making these charges to flaunt that they knew his Social Security number. "That's awful. Who did it? Is this what Ryan meant by Gideon's fans being weird?"

"I assume so. If Autumn's fans had this kind of skill, it would have been happening all along to the different Ariels and to the Gary Vogels."

"But how did they find you so fast? How did they know you were Gary Vogel?"

He assumed that Gideon's fans had found him by hacking into the publicist's phone. "If they were really as good as they seem to be, it wouldn't have taken them long at all. There were so many calls to my number. It never occurred to me to use a burner, but clearly I should have."

His entire online identity had been compromised, but the hackers were doing the oddest little things. There were these tiny charges on his credit cards; his health insurance now said that he had been born in 1943; he was actively commenting on an arborist's website.

"They're making me sound like I am some kind of Druid, that if you worship each tree's individual spirituality, you don't have to worry about pests and drought."

"They could be having you comment on kiddie porn sites," she pointed out. "But what about bank accounts?"

He had talked to his financial person. There had been some attacks on his big investment accounts, but they had been repelled by the wealth management company's security systems. "We froze all my accounts, and actual people are monitoring them continuously, not just the computers. But again, all the amounts have been small."

"If they don't want money, what do they want?"

"They want you."

"*Me?*"

"Of course. The child of their idol. The Lost Princess. They don't yet know that it's you, and believe me, I tried my damnedest to scrub all my data so that they can't find you through my phone. We didn't call and text that much, but you never know what is still out there. I'm afraid you need to freeze your accounts and delete your social media. Do you know your passwords?"

"Sure."

He looked at her suspiciously. "Should I have said 'password,' not 'passwords'? Jesus, Colleen, don't tell me that you use the same password on everything."

"Sometimes I capitalize the first letter."

"That's certainly taking security to the next level. Besides your money, what's the worst thing someone could do to you online?"

She thought. Her father? Her brothers? "My students. Their grades." Monkeying with kids' transcripts could make a joke of all their hard work and potentially ruin their college plans. It was a horrible thought. She couldn't let that happen.

Ben logged on to the school system with her access code. After a few keystrokes, the familiar screen changed to lines and lines of code. They meant nothing to Colleen, but Ben was looking at them intently.

After a few minutes he shook his head. "Your school's good. The transcripts are locked up tight. A person would have to be a thousand times better than me—" He broke off. "Of course, that is what we are dealing with, people who are a thousand times better than anyone. The safest thing is to delete your access and everything associated with you. Then if they do find out who you are, they will leave the school alone."

She certainly didn't want the school's website to flash the sort of pictures that Autumn's was. Ben deleted her name and photo from the faculty list. Then the French and Latin clubs lost their sponsor. She was gone. It was as if Colleen Ridge had never existed.

But she had existed. Judge Rutherford's signature had made her herself.

Deleting her social media accounts was equally painful. All those pictures, years and years of pictures, her travels, her friends, a series of keystrokes and they were gone. And her contact information, all the phone numbers and email addresses. What was she going to do when this was all over? It wasn't like you could open the phone book anymore and find people.

"I guess we've done what we can do," he finally said. "You probably need to get in touch with the school and tell them what you had to do."

She reached for her phone and then remembered that it didn't have a battery. That was okay; the offices would be closed by now. She could send an email. No, Ben had closed her email account. It would have to wait until morning.

"I think it's okay to use your grandmother's landline," he was saying. "The connection is so old that to tap it, these people would have to leave their mothers' basements, and I bet that Gideon's fans don't do that much."

Ben said that he had also parked at the school. Outside the arcade the sidewalk was crowded with the summer visitors. Someone bumped against her. Ben reacted quickly, putting his hand on her back, steadying her. But she was fine so he let his hand fall away.

Twenty-four hours ago she had been sitting on the library table, her legs spread, feeling the scrape of his belt buckle against her inner thigh. Now he touched her only as long as was polite.

This was worse than the miserable awkwardness she had felt last night. At least the awkwardness said that the sex had mattered. Yes, it had mattered in a bad way, but now it had no significance at all. They didn't even feel awkward about it. He probably hadn't thought about it.

Four years ago the story had been about them. Their relationship was the most important thing in their lives, and everyone else was encouraging and happy. But now the story was about everything else, Grannor's will, Autumn, Gideon, her adoption, the hacking. What was between them was sitting at the edge of the room, not even trying to be heard.

There didn't seem to be anything to do about that.

They crossed the playing field. As they got closer to the school parking lot, Ben cursed. "On top of everything, we just got parking tickets."

Colleen looked at her car. There was a yellow slip tucked under the windshield. Apparently it wasn't legal to park here even in the summer. She should have known. "At least the fine isn't much," she said as she looked at hers. "And we can pay them online…oh, no, we can't get online unless we go back to the arcade."

"And we don't have any credit cards to pay them with. In fact, how much cash do you have?"

"Not a lot. Grannor had a stash, but Dad had me put it in the estate account."

"I'll call Nate." Nate was one of his longtime friends. "He's in West Virginia, just a couple of hours from here. He can go to the bank in the morning and get a couple thousand to tide us over."

A couple *thousand?* How long was he thinking this would last?

Back at the lake, he went to the extension in Grannor's room to make his call while she tried to figure out something for dinner. They hadn't done a proper grocery trip in days, and now they had no way of paying for anything.

Nate Forrest had apparently thought nothing of lending a friend that kind of money. Ben had offered to drive to West Virginia, but Nate had agreed to meet Ben at Mountain Ash, the resort Ben would be working at for a week next winter. "I think he wants to figure out what I am doing. I also had him pay our parking tickets. I knew you would be worried about them."

Parking tickets did seem trivial in light of everything else going on, but Ben was right. Colleen cared about the ticket. Nice girls paid their parking tickets right away. Going back to being a nice girl felt safe right now. "Thank you…and thank him too."

"I will, but actually it was pretty awkward."

"Oh?" Colleen was trying to make out the date on a package of chicken breasts she had found at the bottom of the freezer.

"When he entered the ticket number, the license plate came up with your name."

"So?" Colleen gave up on the chicken. "What's the—" Then she got it. "You never bothered to tell your friends that the place where you've been staying since April belongs to the Ridge family."

"No, I didn't."

She opened the kitchen cabinet. She was pretty sure there was half a box of pasta somewhere. "That's kind of insulting, Ben, that you're ashamed to let anyone know you're staying with me."

"No, no," he protested, but then he had trouble explaining himself. "They all liked you, everyone did that summer. They thought I was crazy to let you go."

Colleen found the pasta. "You didn't *let* me go. You pushed me."

"I know that. They know that, and they didn't let me forget it."

"So what did Nate say when he found out?"

"He asked if I was fucking it up again."

"And?"

"I said that I probably already had." He looked down at his hands. "I hope you can believe that through this whole mess, I've wanted the best for you…except yesterday in the library. I don't know what to say about that."

At least he hadn't completely forgotten. "You can say that you had affirmative consent." Affirmative consent…how romantic was that? "If you're done with the phone, I need to call my dad. Will you start the water for this?" She gestured toward the pasta. "There's a jar of sauce, and I can open a can of corn, which won't add much in the way of interest or nutrition."

"I'll go to the store as soon as we get money from Nate."

Colleen knew that after calling her father, she was going to need to call Amanda. She was keeping a much bigger secret from her friends than he was keeping from his.

Genevieve answered the phone. Colleen asked her to stay on the line. Her father was going to need his wife to help him through this. While they were waiting for her father to pick up the phone, Colleen asked Genevieve if she would call Patty and Liz later tonight and tell them everything. Colleen figured that the story would be more complete if it went through the women.

She now knew how to get what she wanted from her family. In a perfect world her father and brothers would have worked with her to fill the holes after her mother had died, but the world was still many degrees south of Eden. She should stop waiting for the men, but work with their wives. Together, she, Genevieve, Patty, and Liz would create an extended family whose bonds would be as strong as if Mary Pat were still alive. She was very lucky that the other three would want that as much as she did.

"Good God, Colleen if they are doing this to Ben," her dad said after she had explained the situation, "what would they do to you?"

"I don't know, Dad. That's what makes it sort of scary."

"Is Ben there? Can I talk to him?"

Colleen supposed that her father was in the total "women and children in the lifeboats first" mode, wanting to talk to Ben because he was another man. But this didn't seem like a good time to fight that battle. She handed the phone to Ben.

"Yes, sir…I agree…I'm sorry, Dr. Ridge, but I've had to close my accounts. I'm sure I'd need a credit card to do that…"

The conversation continued with Ben agreeing to everything her father said.

"What was that about?" she asked as soon as the call was over.

"He wants a security guard at the end of the driveway and one on the waterfront. He'll set it up since we can't."

"Are you kidding? Is that really necessary?"

Ben shrugged. Clearly he thought so. "If you were a prize yesterday when it was only Autumn, think of what you are today."

No. If Colleen were a prize, it was because she was a good teacher, a generous friend, a reasonably faithful Catholic, and a far better granddaughter than her grandmother had ever deserved. It wasn't because a drug-addicted rock star had had sex with an emotionally starved teenage film star.

"How does this end, Ben? We can't go on forever without credit cards or phones."

"I know we can't," he admitted. "Let me make another call. Back at the thrift shop, I called a guy I know from school. He used to be a 'black hat' hacker, the sort who would have done this to other people. He's gone legit, but he still knows a lot. I called him right away and asked him to see what he can find out about who is doing this. I told him that you wouldn't want him to do anything illegal or unethical."

Colleen wasn't sure she cared as much about that as she once had.

She sat the table while he called. They were eating in the kitchen. This meal didn't deserve anything better.

"It could be worse," Ben said after he had hung up. "He called some other people to help, and they are all sure that my information isn't on the dark web, at least as of fifteen minutes ago. As best they can tell, there are only two, maybe three, people at work, but as good as my guys are, they say that this group is better."

"Could they tell what the hackers wanted?"

"Not entirely. Obviously they wanted to punish Autumn for giving up Gideon's baby, but what they did to the Find Ariel site was worse. Anyone who logs in with an admin account is going to have their computer so infected with malware that they are going to lose everything."

Colleen wasn't sure she could trust herself to drain the pasta without saturating herself with boiling water. She gestured for Ben to do it. "I understand why Autumn wanted to find me, but why do these people? Do they think I have some kind of magic? I had never heard of Gideon Forbes until this morning."

"They don't know what they want." Ben deftly tilted the pasta pot over the colander. The long strands of spaghetti slithered out along with starch-laden water. "That's what makes them so dangerous."

* * * *

After dinner Ben said that he would sleep in the house until the security guards arrived. He would take one of the second floor rooms in the front of the house. With the windows open, he would hear a car drive up. Apparently he had been infected with her father's lifeboat thinking.

He went to the boathouse to get a few things. She took a breath and went to the phone to call Amanda.

Fortunately she remembered her friend's cell phone number. She started with the easy part. Ben had had his identity compromised. The hackers were very aggressive, so Colleen had had to protect herself. She explained about deleting her identity from the school website.

"Isn't that a little extreme?" Amanda asked. "This sucks for Ben, and I can understand you're wanting to be careful about your money, but the school site? Really?"

This was the hard part. "There's a lot more to it. You know everything that's been going on with Autumn Chase? It looks like I am Ariel."

"*What?* You? How's that possible? You weren't adopted."

"Actually I was. Until this mess, it never occurred to me that you didn't know."

"But we watched that show together, and you never said anything?" Amanda sounded bewildered, maybe even betrayed.

Colleen didn't blame her. "I guess I was thinking that if one of those women had had the right DNA, then it wouldn't matter, and we could forget all about it."

"How do you know now? Did you do the DNA?"

"No, but Autumn said that the father was—"

"Oh, my God," Amanda interrupted, "you're the child of Autumn Chase and Gideon Forbes. *You?*"

"I'm going to be a big disappointment, aren't I?"

"I didn't mean it that way," Amanda apologized hurriedly. "It's just that you never expect this to be happening to people you know."

"It's happening to me."

"And that's behind all this hacking?"

"Apparently. They're looking for me. I don't know what they'll do when they find me. I can't stay hidden forever, but my dad is hiring security guards."

"Security guards? Is he worried about people mobbing you? You know what this will mean, don't you? The school is going to want you to take a leave of absence."

Oh. That was right. Last year the husband of one of the teachers was a university administrator involved in a major controversy. It made the national papers, and she had taken leave until things had died down. And this would have far more publicity than that had ever had. "I guess it would be distracting to have me there."

"It would be all anyone talked about, but you should wait until the school asks you," Amanda said. "Then you can ask for pay. Margaret Whitmore didn't need the income, but you do."

"Actually…oh, God, Amanda, that's another story."

As briefly as she could, she told Amanda about Grannor's will.

"That's huge." Amanda was having trouble taking all this in. "And you never said a word."

Clearly Amanda was hurt by Colleen's secrets, but she was still willing to be loyal. She would call the headmistress in the morning and tell her the story that Colleen couldn't bear to repeat again.

* * * *

Ben didn't leave in the morning until the security guards showed up. He showed them around and supervised them posting "No Trespassing" signs around the edge of the property.

"Signs aren't going to stop anyone, are they?" she asked.

"No, but you need to have them visible if you are going to prosecute."

Prosecute? That was Southern hospitality?

When Colleen was growing up, she had noticed how boats slowed down in front of Grannor's property.

"They like the way it looks," her mother had said. "They're curious."

"Why don't we invite them in?" Colleen had chirped. "We can show them around."

Now she had a guard standing on the dock.

Genevieve called to check on her, then Patty and Liz. At the end of her call, Patty had said, "Sean and I are running down to Chicago for a couple of days soon. We were hoping to coordinate with you. We'd like to see you too."

"Oh, God, Patty, I'm sorry. I can't make plans right now. I can't even go to the grocery store."

"Okay. I understand. Really I do. But keep it in mind, will you? We would like you to be there."

After they hung up, Colleen realized that this trip must be for Sean and Patty to tell everyone about the baby.

That was good news, right? Of course, it was. Colleen remembered the spurt of happiness she had felt when she had first realized that Patty was pregnant. But so much had happened since then. Now she was numb.

It was harder to stay numb during the next call. It was from the headmistress. Amanda had given her Grannor's landline number.

Dr. Bettler was familiar with the search for Ariel, and she knew who Gideon Forbes was. As Colleen expected, she dreaded the publicity. "With our grounds mingling with the church's, it is difficult to make our campus secure. And our carpool line is on a public street. We can't keep strangers from harassing the staff and students. But if all the publicity has died down, we would be happy to have you back in January."

January seemed so far away. "I assume that you won't have trouble replacing me." Charlottesville was a university town, and behind the counter of every coffee bar and bagel shop were foreign language majors who hadn't wanted to leave town after graduation. "I have my lesson plans."

Twenty minutes later it occurred to her that she might not have her lesson plans. They had been stored on the cloud, and her account had been scrubbed. She had no idea if she had backup copies on the hard drive of her computer. That wasn't the sort of thing she paid any attention to. Maybe she should have had a few more trust issues.

* * * *

Ben called around noon. "Nate brought the cash. He also opened a new credit card in his own name and gave me the number."

"Really? Even I wouldn't let anyone else use my credit card. He is nicer than me."

"I would describe him as more oblivious to risk."

Ben said he was going to be at the resort longer than he had expected, probably most of the day. "I want to add a couple of extra layers of security to their systems if I can."

"Oh, no," she sighed. "Have they been hacked too?"

"Not yet because they haven't put my name up, but Nate and Seth have been opening their big mouths about me giving privates. They are all gung-ho about it. I told them to blame you."

"I appreciate that." It couldn't have been easy for him, telling his friends that she was still living up to the good opinion they had of her.

"Listen, Colleen, I need you to believe something. If I can't go through with this, it isn't because I don't want to. I do. The more I think about it, the more I do, but I might not be able to."

She didn't understand. "Might not be able to do what?"

"These lessons. I am not going to put this resort in jeopardy. It's not fair. It's not right."

Colleen felt as if she had been kicked in the stomach. He was talking about giving up this coaching opportunity, his first chance to get back in the game. He was finally realizing that this was what he wanted, and now he might not be able to. Because of her.

Everything that was happening to him was because he was trying to help her, protect her. And now the one good thing he could have done for himself might blow up in his face.

When was this going to stop? It couldn't go on. The search for Ariel had become a widening whirlpool doing more and more damage. She had to do something, she had to act.

Chapter 16

She would offer herself up if she thought that would work, but playing the kidnapped child stumbling out of the forest was a path full of too much uncertainty. Autumn had said that she could protect Ariel, but look what had happened to her website. Autumn couldn't even protect herself.

The Forbes family must have figured this out. They seemed to have normal lives. Zachary had a website for his film work. Jonathan was listed all over the Duke University directories. The parents were frequently mentioned in their church's online bulletin. They had a lawyer who knew how to issue statements for them.

That statement had made it very clear that the family didn't want to hear from her. Forcing herself on people was not something that nice girls did. Colleen was going to do it anyway.

I'm sorry. I know you want to be left alone. I understand that, believe me. But I don't know what else to do.

Colleen couldn't remember if she had ever called Directory Assistance to get a phone number. She had always used the internet. She dialed zero on the phone. That operator told her to call 411, which she did. The person who answered that line was able to give her the number for the Duke University linguistics department.

Two actual people. Amazing.

The department secretary said she would connect Colleen to Professor Forbes's office. Colleen secretly hoped that he wouldn't answer.

But he did. "This is Jonathan Forbes." His accent was lightly Southern, more North Carolina than Ben's Georgia one.

"Professor Forbes, my name is Colleen Ridge. I am a Norwegian-to-English, English-to-Norwegian interpreter." Why had she said that?

"Yes?"

"I've studied with Keith Alvord." That was her most famous professor.

"He is an excellent scholar. How can I help you? I don't need any interpretive services at the moment."

No, of course, he didn't. "Oh, no, that's not why I am calling."

"Then again, how can I help you?"

"I'm calling about Autumn Chase and your brother Gideon. I think that I—"

"I have nothing to say about that." His voice became formal. "Please give my regards to Professor Alvord."

"Don't hang up. Please don't hang up."

"I have nothing to say. Now I must excuse myself."

"Wait...wait..." What could she say? How could she prove herself over the phone? *I have your mother's eyes.* Anyone could say that. What could she say?

Oh, of course. That was it. She could say anything. "Say something in a foreign language."

"I beg your pardon?"

"An obscure one. Urdu, Pashto, one I don't know."

He paused, then said a string of syllables. She repeated them. And she knew that she had done it perfectly. However fluent he was in this language, that was how fluent she would have sounded.

"You know Portuguese?"

"I didn't know for sure it was Portuguese. Try me again."

He did.

"That's Hebrew, isn't it?" she asked after parroting the sounds. During seventh grade she had attended several bar mitzvahs. "I don't know the Afro-Asiatic languages if you want to try one of those."

"Why are we doing this?" he asked.

"I can repeat any sound that you make. And surely someone else in your family can."

"My older sister, but she isn't as good as you," he admitted. "So what is it that you are suggesting?"

"All I can be sure of is that I was adopted, I have an October birthday, and I look like your mother and sisters."

It was a moment before he said anything. "My mother still thinks about Gideon every day. For all the pain he caused her, she thinks about him every day. Every time someone says that he might have had a child, it's really hard on her. You do understand that we have to be suspicious."

"Of course, and I don't want money. Really. I'm a teacher; I have a job. My father is a dentist, and he is from a family of means. Are you online now?" She gave him her school's URL. "Go to the foreign language department. There are pictures of all the teachers. My name is Colleen Ridge."

He was silent, and then—"Ah...no, Ms. Ridge. There is no listing for anyone by that name."

Oh, shit. Shit, shit, shit. Ben had wiped her off the faculty rolls. How suspicious this must look. "Oh, please, don't hang up. I can explain that. Search for a picture of the Latin club. The teacher...there's no name, but that's me."

She forced herself to wait silently, praying that he wouldn't hang up.

"Yes," he said slowly. "The eyes...the mouth..." Then speaking in Italian, he asked, "Are you my brother's child?"

It was easier for her to answer in French. "Yes, I think that I am." Then she switched to English. "But please believe me, I am not after money." She knew that she had already said that, but she needed to say it again.

"I talked to my younger brother yesterday," he said, "after Autumn named Gideon. He did say that Gideon came to Canada for a few days while he was shooting *Cards*. He didn't have a clue about anything happening between him and Autumn, but I've always suspected that Zachary hadn't liked working with her, so he probably didn't spend much time with her."

"Oh." Colleen had never heard about anyone not liking to work with Autumn. It hardly fit with her public image.

"I hope you won't be offended," he continued, "if we ask for a DNA test."

"Oh, no, not at all. I already sent mine in, although I haven't compared it to Autumn yet." She asked him to hold while she got the information about the lab and her specific code number. "You should probably see if you can get them to tell you about the results. I'm sure that they just have my email and cell phone, and both of those are down."

"I'm not going to bother my parents yet. Can I do it, or should I ask one of my sisters?"

"The sex doesn't matter, and they trace connections through aunts and uncles all the time."

Aunts and uncles. How strange that sounded. This man might be her biological uncle.

"Then I will take care of it right away, but—and maybe this isn't my business—why can't you use your phone or email? Is it related to this?"

"Oh, yes. That's why I called." What a ditz she was being. "I don't need money, but I do need help. Gideon's fans have hacked a friend's identity. Neither one of us can use our phones or the internet. That's why I'm not on the faculty list at school. We've had to cancel our credit cards. I'm hoping that your family has some way to manage things like this, although I can't imagine what it would be."

"Ah, yes"—there was the slightest laugh in his voice—"being related to Gideon Forbes is an acquired skill. We do have people who keep tabs on the craziest of fans. We have to. Zachary oversees everything for the rest of us. I will speak to him and call you back."

"Oh, I would appreciate that. Really I would." She gave him the phone number. "But it's a landline without an answering machine. So you may have to keep trying."

"I will do that. In the meantime, I hope you will refrain from calling our parents. Mother used to get her hopes up so much, and then we would find out that the person was crazy or after money. Now that she has the other grandchildren, she seems to have accepted how completely Gideon is gone. We hope you can respect that."

"Oh, yes, of course, anything."

"There is one more thing. You don't sound as if you grew up in the South. Is that correct?"

"I am from a Chicago suburb, but my father is from Georgia."

"Then you might understand. This was years ago, but the first time the possibility of Gideon having a child came up, my mother asked us to promise that if it turned out to be true, we were to assure that person that there was room for him or her in the family burial plot."

* * * *

Colleen exhaled as she hung up the phone. Ever since she had seen Ben crossing the lawn from the boathouse, things had been getting steadily worse: Grannor's will, the search for Ariel, Gideon and his fans, leaving her job, being cut off from her friends. For the first time she felt hopeful. This man was what uncles were supposed to be like.

Which was more than she could ever say for her uncle Norton.

She needed to call her father. "Is there any way I can catch him between patients?" she asked the receptionist. "I'll be as quick as I can."

She first had to reassure her father that the security firm was here, one man on the dock, another in a car angled across the base of the driveway. Then she told him that she had contacted Gideon Forbes's brother.

"Oh." His voice was heavy. "I thought you weren't going to do that."

"We needed help, Dad." She explained her reasoning. "I didn't know what else to do."

"Oh."

Almost everything on Autumn's message board and the Find Ariel website had been about the mothers. There was some talk about the "bio dads," but little about the man who had raised the children, who had given them his name, who had loved them every bit as much as his wife did.

"Oh, Dad, please believe me," she exclaimed. "This family is no threat to you. You're still my dad. You'll always be my dad."

"They are your blood, Colleen."

"Norton and Laura are yours, and they are horrible people. Of course I got things from my biological parents: my build, my facial features, my ability to learn languages. But my values, my morals, they are from you and Mom. Why do you think I am a good teacher?" She needed him to believe this. "It isn't because of my genes. It is because of you, the way you listen to your patients and try to figure out what they are saying even when they don't have the right words. You respect them even when they are putting Mountain Dew in a baby's bottle. You've always said that they are not bad people for doing that. They just have terrible information."

"That is fortunately improving."

She was not going to let this conversation be about dental care even if he was more comfortable talking about that. "I don't know how you got that way. Grannor was the complete opposite."

"I did learn from her, from both of them," he said slowly. "The one thing I knew is that I didn't want to be like my parents. That's why I left Georgia as soon as I could. I wanted to be the opposite of them. Until I met your mother, that was my map, my only map, not being like them."

"My version of the map was a whole lot easier to follow. I never had to read it upside down like you did. That's true of Sean and Finn too. You have been their role model, Dad, not the Bannings, but you and Mother."

"I've always given your mother the credit for how well you three turned out."

"Well, don't," she said bluntly. "Take some of it for yourself."

"That is very sweet of you."

"No, it isn't. I'm not being sweet or nice. I am telling the truth, and Mother would agree. Ask Genevieve. She knows what was in Mother's heart."

"Yes, she does…but, Colleen, you know what probably bothers me the most about your calling that other family? You needed help, and it was something I couldn't do."

* * * *

There were two more eggs in the nearly empty refrigerator. Colleen used them to make cookies for the security guards. She could feel her natural optimism returning. She didn't know how this would end, but it would. By next January she would be back in the classroom. The heirlooms would have been shipped to wherever her cousins wanted them. The ownership of the lake house would be settled. Things would be normal. Maybe not pre-Ben normal, but everything else would be just fine.

When she stepped out on to the patio to take some cookies to the guard on the dock, he frantically waved at her to get back inside.

Waiting for normal might be tedious, but she was willing to humor the overprotective men in her life for a few more days. Her father loved her; the Healy family loved her in a different way. Ben might not love her in the way he used to, but he did wish her well. So she was going to accept her role as a fragile blossom because rationally she did know that there was a danger out there, and this seemed like the best way to handle it.

In the middle of the afternoon Ben called. He was finally leaving the resort. Did she have anything to add to the grocery list? She told him to be sure and get eggs. Around five the phone rang again. She assumed that it was Ben calling to find out about salted or unsalted butter, large or extra-large eggs.

"Ms. Ridge? Colleen?"

It wasn't Jonathan Forbes; the voice was similar, but the accent was more muted. It must be his brother Zachary.

"Oh, thank you. Thank you for calling."

A quick, soft laugh came across the phone line. "Jonathan said that you'd know my voice, that you can do the things our sister can. She teaches French just like you."

"Really?" That couldn't be a coincidence.

"But she doesn't know Norwegian. At least she didn't at Christmas. She probably could have learned it by now."

This was how the O'Connells, her mother's family, talked about each other, lighthearted, teasing, and warm.

"First," he continued, "I have to apologize. Getting tied up with Gideon is not easy, but I think we're on track to clearing things up for you and your friend."

"Just like that? That fast? You knew who the hackers were?" She couldn't believe it.

"We have a pretty good idea of who are the ringleaders among Gideon's fans and who has this kind of skill. So we made a deal with them."

"A deal? What did they want? We haven't been able to figure that out. They are going to be so disappointed in me. I'm really ordinary."

He laughed again. "They're disappointed in all of us. They want us to be Gideon reincarnated or to at least spend our lives worshiping him."

He explained the deal the family had made. This particular cluster of fans had in their possession some writings of Gideon's, rough drafts of a number of songs and two drug-fueled journals. Not only had the documents been stolen, but the family owned the copyright on them. "We have piles of injunctions to keep them from circulating or publishing anything. We are giving them permission to publish one of the rough drafts in a week if the hacking stops within the next twelve hours and another one in six months if there is no reoccurrence."

"But this was so fast. How did you do everything so fast?"

"We have a number of different plans in place because we have always worried about the fans messing with the grandkids, and it sounds like you are the oldest of their generation."

The grandkids' generation? Did she have even more cousins? "But you don't know that," Colleen protested. "I know I look like your mother and sisters, but people resemble each other sometimes." The first candidate on Autumn's TV show had been a woman who randomly resembled Autumn. "Why are you doing this for me before we have gotten any of the results?"

"Whether or not you are related to Gideon, you are struggling because of him. Mom and Dad have been cleaning up after him since he was five, and now the rest of us do it. But I should warn you that if the DNA is a match, this is all just a start. Gideon's normal fans are going to be interested in you, and then there are all of Autumn's. You have to manage the publicity. We can help you through the worst of it, although I suppose Autumn has offered too."

"Yes, but my goal is to avoid publicity. That doesn't seem to be hers."

"No, it wouldn't be. But you've done a great job so far. The hackers think your name is Leah or Leia, something like that. Someone in the office has it written down."

"Leilah?"

"Yes, that's it. But they keep hitting a brick wall with her. They can't even find anything associated with a Leilah who would be the right age, but they still seem to think it is her. Do you know who she is?"

"Yes, but she doesn't have anything to do with this, and she is a lot older than me."

So Leilah had ended up doing Colleen a service, distracting the hackers in their search for Ariel.

"Do you all have a way of figuring out if the hacking has stopped?" he asked.

"I don't, but I'm sure Ben—my friend—will know."

"As soon as you check, get back in touch so we can authorize the first release of the rough draft." Then Zachary said that he had to leave for a meeting, but that the DNA results should come soon. There was a branch of the lab not too far from the Duke campus. Jonathan had driven over and given his sample in person.

Colleen was still staring at the phone when she heard Grannor's car come up the drive. Ben pulled around to the kitchen door. That's what they did after going to the store.

She hurried to open the kitchen door. She had so much good news to share. Ben got out of the car and came around to the rear. The cavernous trunk was full of grocery bags. "Good God, you got a lot."

"I had Nate's credit card. Why not let him buy us raspberries and prime rib?" Then he grew serious. "Did your headmistress call? Does she want you to take the leave of absence?"

Had that call only been this morning? So much was happening. "Yes, but maybe I won't have to now." She didn't want to start telling him until they had the groceries inside. She reached in the truck and picked up two of the bigger bags. Ben scooped up the handles of several bags at once and shoved those up over his arm so he could carry more. He followed her in the kitchen. Once she had set her bags down, she helped him untangle himself.

"I have news. I called one of Gideon's brothers, and—"

"I thought that they didn't want to hear from you." Ben started to unload the groceries.

"He did want to hang up on me, but once I could recite what he said in Portuguese, he was really wonderful."

"Portuguese?" Ben had been about to get the rest of the groceries, but he stopped, a little bewildered. "What does speaking in Portuguese have to do with anything?"

"I never said I could speak Portuguese. That's what I had going for me, that I couldn't. Here's the good part, he—actually, the other brother—thinks that they have stopped the hackers."

Ben drew back. "How? Between my guys from school and the team at the money managers, where did they find people better than that? And so fast?"

"They aren't doing anything fancy-schmancy technical. It's plain, old-fashioned blackmail and bribery." She explained the stolen papers and the deal the Forbeses had made with the hackers. "Do you have a way of checking to see if the hacking has stopped?"

"I have an after-hours emergency number for the money people. But if the brother gave them twelve hours to stop, that won't be until the middle of the night."

"Would you try now anyway?" She didn't want to wait.

"Okay, but we need to get the rest of the groceries. There's ice cream in one of them."

She went outside for the other bags and listened to Ben's conversation as she looked for the ice cream.

He was shaking his head as he hung up. "I'll be damned," he said. Ever since the hacking started, there had been a steady stream of pea shooter attacks on his investment account. They weren't creative or challenging, just annoying. "At 3:17 p.m. Eastern time, they suddenly stopped. The guy I talked to is worried that they could be gearing up for something more sophisticated."

"Or it could be over." Why couldn't he be a little more hopeful? "Will you call your hacker friend?"

"Don't call him a hacker. He isn't anymore." But he turned back to the phone.

She quit working on the groceries to watch him. He was shaking his head again, but it was a good shaking, expressing disbelief, not disappointment or disapproval.

"You know those four little charges they put on my credit card?" he said when he was done with the call. "They issued a refund. They added up the amount and credited the account even though the amount was insignificant."

"That was weirdly honorable of them. Or they're trying to send a message to Gideon's family, saying that they were laying down their guns. What about Autumn's website?" She had forgotten to say anything to the Forbeses about that.

"Autumn's people have suspended her site from their end so it's harder to know the status of that, whether or not they got rid of the porn link."

"Did you ask your friend about the other site, the Find Ariel one?"

"The damage has been done. There's no way to make that good without access to the actual computers. One of my friends crashed the site. It's probably best to leave it to its eternal rest and hope that the administrators learned a lesson. I bought one of those rotisserie chickens. Can we have dinner now? I'm starving."

"Okay, but there is one other thing. The hackers thought that Leilah was Ariel."

"Leilah?" He was surprised. "Why would they think that? Oh, right, after she left, I did a pretty deep search for her. That would have looked suspicious, much more than the couple of calls I made to you. Do you know if they harassed her?"

"They were looking for someone my age, so apparently not. Do you have any idea where she is?"

He started to cut up the chicken. "No. She doesn't want to be found. I am going to respect that. Now tell me about the Forbes family."

As they ate, Colleen told him everything she had learned.

"They have a point about the publicity," he said eventually. "This hacking may be over, but remember all those people outside the hotel, they are still going to think that they own you. I imagine that your school isn't going to want you back until things die down."

She supposed he was right. If the DNA came back as a match, it was foolish to suppose she would be teaching the fall semester. "Zachary says that the people who manage Gideon's affairs will help me."

"What about Autumn?"

Colleen dropped her napkin across her plate. It had been such a relief to deal with the normal-seeming Forbes brothers that she hadn't thought much about Autumn all day. But the start of all this had been a young girl who, however successful she had been, had been vulnerable enough to be seduced by an older man.

"I don't know, Ben. I feel so conflicted. Why can't she and I meet like two normal people?"

"Because she doesn't have a normal life. She's dangerous, Colleen. You need to be careful."

"Dangerous? You aren't serious, are you? That's so harsh."

"Remember what happened in DC."

Oh, Lord. He had lost control for ten minutes, and now he was never going to let go of it.

But she had to admit that she had been scared that day. "I think a lot of that was all the mystery associated with not knowing who Ariel was." As usual she was trying pretty hard to look on the bright side. "Once everything is out in the open, what is there to worry about?"

"It will be a different kind of danger. She will try to turn you into her mini-me. She's going to want you to go to appearances with her. Her stylists will do whatever stylists do, hair, makeup, designer gowns."

Colleen actually liked the sound of a makeup artist and a designer gown. That would be fun. "Why does that worry you?"

"I wouldn't want to see you taken over by that relationship. It wouldn't make you happy to go to LA and live in her shadow."

This was annoying. Here they had had all this good news, and he was being Mr. Doom and Gloom. "Why are you so sure you know what will make me happy? What are you asking of me, Ben? To repudiate her? Not to give her a chance?"

"Not to let her break your heart."

He was asking that? Hadn't he been the first person to break her heart?

"Don't you trust me to make those decisions for myself?" She stopped, her hands suddenly dropping to the table. "That's it, isn't it? All this, and you still don't trust me, do you?"

Chapter 17

They were back to the wearying politeness. Why couldn't one of them be like Leilah and disappear?

Because we're better than that.

She cared about him. No, she loved him. For all his stupid, pigheaded, testosterone-poisoned, worst-case-scenario blindness, she loved him. She also trusted him. As long as he thought that he could help her, he would never leave.

But she wasn't going to stand on her ear trying to prove herself to him. She wasn't as desperate as she had been four years ago,

Over the weekend he and his friends restored her access to what she had filed on the cloud; she got back all her lesson plans, her work on the grant, letters she had written to her grandmothers. Most of the data from her phone was also there. Apparently she had a setting that did back things up. That was a surprise to her. She was going to be more careful in the future.

She couldn't restore access to her checking account online. Ben said she might be able to do it over the phone on Monday.

"I'll do it in person." She had to go into Charlottesville anyway. She needed to check on her apartment and return her summer tenant's security deposit.

* * * *

Her apartment was fine. The bank urged her to open a new credit card and sign up for more services. She kept saying no, and they finally restored everything to how it had been before.

But it was strange to be in Charlottesville. The whole town was gearing up for the start of classes, the secondary schools and the university. The shops had washed their windows and were displaying new merchandise. The bars were offering coupons, hoping to lure in the students. Her friends were comparing course schedules and fussing about changes. Everyone else was busy; she had nothing to do. For the first time in her life, Colleen felt that she was someplace that she didn't belong.

On her way out of town she stopped at the university's housing office and put her apartment on their Off-Grounds Housing list, offering it for fall semester. Her father hoped to settle her grandmother's estate by the end of the year. By the start of second semester her cousins would have had to take possession of their heirlooms, whether they wanted them or not; the lake house would be emptied; she would know how much money she was going to have. Her life could go back to normal.

Although it might be a different normal. She would be known as the biological offspring of Autumn Chase and Gideon Forbes.

She still didn't have actual confirmation yet. The website for the lab said that even with expedited service, processing for a DNA match would take three to five business days. Jonathan had given his sample on Thursday. So tomorrow, Tuesday, would be the absolute earliest the report would come back. But as it was August and people might be on vacation, next Friday was more likely.

She stopped in the village for gas. As she was waiting for the tank to fill, she automatically took out her phone and checked her email.

There it was. Today was still only Monday, but there it was—the lab report for an "avuncular test," which matched aunt/uncle and nephew/niece pairs. The email message itself said nothing about the results. She had to click on the attachment. There were dense blocks of numbers, columns for the child—that was her—and columns for the possible uncle—that was Jonathan Forbes. It was impossible to make sense of the numbers on her phone. She scrolled down to the end of the report. The "combined first order index" was over 17,000. The statistical probability of the "untested person"—that was Gideon—being her parent, child, or sibling was 99.4 percent.

Gideon Forbes was her "bio dad." She was the Lost Princess, she was Ariel.

It felt anticlimactic. Ever since she had seen the pictures of Gideon's mother and sisters, she had been sure.

And truly, truly, in this moment—whatever might happen in the next few weeks—it changed nothing. She was still herself, Colleen Ridge, a good teacher, a generous friend, a reasonably faithful Catholic, etc., etc., and a woman in love with a man she couldn't share her life with because he was too much of an emotionally stunted, pigheaded, gorgeous jackass.

The landline was ringing when Colleen got into the house. She rushed to answer it.

"Hello, may I please speak to Miss Colleen Ridge?"

It was a woman's voice, and not just any woman, but one whose vowels glided and lingered with Carolina grace. "Mrs. Forbes?"

"Oh, you dear girl, you darling child, I have so much to say that I don't know where to start. We didn't know about you. We would have never abandoned a child."

"Please don't feel bad, please don't. I grew up in the right family. Truly. My mother always said that my brothers and I were gifts from God, that God had put us in the only place we belonged."

"I hope that that is true. We have no business criticizing Autumn when Gideon took such advantage of her, but I can't help wishing she had come to us. We could have helped."

"She said that she wouldn't even tell her parents who the father was." Colleen struggled to reassure Mrs. Forbes. What guilt and sadness she must be feeling. "And there's no reason to dwell on any of that. It's all in the past."

"I know," Mrs. Forbes sighed. "But I can't help wanting to make up for lost time. The boys just told me. I wanted to throw myself on a plane and come to you wherever you are, but they said that they didn't know."

The "boys" were a distinguished linguistics professor and an Academy Award–winning sound editor. That was how families talked about each other.

"I'm in Virginia near the West Virginia line."

"Virginia? That's so close. I hope you will let us come see you very soon."

"Of course," Colleen answered, "or I can come to you. I'm not teaching this fall."

"Zachary said that you teach French, just like my Mary. That's amazing. You seem like family already, but first, tell me about your family, your people. I want to know everything about you."

Mrs. Forbes had not said "your adoptive family" or "the family you grew up with," but "your family." That meant a lot. Colleen told her about growing up in Chicago, about her mother dying. "But my father married a woman who is very good for him, and while I'm not supposed to know this yet, I'm sure that my sister-in-law is pregnant."

"That's wonderful. We love babies, don't you? But what about you? Do you have someone significant in your life?"

"It's complicated." That was the best Colleen could come up with.

"I understand…I mean, obviously I don't, but I raised two girls. I tried not to push even when I was dying to know."

She told Colleen about her family. All four of her surviving children were married with children of their own. "There are twenty-one of us at Christmas and you should know that they are all going to want to meet you."

"I'm not afraid of crowds. My mother came from a family of eight kids, and so I have a million cousins on that side."

"Are you—and I know I shouldn't assume this—but with all those brothers and sisters, your mother, was she Catholic?"

"She was, and I am."

"Oh, my." Donna Forbes's voice shimmered with a low thrill. "That shouldn't make a difference to me, should it? That you're happy and healthy, that's all I should care about."

"There's nothing wrong with caring about this too."

Mrs. Forbes understood how concerned Colleen was about public attention. "One Christmas when Gideon was home, one of his fans actually climbed on our roof and leaned over the gutters, trying to see in the windows. He got stuck and couldn't come down. If my husband had had anything to say about it, we would have left the boy there."

They went on talking for at least another hour. Ben returned to the house around six because Colleen had said that she would make dinner. When he saw that she was on the kitchen phone, he quietly brought a chair over to the kitchen counter so that she sit down. Colleen, used to talking on cell phones, could feel her ear throbbing from the pressure of the telephone's handset.

When the call was finally over, she found Ben on the patio on the lake side of the house.

"I take it you were talking to Gideon's mother. The DNA match came back?"

She nodded.

"How do you feel about that?"

"Like I already knew, but she is wonderful. She feels terrible about them not knowing about me. But I kept telling her it was all for the best."

"So what happens next?"

"I'm going to go down and visit them. The real estate appraisers come tomorrow so I'll go on Wednesday."

"Do you want me to go with you?" Ben asked. "Help with the driving and all?"

"It's an easy trip. I don't need any help."

"I won't be in the way. I'll go hang out with Seth. He's not that far away."

"No, Ben. I don't need your help."

And she didn't. While the Forbeses were not as noisy as the O'Connells, they were still a big Catholic family, and Colleen felt at ease…although she did wish that Donna Forbes would stop apologizing for not knowing about her.

Jonathan came in from Durham, and even with this very short notice, a PR representative flew down from New York to plan the "rollout" of her identity. There would be a lot of interest in her. The PR person said that the best way for her to end up with a relatively normal life was to be widely available for a few weeks and be so pleasantly boring that people would lose interest.

"Pleasantly boring? I can do that," she assured them. All the years of being a nice girl would be good training for that.

She would first appear on one of the morning network shows a few days after Labor Day when viewers would have settled back into their normal habits. She would also sit for several print interviews.

She was to come to New York City a few days before the first interview. She would meet with a stylist who would help her with her wardrobe and get her to the right hairdresser. Gideon's estate would pay for all that.

"Actually," Colleen said, "I think my father would want to do it." Although Colleen supported herself, never asking her father for money, she knew that at this moment he would like to be the daddy who was buying his little girl a new party dress.

She could only stay in North Carolina for two nights. The silver appraisers were coming over the weekend. She left North Carolina with hugs, kisses, and a list of questions she was to practice answering.

How had it felt growing up adopted? That one was easy.

Why hadn't she come forward earlier? That was harder because she didn't want to be seen as criticizing Autumn.

What would you say to women who relinquished children? Do birth fathers have…What does it feel like…Why did you…Would you…

She had no idea that people did so much work before an interview.

* * * *

It was exhausting having the silver appraisers in the house. Their voices were loud; they were in and out of the kitchen all day, getting more coffee, asking Colleen if they could have a piece of fruit from the fruit bowl or a cookie from the cookie jar. It took her a while to note that Ben was using the fax machine more than he ever had before.

Next time he was in the library, she took him the last of the cookies.

"What's going on?" She nodded toward the fax machine.

He took another cookie. "Are you ready for a huge 'I told you so'?"

"Oh, crap." She sat the plate down so that she could make a quick getaway if she needed to. "What do you think I have done this time?"

"Oh, no. No." He had just taken a bite of the cookie; he had to swallow hurriedly. "It's the other way around. You were right, and I was wrong."

She liked the sound of that.

Apparently Nate and Seth had been gone back to "blabbing" throughout the entire free world about him giving private lessons. Chloe in his agent's office had had a more focused approach. She spread the word among East Coast families who didn't yet care about the politics of the winter sports establishment. Their kids weren't advanced enough yet to have sponsors. What the parents knew about Ben was that he cared more about their kids' health than their short-term success. An added benefit was that his sessions, priced to bring little kids at a small resort, were a whole lot cheaper than anything with the established coaches.

His entire week was already blocked with some pretty talented youths.

"And yes," he said, looking straight at her with his Irish green eyes, "I am happy about it, very happy. I figure if I bust my chops until December, I can finish my degree. Then I told the resort to set up as much time as they wanted. Nate says the Almost Heaven people are maybe interested now, but I owe something to this place for giving me a chance."

Colleen was not going to gloat. "I'm glad it's working for you."

"It's a long way from working with the top competitors, but the right couple of kids with the right coaching...who knows?"

I know. Colleen was as boundlessly optimistic as always. *And when you start your own program, Amanda and I are going to run the scholastic component.*

* * * *

Negotiations had begun for Colleen's appearance on the network show. Her name and identity were being kept secret, but Autumn's team heard that such an appearance was in the works. They contacted Colleen's representatives, demanding to know Colleen's name and insisting that Autumn be included in Colleen's appearances. Autumn's show in July had been on a cable channel on a holiday weekend; Colleen was appearing on a network in a much more desirable time slot.

"It's your call," the PR rep told Colleen. "But if we include her, we will have to rethink the pleasantly boring strategy."

"Then no. No, thank you."

Autumn's website was back online. The opening letter acknowledged how offensive people must have found the site when it was hacked. Even though she, too, had been a victim, she wanted to apologize. Anyone purchasing one of her purses through the website in the next month would receive a free clutch. There was no mention of Ariel.

Ben reported sales of Autumn's products continued to sag.

The weather turned bad again. August in the mid-Atlantic could be unpleasant even this near the mountains. The sky was stormy, the atmosphere close and humid. Colleen had been staying on the third floor ever since her grandmother's stroke. Those rooms were now too hot and stuffy. She moved down to the second floor. She paused at the door to the spacious room over the kitchen, the one her grandparents used to stay in. She could see why they had liked it. It had a private feel, being separated from the other four bedrooms by the back stairs. It had windows on three sides and its own bathroom. But there were still crated artworks leaning against the wall and a maze of rolled carpets on the floor.

A week before Colleen was to go to New York, the rain came, bringing some relief from the heat. It was still raining in the evening, and the light disappeared early because the clouds were low and dense. The darkness wrapped around the house like a blanket, holding in the quiet. Suddenly the doorbell rang, echoing through the unused rooms in the front of the house.

Colleen and Ben looked at each other. No one ever turned up here unexpectedly.

Ben stood up. "Let me get that." He turned off his reading light and gestured to Colleen to flick off the wall switches. She followed him as he turned on the hall lights. He glanced through the sidelight window along the edge of the big wooden door, then instantly jerked back out of view. "It's Autumn."

"Autumn? How did she find us?"

"How would I know? But I'm not letting her in."

"That's not your decision to make, and you know it isn't."

He did know. "Okay, but will you stay back for a bit?"

Colleen was willing to do that. She stepped back into the shadows of the arched opening that led to the sitting room.

The bell rang again as Ben was flipping on the front lights and opening the door. There, her chestnut hair lit by the exterior sconces, the rain at her back, the light from the hall falling on her face, was Autumn.

She threw up her arms, the sleeves of her shimmering sapphire raincoat fluttering from her wrists. "Look, I am alone. All alone. Just me. They told me I had to come to the door alone. You're Gary, aren't you? Gary Vogel? Where is Ariel? Where is my Ariel?"

"How did you find this place?"

She flipped her hand. That didn't matter. "Is she here? They told me—" She broke off. "Oh, my, you are a very handsome man. Do you know that? Oh, you must. People always know that about themselves."

Colleen could see the back of Ben's shoulders draw together. He must be surprised. He wouldn't know what to say.

"But we can talk about that later," Autumn said, her voice as lovely as her face. "I'm here to see Ariel, my darling Ariel. She is here, isn't she? I've come all this way. You have to let me see her."

Colleen stepped through the arch into the light of the hall.

Autumn gasped and moved toward her. "Oh, is it you? Is it really you? Are you Ariel?"

"I'm Colleen."

"Come into the light," Autumn took her by the shoulders. She was only a little taller than Colleen. Her touch was light. Her scent was floral and powdery without being sweet. "Let me look at you. Oh, how pretty you are. And if you highlight your hair...oh, listen to me, already telling you how to wear your hair."

"I do need a haircut. I know it." Colleen felt Autumn's charisma like a natural force, even more essential to the earth than electricity or chemistry. It was as if Autumn carried within her a little piece of the magnetic North Pole, drawing everything to her.

Or was it more? *We were together for nine months. I was a burden, a tragedy, but we shared your body.*

"Can I take your coat?" It was Ben.

"Oh, yes, thank you. Oh, my, what a nice watch that is," she exclaimed. Ben was in a T-shirt; his forearms were bare, and Judge Rutherford's elegant watch encircled his tanned wrist. "And what good posture you have. Have you ever modeled? I could get you to the right people."

Ben was still standing there, his hands out. "Your coat, ma'am."

"Oh, goodness, don't you go 'ma'am'-ing me. I'm not that old." But she turned and let him lift the coat off her shoulders. It was a beautiful coat. The fabric was lustrous and a glowing shade of blue. The buttons were silvery and black braid scrolled in a military design.

"Would you like a cup of tea?" Colleen didn't know what else to say.

"Oh, yes. That would be lovely. Herbal please. With lemon. Stevia if you have it. Otherwise the tiniest bit of honey."

Colleen went into the kitchen and filled the teakettle. She had put too much water in. It would take forever to boil. She dumped half of the water out. The tea bags were in the far cabinet. She didn't think that they had any lemon. And Stevia? It was an organic natural sweetener. Leilah might have left some, but Colleen wasn't sure where to look.

A moment later Autumn was in the kitchen. "I'm terribly sorry, asking you to wait on me. I didn't mean to sound so demanding. Anything will do. Is this your home? It's charming."

"It belonged to my grandmother."

"Your grandmother?" Autumn looked puzzled. "Gideon's mother?"

"No, I mean *my* grandmother." It felt good to say that. "My father's mother." *This is my family's home. This is where I come from. These are my roots.*

And suddenly Colleen knew exactly what she wanted from Grannor's estate: this house and enough money to maintain it…and maybe enough silver and china to set a pretty table. It could be her weekend and summer home as long as she was teaching in Charlottesville. Or maybe she could get a closer job and live here year-round. This would be her legacy, what she would pass on to her children. Let Kim pry the diamonds out of the fox head brooches, wear the pearls without restringing them, watch the silver tarnish. She was going to have this house. She would take over the big bedroom. She would be the owner, the hostess, the chatelaine.

"The house has been my family's summer home since before I was born," she continued. She felt strong and confident, very certain of who Colleen Ridge was and what she stood for. "I never met the Forbeses until this month."

"Oh, of course. I'm sorry." Autumn apologized. "I wasn't thinking. It's hard enough not to think of you as a baby, much less as having been brought up by strangers. After you were born, they told me I would never see you again so I could only think of you as a baby. I want to know everything about you. Tell me everything. But, first, you need to understand that I never meant for things to get so out of hand. I just wanted to find you, no differently than any first mother wants to find her child. People were using me. I mean, I should have expected it. People try to use me all the time. They've been doing it since I was eight, but I'm always so surprised when it happens."

"How did you find me now?"

She waved her hand. "I'm not sure. Something about an intern at the network or something. I was on a plane within an hour. I've been so nervous about meeting you, wondering what you would think of me. I hear that you are a teacher."

Colleen nodded.

"I never had an education. I was working. There were tutors and such on set, but there was never really time. I didn't learn anything. I am always a little ashamed of that. I don't even have a high school diploma, and here you are a teacher. You must have all kinds of degrees."

"A BA, an MAT, and various certifications."

"I don't even know what you are talking about. That's how ignorant I am. You will have to explain it all to me, but we do need to talk about these network bookings. I know you're doing the morning show soon, but there's still plenty of time. I hope you'll use my stylist and my hairdresser. They're both so good. And we don't want to show up in colors that clash."

"Clash? We aren't appearing together. That has been set."

"Of course we are going to be together. That's what you want, isn't it? Isn't that what everyone wants? To see us together? That's really important, and if you ask, the network will schedule it. They will have to."

Colleen pushed her scraggly hair off her face. "This has been very difficult for me."

"I know, I know. But my people can all make it so much easier for you. You won't have to worry about a thing." Autumn's eyes were warm and overpowering. "You will be thrilled with what we can do with your hair."

Colleen was not going to apologize for her hair. Yes, it was straggling and shapeless, but she was going to get it cut in New York next week. And why was Autumn talking about her hair? Where was the loss and the emptiness that Autumn had said she had felt? Where, amid all this charisma and energy and warmth, was that?

"I think it would be better for me to do this alone," Colleen said quietly.

"Oh, but why? You're my daughter. We should do things together."

Ben was standing in the corner of the kitchen, not saying anything.

"Is this why you are here?" Colleen asked. "To get on the show?"

"No, no, no, *no.*" Autumn's beautifully trained voice trilled through the syllables, making each one different. "I'm here to see you, my darling, you."

"It does seem that you care more about the publicity."

"Does the publicity make you uncomfortable?" Autumn didn't seem to have heard what Colleen had really said. "It's nothing to worry about. You'll get used to it. After a while you won't even notice the cameras, and talking to reporters, you simply think of them as friends. That's all there is to it. Most of them are lovely people. And that's all the more reason we should do it together so I can help you if you run into trouble."

Anyone who could think of reporters as friends must not know much about friendship. "I am going to follow the advice I am getting."

"Gideon's family hired those people, didn't they? I should have realized that I would start having to compete with him even though he is dead." She swiveled, looking back at Ben. "Please, Gary, you're her friend. Tell her that she and I need to appear together. That it really will be the best thing for everyone."

"No, ma'am, I don't tell her what to do," he said.

"Oh, but you must," Autumn pleaded. "You *must*." When Ben shook his head, she turned back to Colleen. "You have to understand how much I have sacrificed to find you. I don't care about all those numbers and sales, but they say that the brand might never recover, that we might have to close it all down. And I did it for you."

Colleen was not going to let anyone make her feel guilty. "I believe that the most dignified route will be for me to appear alone."

"Dignified? What are you talking about? You're trying to punish me. I was told about that, some children are so angry about being relinquished that they try to punish their mothers."

"I am not angry, and I'm not a child."

"But if you go on alone, what are you going to say? How are you going to explain why I'm not there? People are going to wonder. You're going to be asked."

"I will tell them the truth. I don't need a mother. I had a wonderful mother. She died, but thanks to my father marrying again, I have a wonderful stepmother."

"Is that what you are going to say? That you have no room for me in your life? You shouldn't say that. You will come across as so cold."

"I know that I am not cold. It doesn't matter what other people watching me on TV think. And I'm not saying that there is no room for you. I hope someday that I will have children, and my children will need a grandmother."

"A grandmother? Who, me? A grandmother?" Autumn was genuinely stunned.

"I'm almost twenty-eight. I could have had four children by now."

"You aren't going to go on the network and call me a grandmother, are you?"

"No, because you aren't, but if someone asks what I hope for in terms of our relationship, it will be that."

"You can't do that. You simply can't do that."

As quickly as Colleen had realized that she wanted this house, she realized something else. She would not tell her children that Autumn was their grandmother.

For all that had been wrong with her as a human being, Grannor had been, at least until her will, predictable as a grandparent. She didn't make many plans or promises, but if she did, she followed through completely. She wasn't sunny one day and critical the next. She was critical all the time, but at least the grandkids had known what to expect, and children needed that.

A grandchild of Autumn's would have to walk on eggshells. She would promise an all-access pass to the secret places in Disneyland and then cancel at the last minute, leaving a child wondering if it were their fault. She would fawn over grandchildren when they were adorable toddlers dressed in perfect clothes. But when they started to choose their own clothes, wearing a fluffy pink ballerina skirt with a red Wonder Woman T-shirt, the rejection would be instant.

If Colleen only had herself to consider, she would go on forever wanting to believe in an Autumn who wasn't really there. She would risk the soul-deep disappointment for herself, but only for herself.

Not for a child. Her sometimes unthinking optimism would stop there. Never for a child.

She was ready for Autumn to leave. "B—Gary, would you please get our guest her coat?"

Autumn was still staring at Colleen speechless when Ben returned. He held the coat open, but Autumn didn't seem to see him.

"It's raining, ma'am," he said. "You need your coat."

"You aren't really asking me to leave, are you?" she implored Colleen. "I'm your mother."

"I do think it would be better if you left now."

Ben draped the coat over Autumn's shoulders and took her arm. "You need to come with me, ma'am."

A minute later Colleen heard the door open and close just as the teakettle begin to whistle.

Autumn hadn't been here long enough for water to boil. This was the supposedly legendary meeting, the one that fans everywhere would be aching to witness. It hadn't lasted long enough for water to boil.

Ben's footsteps grew louder as he approached the kitchen. "Grandmother... that was a zinger."

"She would be on probation. I don't trust her." Colleen turned off the burner under the teakettle. "You can say 'I told you so' because you didn't trust her from the beginning."

"I'm not going to say that, not after what I just saw."

That didn't make any sense. "What are you talking about?"

"You. The way you handled that. Your dad, my dad, my brother, me... we've all been thinking that you couldn't handle this on your own—"

"I have needed help."

"Maybe we are good at the planning and the logistics, all that, but when it comes to relationships, you're better than anybody. If we had followed your instincts and gotten you and Autumn in a room together right away, this all would have played out very differently. We should have done it your way."

"But then she would have never revealed Gideon's name. She dribbled information a bit at a time to keep people interested in the search. It worked out as it should have. As much conflict as you and I had with each other, we make a good team, Ben."

She put out her hand, but she didn't cross it across her body as she would in a handshake. He took it, slipping his fingers under her palm, and started to raise her hand as if he was going to kiss it.

The doorbell rang again.

"Do you think that's her?" Colleen curved her fingers around his so that he couldn't let go.

Ben shook his head, still not letting go of her hand. "She couldn't have actually come alone."

"She probably never does anything alone." How warm his fingers were, how strong.

The doorbell rang again. And again. "They aren't going to leave," she said.

"No," he said. They let their hands drop. When they got to the door, he glanced through one of the sidelight again. "It's someone from her entourage."

Without him telling her to, Colleen retreated into the dark dining room. Ben opened the door to a man who was middle-aged and slightly overweight, an aging pretty boy. He had a large, shiny shopping bag in his hand. Colleen recognized the logo. It was from Autumn's handbag collection. "I had to come talk to you," he said, his voice a little shaky. "Autumn is so upset. You can't do this to her."

"Why not?" Ben asked.

The man was even more startled. "Because..." He didn't know how to answer that. "She's Autumn, Autumn Chase. People love her."

"I know they do." Colleen stepped forward. "And that's good. Everyone needs to be loved, but I'm not part of that."

The man looked at her. "You're Ariel? Here, she wanted you to have this." He held out the bag. When Colleen didn't take it, he tried to give it to Ben, who had his arms folded. The man then set it on the floor. "Why didn't you come forward?" he asked Colleen. "Do you have any idea how much you hurt her by hiding? Why would you want to hurt her like that? She's your *mother*. You owe her. She could have had an abortion."

Colleen lifted her hands, shrugging.

"And she said something about you calling her a grandmother. Don't you understand that you can't do that? You simply can't."

"She can't declare herself to be my mother and then say that when I have children, she's not a grandmother. It doesn't work that way."

"But that's not right," he insisted.

Colleen couldn't see the logic of that. "I don't think there's any reason to invite you in," she said even though the man had already taken a few steps in when he was trying to give one of them the bag.

"But I can't leave. Autumn told me that I had to stay until you agreed to talk to her."

For a moment Colleen felt a little sorry for him. But he was not her problem.

At least he wouldn't be once she got him to leave. "This is a Southern home," she said. "We have guns. In fact, Gary, you're armed, aren't you?"

"Yes, ma'am." Ben had the sense to take a menacing step forward, but then moved his hand toward his hip as if he were a gunslinger in an old Western.

Except it was obvious even to a person as distressed as this man that Ben hadn't gotten up this morning and buckled on a leather holster and a Colt .45.

The man looked confused. Colleen took advantage of the moment to announce, "The door is heavy. You best take a step back."

Instinctively the man did so. Ben reached around Colleen to slam the door shut with such force that the floorboards vibrated.

She turned her head to look at him. "Your hip, Gary? Reaching for your hip didn't fool anyone."

"I'm wearing jeans and a tee. Where would I be hiding a gun? And do we have guns?"

"I have no idea. Maybe in the basement somewhere. But you had a good time with the 'ma'am' thing, didn't you?" Then she noticed the shopping bag. She crossed the hall to pick it up.

"Oh, crap," Ben said. "I wish I had thought to throw that after him."

"Let's look at it first. My sister-in-law says there's a blue purse that she wants."

Colleen sat the bag on the round center hall table. There were two purses inside, one was an all-purpose black, the other an all-purpose summery taupe. They were from the highest end of Autumn's collection. The only brand identification was a little pewter-toned maple leaf dangling from one of the zipper pulls. Autumn's lower-priced purses had her name and logo splashed all over them.

She would have liked to have hated these purses, but they were absolutely, totally, and completely perfect. Made of a microfiber so that they were light, carefully constructed with pleats and gussets, they didn't look anywhere near as big as they actually were, but you could carry a small laptop or even a pair of heels in them.

She lined them up on the hall table, admiring them. She wondered how much Autumn had had to do with the design.

"You're keeping them?" Ben sounded surprised.

"No. I'm going to send them to Patty and Liz. It's the least they deserve. They've been so good at keeping their mouths shut, and it's been hard for them."

Ben cleared this throat. "Are we done talking about handbags?"

Colleen gave the black bag one last little pat. "I suppose."

"Then can we go back to talking about how amazing you were, so clear and firm, so definite."

"I'm pretty pleased with myself," she admitted. "I felt like my grandmother. Grannor, I mean. Not the mean, nasty part, but the strong, lay-it-on-the-line, be-in-control lady. Grannor herself would have called it 'being a Ridge.' It felt good."

"Your behavior and this house did put a crimp in any rescuer fantasies that Autumn might have had."

The hall chandelier kindled all the copper highlights in his hair. Autumn was right about one thing. He really was a very good-looking man. But that wasn't why she loved him. "Fortunately in all this Grandmother Ridgeness, I've held on to enough of Grammy O'Connell to believe in love."

"Your family is a loving one."

"For God's sake, I am not talking about that. I'm talking about you and me." She laid her palm against his cheek. His skin was warm. His eyes were jade, soft and lustrous. "There are good things you can believe in, Ben, especially me. You can believe in me."

She lifted her chin. She was going to kiss him. She didn't need him to go first. She was going to do more than kiss him. She was going to propose. Nice girls might wait to be asked, but Colleen wasn't all that nice anymore.

Suddenly he stepped back, leaving her hand dangling. He was pulling his phone out of his pocket.

"What are you doing?" she demanded. "I'm being all gushy and romantic, and you're making a phone call?"

"I'm making a flight reservation. I'm going to Chicago tomorrow."

"Chicago?" She was bewildered. "Why?"

"Because I'm a good Southern boy, and we ask the father first."

It took her a moment to figure out what he was talking about. "You aren't serious, are you?"

"Of course I am. Ryan did it. Tommy too, even though Megan's dad is a worthless drunk. I'll need to take your grandmother's car to the airport."

"You'll do no such thing. In fact, don't you dare confirm that reservation." She tried to grab the phone, but he turned and quite easily held it out of her reach. Tilting back his head, he raised his other arm to try and complete the reservation overhead.

His ribs made a tempting target. Colleen started poking at him. "At least call him. Don't fly halfway across the country." She continued to poke. "And what will you do if he says no?"

"Would you cut that out?" He swatted at her hand. "I'll be sorry if he refuses permission because I know you would hate going against his wishes."

"But you know I'd do it anyway, don't you?"

"Can't you at least humor me and pretend that we men still have some patriarchal authority?"

"No." She moved in front of him so she could poke at his ribs with both hands.

"I'm serious, Colleen. That's annoying."

He wasn't paying attention to how he was holding his phone. She stood on her toes, stretched up, and grabbed it. She brought up the keypad and dialed her father's number. "Dad, it's me. Ben Healy wants to talk to you about proposing to me. Here he is."

She smiled sweetly and, after pressing the speaker button, handed his phone back to him.

Ben glared at her. "Dr. Ridge?"

"Ben?"

"Yes, sir."

This was getting off to a great start.

"Ah…" Her father didn't seem to know what to say any more than Ben did. "I appreciate how willing you have been to stay at the lake. We were all worried about Colleen being alone there."

Clearly the two of them needed someone else to get this party started. "Will one of you get to the point?" she prodded.

Ben still looked like he needed someone to hand him a script. After a moment, her father spoke. "Genevieve told me that this might happen. Colleen's right there, isn't she?"

"Obviously," Colleen said.

"So this isn't exactly the man-to-man conversation you had envisioned."

"No, sir," Ben answered. "I was in the middle of making a reservation to come to Chicago when she took my phone."

"Why don't you both come this weekend before Colleen goes off to New York? The boys and Patty and Liz are coming."

"We'll be there," Colleen said instantly. Sean and Patty would be sharing their big news. "So is that it? Does Ben have your permission?"

"Hold on," Ben said. "I want to sign a prenup. I don't want Colleen to sign one, but I know that she's coming into a lot of money, and I want to be sure that it is hers and always hers."

"You have money too," Colleen said. "Why would you want to sign one and not have me do it too? That's the dumbest thing I've ever heard."

"Perhaps it is," her father said. "But it was gallant."

"Exactly. Gallant, dumb. They aren't all that different."

"Are you trying to get him to drop the proposal, Colleen Marie?"

"I'm not going to," Ben said, "even if she doesn't respect me as a fine flower of Southern chivalry."

"Oh, lay off it," Colleen ordered. "Your family had nothing to do with the Confederacy. You were still hoeing potatoes in Ireland."

Ben acknowledged the truth of that.

"So, Dad, do we have your permission?"

"Your mother and I raised you to make your own decisions. You don't need my permission, but I can tell you if she were here, she would be thrilled. She and Ben's mother really were soul mates. Furthermore Genevieve says that your mother would not approve of the way I have handled everything associated with your birth families. I suppose this is as good a time as any to begin apologizing."

"Oh, Dad..." She didn't care about an apology. "I love you. You're my dad. Nothing will ever change that. All this stuff with Gideon and Autumn doesn't change that."

"I know that."

Colleen disconnected the call and handed the phone back to Ben. "See, that was a lot cheaper than doing it in person. So do you have something to say to me?"

"Do you still want to have a five-foot-nine, red-haired daughter? Your chances improve if you reproduce with me. Mom and Kate are both tall and have red hair. Nina's tall too, but her hair is the same color as mine so you do risk that."

"Reproduce? Wow, Ben, that is the most romantic proposal I've ever had."

"I thought you said that you hadn't let anyone propose to you before. So this *is* the most romantic proposal you've ever gotten. I used to only get a gold medal when some other dude screwed up. Same now. All those other fellows didn't show up so, once again, I win."

EPILOGUE

"Okay, let's get a picture of two fathers at the grill."

Charles Forbes and Colleen's father were already at the grill set up on the grounds of the hotel in the village.

"I'm the grandfather," Charles Forbes corrected the photographer. "Dr. Ridge is the father."

The two men were only eight or nine years apart in age so they had felt like comfortable contemporaries.

"Yes," Colleen's father added happily, "but I'm going to be a grandfather soon."

It was a faux-picnic, a photo op staged on the grounds of the inn over Columbus Day. Colleen had learned that one does not do these things in one's own home.

Colleen had rocked the "pleasantly boring" tone of her media appearances. There was a lot of flurry for a month or so. She was barraged with interview requests, and Amanda said that it was all anyone was talking about at school. But the carefully staged banality of every word that had come out of her mouth left Gideon's fans feeling betrayed and everyone else uninterested.

She had invited Charles and Donna Forbes to come to the lake over Columbus Day to meet her father and Genevieve, but her brothers and sisters-in-law wanted to come, as did Gideon's siblings and spouses. The weekend was smelling enough like an engagement party that Ben had wanted to include his family. Every room in the house was full, and the overflow was in rooms at the inn.

Colleen hadn't wanted one of the Ridge family diamonds. She said that they were all so expensive that she would be afraid to wear them, and Ben liked the idea of buying her ring with money he had earned himself. She did ask her cousins' permission to take the three wedding dresses to a seamstress who was taking the beading off of one, the lace off of another, and using the beautiful textile from the third to create a gown that was flattering to Colleen's petite frame.

"Leave a big hem and huge seam allowances," she told the seamstress. "If I have a daughter, she is likely to be bigger than me."

The wedding was to be over Christmas. Both Colleen and Ben had so much family and so many friends that they decided to have only one attendant each. Seth and Nate flipped a coin to see who would be best man, and Colleen asked Amanda. Amanda said that she would wear anything, but it would be great if Colleen could remember that her maid of honor was tall with an athlete's square shoulders. She would look horrible in anything frilly or strapless.

"I have just the thing," Colleen said, "but you have to give it back."

So Amanda would be walking down the aisle in an emerald green silk suit that had belonged to Colleen's real mother.

"Will you be asking Autumn to the wedding?" Donna Forbes asked her.

Autumn's publicist had tried very hard to get Autumn into this photo shoot. She would only come for the shoot, her publicist said. Her schedule wouldn't allow her to come for the other family gatherings, he had said, but she could certainly make arrangements to come up for the afternoon.

Of course, to Colleen the photo op was the least important part of the weekend. If Autumn ever wanted to come without the cameras, Colleen would have welcomed her.

"Yes, I will invite her," Colleen told Donna, "but I don't imagine she will come."

Space at the inn was going to be scarce for the wedding; Colleen had blocked every room that hadn't been reserved by the guests who came Christmas after Christmas. The "plus one" invitations were being extended only to people known to be in serious relationships. Like every other single guest, Autumn would be allowed only one room. There would be no space for her entourage. She would be getting exactly the same treatment that Colleen's much-loved aunt Eileen was getting.

Maybe someday that would be enough for Autumn. Maybe someday Autumn would understand how much that actually was.

We hope you enjoyed

AUTUMN'S CHILD
By
Kathleen Gilles Seidel

All three of the STAND TALL books are available
from your local bookseller or ebook retailer.

Please turn the page to get a sneak peek at

Book 1 of the STAND TALL miniseries.

CHAPTER ONE

"I'm so screwed." Seth stared at his phone.

Nate grabbed the device and looked at the screen. "Oh, yeah, you are. Didn't your mom warn you about this?"

Ben was on the sofa, his feet on the coffee table, his hands linked behind his head. "I don't know how you clowns ever get women when you still count on your moms so much."

"I don't know either," Nate replied cheerfully. "But we do."

The three guys were hanging out in the chalet they shared on the grounds of the Endless Snow Resort on Oregon's Mt. Hood. They were wearing long-sleeved tees and hoodies, low-slung pants, and knit caps pulled over their shaggy hair. A snowboarding video was playing on the newest-model, wall-mounted TV. The front hall was carpeted with boots and wet coats. Medals of every color were draped over the necks of empty beer bottles.

They were professional snowboarders, three friends in their midtwenties who had trained together since they were kids. On the mountain they were disciplined, dedicated, and determined. They had to be. Snowboarding is dangerous. The rest of the time they felt contractually obligated to have fun. Fans expected snowboarders to be the pirates of winter sports: brash, reckless, and a little weird. This came quite naturally to these three.

"This isn't a joke." Seth shoved his phone back in his pocket. "Have some sympathy. You don't have to go home and report for jury duty."

"Because we already are home," Ben pointed out. "We changed our addresses. We are officially Oregonians. Have been for a couple of years."

"My mom did it for me," Nate admitted. "But relax. Why would anyone ever want you on a jury?"

Despite living in Oregon, Seth was still registered to vote in North Carolina where his parents lived, he carried a North Carolina driver's license, and he paid his income tax to the Tar Heel State. He had already burned through two postponements during the winter competition season. Now he was stuck. He either faced a contempt of court citation, or he went home, spent the night on the Luke Skywalker sheets in his old bedroom, and reported for jury duty. Luke Skywalker it was.

So on the last Sunday in June the male twig on the Street family tree flew home and spent the evening with his parents and his sisters' families. Monday morning he drove to the courthouse, found the jury assembly room, and got in line to check in like an actual adult. As he waited, he scanned the room, looking at—let's be honest here—the young women.

One blonde, pretty in a popped-collar-and-pearls way, nudged her companion, also a blonde, also with the popped collar and pearls. They recognized him. Seth tried to make eye contact; they looked away nervously.

He took another step forward in line. A dark-haired girl, wearing headphones, was working on her computer, using a wireless mouse. Her elbow was propped up on the table; that hand blocked a view of her face. The rest of her looked petite and hipster cute. She was wearing a short black skirt, retro sneakers, and a big man's watch on her narrow wrist. There were empty chairs at her table. He would go sit there.

Then she straightened, dropped both hands to the keyboard, and started to type...well, hello, was this possible? Yes, she was Caitlin, Caitlin McGraw, from the summers.

Suddenly he was a kid again, in his mother's kitchen, staring at the clock, desperate to have the minute hand move faster. *The bus from Charlotte gets in at...then her grandmother will pick her up...and it takes twelve minutes for me...* But he would still get there too early and have to sit on her grandmother's front steps, waiting.

An instant later he was at her table. "Caitlin?" He touched her shoulder in case she couldn't hear him over her music.

She looked up, pulling out her earbuds as she did. One of the cords got tangled in her hair.

Those eyes, those beautiful brown eyes...how could he have forgotten them?

"Seth." She stood up. "I heard that you were in town."

She had? Why hadn't she gotten in touch with him?

He wanted to sweep her up, spin her around, tell her great it was to see her, but they were in public, and for all he knew, she might not be so happy about seeing him. He shifted his backpack and pulled her into a quick one-armed hug, the kind you'd give anyone. "Why are you here? You don't live here, do you?"

"Only technically. I'm a twenty-four-year-old adult still using Mommy and Daddy's address."

He could hardly criticize her for that. "But your folks don't live here, do they? You were visiting your grandmother those summers."

"My dad retired, and they bought a house in that new golf-course community outside town."

He nodded. "My folks said that lots of retired military are out there. The golf course is supposed to be really good." Why were they talking about golf courses? He didn't give a crap about golf courses. "What about you? Where are you living?"

"Hadn't you better go check in?"

"I suppose." He dropped his backpack on the chair next to her. "Hold this place for me."

He returned to the line, and as he checked in, it occurred to him that if she knew that he had left the line without checking in, then she had seen him, been watching him.

When we were kids you said that you wouldn't play games. Let's not start now.

It took him a while to get back to the table. Too many people knew who he was. He sat down just as the jury coordinator called for their attention, welcomed them, then dimmed the lights in order to show a video. The screen was behind Seth so he had to turn his chair away from Caitlin. The video explained the court procedures and talked about how important it was for them to serve, how a trial by jury was a right first guaranteed by the Magna Carta, and—

Caitlin touched his arm and whispered. "You aren't supposed to say *the* Magna Carta. It's Latin so no article. Just Magna Carta."

He looked over his shoulder. "How do you know that?"

"I'm kind of nerdy."

One of their other tablemates gave them a stern look so they shut up and learned that if they were admitted to a jury, they would be issued red tags that they needed to wear whenever they were in the courthouse.

At the end of the video, the jury coordinator flicked the lights back on, and a different person, the Clerk of the Court, told them that there were two trials scheduled for that day, one civil, one criminal. He explained the difference between civil and criminal trials, repeating pretty much the same words that the video had just used. Then he told them about the little red tags, again using the same words as the video.

Within a few minutes fifteen people were called for the civil trial. Neither he nor Caitlin was called.

During the presentations he had been wondering if he should say something about what had happened. No, it hadn't "happened." He had done it. But, come on, it had been years ago, high school shit. There was no reason to mention it. Pretend that everything was fine. That worked for him. Ignore the sticky stuff, and it usually went away. Avoid the edges of the map; just have a good time with other people who wanted to have a good time. He was a snowboarder, after all. Having fun was part of the job description.

But when she started to lift the screen on her computer, he spoke quickly. "I kind of disappeared on you, didn't I?"

"You didn't disappear at all," she said evenly. "I knew exactly where you were. Your face was on the front of the Wheaties box, and you did start sending me form replies to emails."

"Oh, man, those autoreplies." He didn't like being reminded of them. *Hi, the Olympics were a great time for all the US teams, weren't they? Thanks so much for...* "I wish I hadn't done that. But it was a pretty bad time for me, and I did a lot of things wrong."

"Bad time? You had just won an Olympic medal."

"Yeah. It was complicated. But tell me about yourself. What are you doing? Where do you live?"

She was a freelance graphic artist living in San Francisco. Yes, she liked it out there. And her parents and her grandmother, they were all fine. Her sister? "And her baby...who's probably not a baby anymore."

She smiled. "No, he's not. He'll be in fifth grade next year. My sister and Trevor, Dylan's father, actually got married a few years ago."

"They got married? After all the crap you went through, they're married now?"

"Yes, but if they had gotten married back then, they would be divorced by now."

Good point.

Seth noticed someone hovering by the table. He looked up. The man said that he worked for Seth's dad. Seth stood up and made nice. Caitlin put her earbuds in and went back to work. She didn't look up when he sat down.

He watched her work. Her fingers tattooed across the keyboard. Sometimes she would stop, hunching forward, staring at the screen, one hand over her mouth, obviously thinking. Then most of the time she sat back quickly as if she had had an "aha" moment and started the rapid-fire typing again. Other times she'd type slowly as if she wasn't sure of her solution.

The morning was starting to drag. He had stuff he could do, but he couldn't get started. This sucked. Such a waste of time. Since the assembly room had Wi-Fi, most people were on their phones or computers. A few older people had newspapers or actual books, the kind with paper and all.

Caitlin eventually took out her earbuds and stood up to go to the ladies' room. When she got back, he asked her what she was working on. She said that a lot of her clients designed video games, and she helped with the art and some of the coding.

"I had a game out there for a while." Kids were supposed to be able to get the experience of being Seth Street snowboarding.

"I know."

She did? "It wasn't very good."

"I know that too."

"We weren't on the same page as the developer." His family didn't make many mistakes, but that had been one.

The jurors were given an hour for lunch. He walked down to the basement cafeteria with Caitlin, but the other people eating there recognized him, and he had to go back to being the Olympic medalist, the face of Street Boards. Seth Sweep, the media had dubbed him after he had won Olympic bronze in a shocking upset. His bronze meant that the United States had swept the event, taking all three medals.

"You're certainly sounding grown up," Caitlin said when they were gathering up their trash.

"It's an act. If I were really grown up, I wouldn't be here. I'd have changed my address."

"They don't have jurors in Oregon?"

She knew where he lived. "Undoubtedly. And actually scruffy riders are a lot more mainstream out there. Someone might actually want one of us on a jury. So maybe procrastinating was a good choice."

"You don't want to serve?"

"God, no. Deciding if someone is innocent or guilty? If they deserve to be in jail? Talk about grown up, that's above and beyond."

He had to go out and feed his parking meter. He offered to take care of hers. No, she hadn't driven. Her mother had brought her; her grandmother would pick her up. "It's like being fifteen again," she said, "and having to call for a ride."

Oh, good, she didn't want a car. He had been looking for an opening. "Remember if you're fifteen," he said lightly, "then I'm sixteen and have a license. I can run you home."

Sixteen... Memories suddenly started swirling in his brain, shapes in a snowstorm. *Look up at me. Look at me with those dark eyes of yours and admit that you're remembering too, remembering how great that third summer was because I could drive and we could go anywhere.*

What was going on in his brain? All this past stuff...he was a here-and-now kind of guy.

But it was good stuff, wasn't it?

"It's completely out of your way."

What? Oh, she was still talking about him driving her home. "All of ten minutes. And then maybe you will let me take you out to dinner."

He hadn't been able to get a read on her. Was she going to agree to have dinner with him? He wouldn't be surprised either way.

"They are paying us a whole twelve dollars for our service today," she answered. "I can buy my own food."

So it was a yes to spending the evening with him, but no to something that would make it seem like a date. He could live with that.

The afternoon dragged on. People were talking to each other more, complaining. Seth looked at his email, then his social media accounts, watched a few videos that the up-and-coming kids had made and were always trying to get him to watch, checked on a couple of games he had going with friends, and then went back to his email.

He could handle stress. Pressure, fear...bring 'em on. But boredom? He wasn't so good at that. He wanted out of here. He'd take Caitlin with him if he could, but most of all, he wanted—he needed—to leave. Snowboarders weren't supposed to be model citizens. They were rebels, outsiders, countercultural iconoclasts, not jurors.

But Seth was the public face of his family's company, Street Boards. It manufactured snowboards and skateboards. His parents, his sisters, and his brothers-in-law worked there; it supported all of them. So there was no way that Seth could be a jerk here in the jury assembly room. If the moms and dads of America thought Seth Street was an asshole, they wouldn't let their kids put his poster up on their bedroom walls, and they certainly wouldn't buy a Street Board to put under the Christmas tree. Seth had to act like a good citizen even if it was driving him nuts.

There was a beverage station at the back of the room, just coffee and water. Seth didn't drink much coffee, but he kept getting water just to have something to do. Caitlin was still working.

By two thirty people were saying that if you didn't get called for a trial on the first day, you weren't likely to have to come back.

At three o'clock there was activity in the front of the room. The clerk came back in and started talking softly to the jury coordinator. Surely they were going to be dismissed. A trial wouldn't start at three, would it? People at the tables started to put away their stuff, clear up their trash.

But when the jury coordinator stood up, she asked them to line up by the door as she called their names. She kept calling name after name until everyone in the room was standing in a line that snaked toward the back of the room. Caitlin's name had been called before his. She was too far ahead in line for them to talk.

And then they waited. And waited some more. Someone stepped out of line to get chairs for the older ladies. Seth winced. He should have thought to do that.

At three thirty, the jurors were all told to sit back down. At four o'clock, they were excused for the day. They could go home as soon as they signed for the little brown envelopes with their twelve-dollar payment. But the coordinator emphasized that they had to call the hotline or check the website later in the evening to see if they had to come tomorrow.

"But we won't have to come back, will we?" someone asked. "If you don't get a trial the first day, you're done, right?"

The coordinator said that that was not necessarily so and that they needed to check with the hotline or the website. Seth didn't like the sound of that.

"I came thinking that this might be kind of interesting," Caitlin said as they walked to the parking lot. She was carrying her computer in a messenger bag crafted out of an old Cub Scout backpack and a worn leather bomber jacket. "It wasn't."

"You got a lot of work done."

"It probably looked like it, but what do you know about the trajectory of bullets on a gravity-heavy planet?"

"Me? Nothing."

"The guy who designed the game apparently didn't either. Now it's too early for dinner. Do you just want to get a cup of coffee or something?"

No, he didn't want to get a cup of coffee. He wanted to spend the evening with her. He had already made a plan. That was one thing about three guys hanging out together. Someone needed to have a plan, or you never got out the door. "You remember the lake?"

"No. Why would I?"

She was being ironic. Of course she remembered the lake. "Let's pick up some barbecue and go out there. My parents have a lake house now."

"Their own place? So we don't have to trespass and eat on someone else's dock?"

"No." *Or have sex on a blanket back among the trees.*

Except they hadn't "had sex." They had made love. They had been in love.

That last summer he and Caitlin had been together, he had feelings for her that he had never felt again. Of course it was probably that your first love always did feel the most intense, the most consuming, but still...

* * * *

They had had three summers together from the time he had been fourteen and she thirteen, until he was sixteen and she fifteen.

He had grown up in the High Country of North Carolina and had started snowboarding when his uncles still had to lift him over the drifts at the edge of the parking lots. He had been a little meat torpedo in those days, fearless about height and speed, clueless about danger. At fourteen he had already been competing professionally for a few years. At the time he didn't—he couldn't—appreciate what sacrifices his family was making for his snowboarding. His dad worked in the furniture factory; it was a nonunion shop, and there wasn't ever any overtime. His mom had done alterations for the local bridal shop.

He had developed so quickly and so early that a lot of doors had opened for him. His mother had been great at negotiating tuition-free deals for him, but there was still travel and living expenses for both of them. In those days, few programs were set up for unescorted school-aged kids, so his dad had outfitted a pickup with a camper, and she made endless long drives, preparing meals in the little camper while he worked his way through the homeschooling curriculum. Pretty soon she had started escorting Ben and Nate too. Nate's mother was a schoolteacher; she couldn't take off during the school year. Ben's mother had five other children; she couldn't leave either. So the arrangement helped a lot with the expenses and certainly made everything more fun.

Although there was snow on Oregon's Mt. Hood year-round, his parents drew the line at the summer programs. Seth's two older sisters needed their mother too. So starting in April, Seth was back in North Carolina, attending regular school, trying to keep up his skills by skateboarding, while his mother turned her attention to the girls.

Each year it was harder to connect with other guys at school. Seth wasn't interested in ball sports, and this was a ball-sports kind of town. Of course he was better than the chumples, the slow, fat kids in glasses, but Seth wasn't used to being in the middle of the pack. He liked being the best, and although his mom kept preaching about this to him, he just didn't have as much fun when he was ordinary. What was so wrong with that?

The county had built a little skateboarding park back when skateboarding was a hotter fad. In the summer Seth was there all day every day, riding his bike over, often providing free unplanned entertainment for the little-kid birthday parties that were the main source of the park's revenue.

One day he noticed a kid, maybe eleven or twelve, on the other side of the fence. The kid was perched on his bike, with one foot on the ground and his helmet still on. Seth showed off for a bit—so what if this was an eleven-year-old kid, it was still an audience—then glanced over his shoulder to be sure that the kid was watching. The kid still was there, but he had taken his helmet off.

And he wasn't a he. He was a girl, slight in build but much closer to Seth's age than Seth had first thought. Okay. That was a better audience. Seth showed off even more, finishing a trick close to the edge of the skate park.

"Hi, I'm Seth," he said through the fence.

"Caitlin."

She was pretty with these really dark eyes. Seth wasn't sure what to say next. It was kind of awkward for a moment, but she spoke. "That's pretty amazing what you do. I suppose you've been doing it for a long time."

"Yeah, but some things aren't that hard to pick up. Do you want to try? I am happy to show you how."

"I don't have any of the stuff."

"That helmet will work. I'll bring a board and pads for you if you want to come tomorrow. And you need to grab a waiver from the front desk. Your folks will have to sign it."

"I'm spending the summer with my grandmother, but I don't suppose they'll care if she signs it."

"They won't notice."

They agreed to meet the next day. That night Seth started to have second thoughts. What if she were a major biff, a total Betty who couldn't learn anything? And what if she kept coming back to the park day after day anyway? What then?

He hoped it would rain, and the whole thing would fall apart. But it didn't. She showed up right on time wearing the same sort of cutoffs and T-shirt that she had had on the day before. Then she took off her helmet.

Oh. He had forgotten how pretty she was. Maybe this would be okay.

She handed the waiver to the kid at the counter and then took some dollar bills out of her pocket. Behind her head Seth waved a hand, and the attendant told her to go on in.

"How come I didn't have to pay?"

"Because you're with me. I don't pay."

"You don't? Why not?"

"They know me. I started here when I was four."

"Okay." She clearly didn't see how that added up. So she reached for the pads. "How do I put these on?"

She was a quick learner. She had strong legs and a good sense of balance, and since his mom was also nagging him to praise other people more, he told her.

She shrugged. "I've taken a lot of ballet."

"Really? Ballet?" She didn't seem like the type.

"My mom thought it would turn me into a lady."

"So how's that working?"

"Incredibly well. Can't you tell?"

He laughed and then showed her how to make a turn sharper. An hour later the park manager—an older man, a regular city employee—arrived, and he called them over to ask why "Mrs. Thurmont" had signed Caitlin's waiver. He seemed to know who Mrs. Thurmont was.

"She's my grandmother, but my parents signed a bunch of forms so that she can take me to the hospital or whatever."

The man smiled. "Let's not have any hospital trips from here, okay?"

A while later he came out again. "Seth, she's getting tired."

"No, I'm not," Caitlin protested.

Seth hadn't noticed, but now that Mr. Kendrick mentioned it, yes, he could see that her ankles were wobbling and they hadn't before. "Then we need to stop. Doing stuff when you are tired is the way to get injured."

How many times had he heard people say that to him? His coaches, his mom, they were constantly on him to stop practicing.

"I'm fine," she said. "Really I am."

"No you aren't." How wack for him to be acting like the grown-up. "We're stopping."

They met up every day for the rest of the week. He learned that her last name was McGraw and that her family lived in Norfolk, Virginia, but they had moved all the time because her dad was in the navy. He was a lawyer, a judge. Seth hadn't known that the navy had judges. Caitlin had an older sister who also took ballet. She was a million times better than Caitlin, but no—and suddenly Caitlin had gotten a little awkward, sending out all kinds of "I don't want to talk about this" signals—she didn't think her sister would try skateboarding.

She continued to improve, but it clearly bugged her that Seth was so much better than she was. She was pushing herself, and Seth didn't need Mr. Kendrick to tell him that she was trying too much too fast. She was going to hurt herself. "You're not ready for this kind of thing, not without a foam pit."

"Are you saying that because I'm a girl?" She looked pissed off.

"No," he lied. "I'm saying that I first got on a skateboard when I was four. And now snowboarding is, like, what I do. I am *sponsored*. That's why I don't go to school and shit." *So how can you think you could be as good as me?* He didn't say that last part.

She glared at him for a moment. Then she stepped up on her board and started again.

A second later he shouted at her. She was going too slow.

But she wasn't. She was so light that she didn't need tons of speed, and when she took off in the air, she didn't get much height, less than she had been getting, but she did something with her arm, letting it trail around her body, her eyes following her hand. Her fingers were gently curved, and halfway through she flipped her palm over. Her landing was soft, only the lightest sound.

When you analyzed it, it was nothing of a move, but he hadn't thought about it. He hadn't thought about anything. He hadn't been able to take his eyes off her. That's what it was like with the really epic guys, the top boarders. Whatever they were doing, even just their warm-ups, you had to watch them. You just did.

He wanted to be like that.

Long bike rides were a part of his summer training routine, and pretty soon she started to come. As long as she didn't do the sprints—he would do one sprint forward and then another back to her—she could keep up even through this hilly country.

The hills' winding roads would be dark with the shade from the birch and ash trees until around a bend everything would suddenly be open and light, and they could see, below them, town and the two ribbony rivers that met there. Further on was a Christmas tree farm with its regular lines of carefully trimmed Fraser firs marching up the lower slope of a mountain where Seth had first snowboarded. They would ride until they reached the lake. They would bring towels and wear their swimsuits under their clothes. In shadows of trees he tried to kiss her once, and she shoved him away.

Her grandmother, whom she called MeeMaw, lived in a big modern house on Pill Hill, which was where all the doctors lived. Caitlin's grandfather had been a doctor before he died. On wet days Seth would ride his bike through the rain, and they would sit at her grandmother's dining table, Seth supposedly catching up with schoolwork and Caitlin addressing envelopes for a benefit that her grandmother was running. She used special pens and had this major sick handwriting. Calligraphy, it was called. No one had taught her. She had learned it from a book.

He hated learning things from books.

One evening when he was at home, he heard his mother and one of his sisters in the kitchen talking.

"Mom, Seth is spending a lot of time with Mrs. Thurmont's granddaughter."

"I know," his mother answered. "It's usually the pregnant one who has to leave home, not the sister."

Pregnant? Was Caitlin *pregnant?* That couldn't be right. Of course, she was a girl. She used the girls' bathroom, and she wore a girl's swim suit, but still...pregnant? A baby? That would have meant that she had—

He couldn't think about it.

"Apparently"—his mother was still speaking—"her parents felt like Caitlin wasn't being supportive enough of her sister."

Oh, of course. Caitlin wasn't pregnant. Her sister was.

His aunt had been pregnant last summer. She already had three kids, and she was enormous. Her feet spilled over her shoes. She struggled to get in and out of a chair. Seth tried to imagine that happening to one of his sisters. He couldn't.

As soon as he saw Caitlin next, he asked her. It didn't occur to him not to. "So your sister is going to have a baby?"

"How did you know that?"

"My mom and sister were talking about it."

"How did they hear?"

Seth shrugged. "My mom seems to know everything. It's a pain." He started to put on his knee pads. They didn't have to talk about it.

"That's why I'm here, because of Trina being pregnant. My parents are all about how we have to show the world that we love her and we stand behind her. And they say that I am 'insufficiently supportive,' that I'm being a spoiled brat."

Seth wasn't sure what to say. "How old is she?"

"Fifteen, two years older than me, and I get that it totally sucks for her. I get that. But I didn't do anything wrong and yet everybody at school talks about me like I'm some kind of slut. I got invited to a rainbow party, and I don't even wear lipstick, much less do *that.*"

Seth was not about to admit that he didn't know what a rainbow party was. That was the one bad thing about not going to school with the other kids. Sometimes you felt like a major stupid-ass dork. "Your folks...weren't they mad at your sister?"

"Who knows? My mom would go into their bedroom, she'd close the door and all, but I could hear her crying. And she kept asking my dad what they had done wrong. But they say that family problems stop at the front door. To the rest of the world we have to pretend that everything is okay, which is crazy because it's not."

"Is she going to keep the baby?"

"Yeah. My dad really thought that she ought to give it up, and this social worker came and talked to all of us. But Trina and my mom...so it's going to live with us. They're trying to figure out stuff like health insurance because the military will go on covering Trina, but not the baby. That's all anyone talks about, Trina and the baby. So that's why," she finished, "I'm not going to let a guy do stuff to me."

"It's okay. I get it."

"Good. Then we don't have to talk about it again."

Seth went home and looked up rainbow parties...and then since the whole family used the same computer and his sisters knew how to check browser histories even if his parents didn't, he instantly did some searches on rainbow photos and rainbow physics as if he were suddenly interested in meteorological phenomena, which actually were pretty cool when you learned about them.

But the rainbow parties thing...why would a girl be willing to do that at all, much less on a bunch of guys and in public?

One afternoon at the skate park he looked up and saw that his dad was watching him work with Caitlin. Usually in this part of town you could hear the factory whistle signaling the shift change; Seth must have missed it.

For someone who couldn't afford to come to any competitions, his dad was stoked about Seth's career. Early on he had taken Seth's cheapie boards and tinkered with them in his garage workshop, putting better edges on them and the like. Now he was making them from scratch, layering and laminating the wood.

He also made the skateboards Seth used in the summer, and a week after coming to the park his dad gave him a skateboard he had made for Caitlin. "She's small for her age. This is a better board for her."

And it was.

She had to leave in the middle of August. She was taking the bus to Charlotte, and her parents were driving to meet her there. He rode his bike to the bus station to say goodbye. She was going to keep her skateboard on the bus with her, and her grandmother suggested that Seth carry it out of the terminal for her. Mrs. Thurmont turned away as if there were something on the station's bulletin board that she just had to read. She was chill for an old lady—although it wasn't like he was going to kiss Caitlin goodbye or something. He walked out to the bus anyway, handed her the board, and punched her lightly on her arm.

"Next summer?" he said. Her eyes really were something. He had gotten used to them so he didn't notice them all the time, but now, standing here...

"You'd better believe it," she said.

About the Author

Kathleen Gilles Seidel is a bestselling author of contemporary romances, two of which have won RITAs from the Romance Writers of America. She has a PhD in English literature from Johns Hopkins. She grew up in Kansas and lives in Virginia. She and her late husband have two adult daughters.

The Fourth Summer

Kathleen Gilles Seidel

Printed in the United States
by Baker & Taylor Publisher Services